WITHDRAWN

THE WOODS

THE WOODS

Paul Jones

The Book Guild Ltd
Sussex, England

WAKEFIELD LIBRARIES & INFORMATION SERVICES	
OOOOOOOO88851 1	
Askews	25-Mar-2004
AF	£16.95

First published in Great Britain in 2003 by
The Book Guild Ltd
25 High Street
Lewes, East Sussex
BN7 2LU

Copyright © Paul Jones 2003

The right of Paul Jones to be identified as the author of this work has been asserted by him in accordance with the Copyright, Designs and Patents Act 1988.

All rights reserved. No part of this publication may be reproduced, transmitted, or stored in a retrieval system, in any form, or by any means, without permission in writing from the publishers, nor be otherwise circulated in any form of binding or cover other than that in which it is published and without a similar condition being imposed on the subsequent purchaser.

All characters in this publication are fictitious and any resemblance to real people, alive or dead, is purely coincidental.

Typesetting in Baskerville by
SetSystems Ltd, Saffron Walden, Essex

Printed in Great Britain by
Antony Rowe Ltd, Chippenham, Wiltshire

A catalogue record for this book is
available from the British Library

ISBN 1 85776 736 5

For Nita, Pat and all the Ormies

1

So here I am outside my girlfriend's work, waiting to find out whether or not she's cheating on me. What the hell am I doing here? How the hell did I let myself get into this state? I can't believe I'm actually doing this. Is she cheating me, or is it just my stupid septic imagination . . . again?

Of course she doesn't know I'm hiding here in the pouring rain down a darkened backstreet across the road from the staff entrance walkway. And I couldn't have chosen a better night to do it. It's cold and wet, and everywhere has that damp uninviting look about it.

Cars are roaring by with their headlights blazing, spray hissing off their tyres; the roads are completely soaked, and look like whale skin in the reflection of the streetlights. Everyone's seemingly in a mad rush to get home from this misery, except for me. Christ, I must be mad!

Take a deep breath, you moron, or you'll end up having a nervous breakdown. Deep breaths . . . relax.

Look at that wiry old man shuffling by on the other side of the road, I bet he's not suspecting his wife's at home now shagging the neighbour. I bet the only thing he's thinking about is the sumptuous, steaming plate of mash, sausages and gravy waiting on the kitchen table for him. And afterwards, feet up in front of the telly, a good film on the box, a few hours of escapism, then a cosy snuggle up in bed later on. Lucky bastard!

That icy wind is picking up again; I can tell because the tops of the aspen trees across the road are bowing quite a bit. In the wintertime, when they're bare of all their leaves, they look like giant skeletal claws.

Shit, here comes the rain again; I can see it through the orange blaze of the streetlights, like thousands of tiny needles fired from the sky. If it gets any heavier, I'll have to go under the bus shelter.

Where was I? Oh yes . . . catching my girlfriend cheating. Where did it all begin?

It used to be absolutely fantastic in the beginning, between Sammy and me. I was 29 when I met her, she was 25. That little volcano of excitement erupted in my stomach whenever I used to see her working on the checkouts in the local supermarket.

That was when I was single and lived in a moderately clean flat in the centre of town. I really looked forward to shopping days, which happened to be a Thursday night (imagine someone looking forward to shopping day – what a sad git).

At first, it was easy to get a look at her because she used to be totally oblivious of my existence. By the way, her name is Samantha, and she has this wonderful Jamaica-cake coloured hair. (Well, I imagined it was like the crust of the old Jamaica cake – dark gingery brown. I always thought she dyed it that colour, but later found it to be genuine.)

Every time I saw her it would be tied back in a pigtail, and swishing back and forth as she scanned the items on her conveyor belt, her nimble little fingers tapping in the price codes on her till. Those soft gentle hands that probably smelt of Atrixo hand cream.

And not forgetting that delightful face of hers, plenty of hidden character. Ever heard the saying: pretty in the cradle, ugly at the table, and vice versa? Well, I always got the impression that she was a bit of an ugly duckling when she was young, but has now blossomed into a classically good-looking girl. Just like the ones you see in one of those period dramas on TV, not so much stunning, but handsome, the type that doesn't require much make-up. She reminded me of someone I once knew.

OK, I'm no oil painting myself. I know I'm slightly balding, so I have short haircuts to get used to the idea of one day losing my Barnet forever. I'm about two stone overweight, although my face always seems to remain slim and, if I may say, passable.

However, getting back to when I was on the hunt for Sammy, I would never use her checkout even though it would have been the ideal way to break the ice. I'd always go to the one behind, so I wouldn't have to stand face to face with her.

The idea was to be near her, but not have actual contact, not until I was ready anyway. First, I wanted to see her little idiosyncrasies, funny ways, silly faces she might pull when she doesn't know she's being watched.

Sometimes I would pray for someone to drop a bottle of pickles on the floor. Or for someone to find out they didn't have enough cash to pay for their shopping. Anything that would knock her off machine mode, and allow the real Sammy inside to have a peep out.

One particular amusing trait of hers I've noticed is when she's about to reply to a droll comment from a customer. Her mouth begins to purse as if she's about to drink out of a cup. Like her mouth is ready to speak before her brain has decided what words to use.

Another reason I didn't want to use her checkout was

so she wouldn't see what I carried in my shopping trolley. (Sounds silly, I know! But they say you can tell a lot about a person by what they buy.) It's bad enough standing in the checkout queue, with everyone else having a sly peek.

And besides all that, I was too shy to go up to her checkout anyway. Once those jowls of mine begin to blossom a deep red, everyone in the whole store would have had to put on sunglasses.

Of course I was going to ask her out . . . I just needed to do it when I was ready. I do believe in *carpe diem* but not when it comes to asking the opposite sex out for a date. Chatting girls up has be done with extreme caution, they can smell you coming a mile away. Listen to me the expert, I've only ever had two girlfriends.

Seriously though, women do have very sensitive crap detectors, and very often it seems they can read your minds, so beware!

More often than not, I've known of lads on the pull in nightclubs who dash in like flies on a fresh cow-pat, and usually end up getting blown away just as quickly.

In my case, with Sammy, I wanted her to start recognising me, and once my face became familiar, see if she was pleased to see me. Maybe even give me a bit of the eye? At least it'd let me know that if her train did happen to pull into my station, I would have the necessary ticket to board. Know what I mean?

However, once I remember I did get a smile off her, something that was more than simply a gesture of politeness. There was definitely a sparkle of pleasure radiating from those enchanting features of hers.

At the time, she happened to be scanning a cucumber that, with its cellophane wrapping, looked like a long dick in a green condom. Still, it was me that she turned to grin at, and you know what they say about first impressions. Hang on a minute, it was the cucumber she was laughing at, and not me, wasn't it?

I've never really asked her about that.

Nevertheless, as you will probably be amazed to know, I did eventually go out with her. (How on this earth did he manage a miracle like that? you may ask.)

Well, as it happened, I soon found out that a mate of mine had started work in the fruit and veg department. And I sort of got him to (cringe, cringe) go cap in hand down on one knee for me. (First finding out she was available, of course.)

Well, I mean, come on . . . how many of you out there have actually had the balls to chat up a tasty bit of stuff, stone-cold sober?

Although at first my mate had a bit of trouble trying to describe me to her. After all, hundreds of customers pass through her checkout each week. In the end, he had to more or less point me out to her.

How embarrassing that was. I had to stand in the queue, pretending not to know what was going on, while she checked me out. It was like standing in an outdoor male nude contest, in the middle of winter, in front of a panel of Anne Robinsons. (You know her – you're the weakest link . . . Goodbye!) I might as well have just gone right up to her and asked her out.

How does that scientific theory go . . .? All things being equal, the simplest solution is often the right one, or something like that.

However, the doctrine of science and human psychology don't always make good bedfellows – that is, if you happen to take me as an example.

Yes, the longest and most awkward way around things always suits me just fine! And to cut a long story short, after almost being bribed to go out with me, her reply to my mate was, and I quote, 'Go on then, but if he turns out to be a pervert I'm going to be suing you.' There's encouragement for you!

So there you have it. I wouldn't presume to bore you any further about our early courting days. We've all been there, done it, bought the video etc.

Six years now we've been going out, four of those actually living together. We bought into one of those half-buy, half-rent housing association homes in our home town of Llandudno. A pleasant medium-sized two bed-roomed semi-detached house in a fairly respectable cul-de-sac.

For the last 12 months, I've given serious thought to getting engaged (shame on me). Actually, until all this cropped up, I was going to pop the big question to her this Christmas. I think I'll put that on hold for now.

In the beginning, Sammy and I would make a special effort to spend time together at the end of the day. But over the last year or so, we've sort of slipped into a rut that's becoming increasingly difficult to get out of. Most of the time, we seem to be passing each other on the way out.

I myself work as a drayman five days of the week, delivering stocks of beer to many of the licensed establishments around the North Wales coast. I'm up at 5.45 a.m., to start work at 7 o'clock, which means I normally have to go to bed fairly early, about 11 o'clock at night.

But when she used to finish work about eight, we still had sufficient time together. However, since her promotion to checkout supervisor, she doesn't get home now until about nine which I know is only an hour, but it makes all the difference.

Especially when our sex life begins to take a back seat, he coughed awkwardly. In the past, we'd enjoy a good old roll in the sack or hay two or three times a week, which is fairly normal for a healthy young couple. Nowadays, we're lucky to rumple the bed sheets once a week.

Yes, I know it shouldn't all be down to just sex, but if I said that didn't matter, I'd be lying through my back teeth.

Far too often I hear these bloody so-called relationship therapists and agony aunts regurgitate rubbish about how we should spend our quality time with each other. Switch the television off, and take more time to talk to one another. Relax, give each other a sensual massage. (You've read them in those weekly supplements magazines.)

Listen, I tell you that after Sammy gets home at night, has something to eat, maybe a bath, all she's good for is catching up on the weekly soaps she's taped, or watching that travel channel on the Sky digital to dream about where she'd like to go next.

So who the hell's going to want to talk about what sort of a shitty day you've had at work? Wouldn't that be the last thing on your mind?

And as for that incredibly sensual massage, who'd have the patience or the energy? You'd just put each other to sleep. More on that subject later.

As for going out together at the weekends, over the years, Sammy and I have developed the understanding that it is better to go out on the razzle separately. Or rather, her with her mates, as she used to do before I came along, and me with mine.

Why don't we go out together?

Guys and gals together on a night out is like a volcano erupting opposite a nitroglycerine factory. It's a terrible concoction for disaster.

For some reason or other, whenever you go out in a

mixed group, the night always ends in tears, does it not? Lads get accused of eyeing up someone else, girls get accused of flirting with someone else. People get blamed for not paying enough attention to their partners. In other words, it's a well-known recipe for doom.

When men and women are out in the pubs and clubs, they just can't seem to relax and let themselves go. They feel as though they have to be on their best behaviour all the time. Even back at home when they have their mates over, someone of the opposite sex is definitely persona non grata.

For example, whenever you walk into your living room when your girlfriend has her mates around, they clam up quicker than a German football supporter in an English pub full of yobs. But the second you leave the room, rabbit, rabbit, rabbit. Christ, they can gab. I've often wondered if one of them has a stopwatch and is trying to see who can talk about the most subjects, in the quickest time possible.

The fact remains that every now and again, men and women need the company of their own sex. Women need an outlet for all that hen talk, otherwise they'd simply explode and take their men with them. And likewise, we chaps enjoy the privilege to wind down with a beer, chew the cud, have a good laugh etc.

Getting back to quality time with Sammy, maybe if we had that extra hour or so, we'd probably be able to bond a bit more, if you know what I mean. All we seem to do now is watch a bit of telly, then go straight to bed. It's not as if we don't enjoy each other's company any more; I mean, it's still comforting to know you'll both be there for one another at the end of the day. But with such little time left, it's not worth making the effort, and that's when you start taking each other for granted. You forget about the wonderful things that drew you both together in the first place, and instead pick up on the things that annoy.

For instance, after Sammy has watched her programmes, which I have left her to do, completely uninterrupted, I might put on a video myself, or watch whatever good film there is on the telly.

So what does she do? Starts bloody talking! And especially if it's something I really want to watch, or if I've reached the climax of a cracking movie that I've sat devotedly through for an hour and a half. She'll say, oh yeah I forgot to tell you ... And if I ignore her, she'll persist in calling my name, the way an irritating child does when it wants to annoy you, until finally I'll say, what! for Christ's sake! Can't you see I'm watching this?

Oooo aren't we moody then, she'll sing.

Well, Christ, Sam, I was quiet for your bloody *Eastenders*.

You know, sometimes I get the impression she does it on purpose just to piss me off. I've even tested her on occasions. Another instance, while she's reading one of her *Bella* magazines, I'll be sitting there purposely not watching anything in particular, and giving the impression I'm bored. Will she use that ideal moment to tell me all those things she's been holding in all day? No she bloody won't!

I could sit that way all night without a murmur from her. But the moment I slip in a video, or I turn the channel over and catch something interesting, down flaps the magazines and out pours another sodding encyclopaedic volume.

Even if she happens to be in the kitchen at the same

time as something good is on the box, she'll saunter in at the right moment and stand dead in front of the TV screen to talk to me. Un-bloody-believable!

Although, I confess, there are things about me she's quick to complain about. Like the way I purse my lips when I'm about to take a sip of tea. (Well, excuse me for being born that way. I suppose if I broke my foot, she comment about the way I limped too.) Oh yes ... Sometimes I leave all the doors open on the kitchen units. To name but a few.

But surely to God she wouldn't cheat on me for things so trivial as those? Every relationship has its own little flaws, nobody's perfect; there's got to be more to it than that. And as I stand here in the freezing cold, outside her work, waiting to find out whether she is cheating on me or not, I can't help but think perhaps I was just never good enough for her.

2

Thinking about it now, over the past month or so I have actually noticed a specific change in her ways. First, and the most obvious, was the lack of sex (which I have already explained).

Why is it we men always have to initiate the act of lovemaking? We always have to make the first move, set the scene, get our women in a romantic mood etc. Why can't they seduce us for a change? Maybe it has something to do with the generation they were brought up in, or the social environment. Maybe it's just me, but after being with a woman for six years, I've found in my case it's 'if you don't ask you don't want'. Why do women like to pretend they don't like sex?

According to them, all men think about is getting their end away. They're as subtle about sex as Jack the Ripper would have been about midwiving.

That is not true!

I've always regarded sex as an essential ingredient in any healthy relationship. Sex is a very important outlet for many aspects. It is not just another way of shooting off a bit of dirty water.

Apart from the most popular belief that it is the ultimate affirmation of real love between two people, in addition, sex is extremely useful as a means of venting stress and tension from the body, as well as emptying the surplus amounts of hormones, which, let's face it, has got to be most common use amongst young adults.

Incidentally, sex is also a good solid bridge between couples. The mental and physical intimacy involved when couples indulge allows them the confidence to be able to communicate with each other on every level of human emotion.

What is more, frequently engaging in sex with your partner also reassures you that they at least still desire you – know what I mean?

I do try my best! Every now and again, I go over and give Sammy a cuddle. (Perhaps not as often as I should have, but I've always had trouble showing real affection. I've tried, believe me, I've tried. But things like holding hands, whispering sweet nothings, mawkish feelings – it's just not me, never has been. Perhaps it was because of what happened in my childhood – more on that later.)

Though lately, even when I do hold her, I can feel an odd tension or rigidity in her body. The way an irritated or uncomfortable child would react with a hug from a soppy old aunt or uncle.

And at night, before going to sleep, Sammy and I used to enjoy a bit of a cuddle. The three stages, we call them; Stage 1. Sammy lying on her side, me snuggled up behind. Stage 2. Me on my back, and her draped over me, head on my chest. Stage 3. We both turn over to our own sides.

Now, she just goes straight to sleep, so I think, To hell with her, and leave her to it.

But what confirmed it for me about her seeing someone behind my back was what I heard last night while she was chatting to her friend in the living room.

On Wednesday nights, Sammy usually has a few of her

own mates around for a coffee, so I often nip around to my workmate's house for a few hours. He only lives about a quarter of a mile away. Most of the time I get back just after ten, and by that time Sammy's friends have already left. However, last night my mate Mike wasn't feeling too great, and knowing what it's like trying to entertain when you've got a pounding headache and the shivers, I didn't stay long.

When I arrived home, I noticed Pamela's dark Spirito de Punto parked behind our Fiesta. Pamela, who is an old school friend of Sammy's, is a mousy-looking petite blonde blue-eyed waif. Neither ugly nor great-looking. But whatever she lacks in the looks department, she more than makes up for it with her motormouth. Christ, she can gab!

In fact she enjoys it so much that when it's her turn to listen (which isn't that often) you can almost see her straining to keep her mouth shut, as if that tongue of hers is a wild animal trying to get out. Not only that, she's always pestering me about the availability of any good-looking young men at my work.

Couldn't be arsed for any of that tonight, so in I crept, trying not to make any noise with the front door. Beside me, the living room door was closed, but I could hear them both rabbiting away inside, which meant they hadn't heard me.

Just as I was about to slink upstairs for a while, I heard their voices hush, as if they didn't even want the walls to hear what they were saying.

At first I thought it was only a bit of secret girly chat. But as it was Sammy's voice doing most of the talking, I decided to bend my ear a little.

Stifled giggles, surprised gasps. I smirked to myself, wondering what the hell were they talking about. I was just about to give up trying to figure out what they were saying when I heard, 'Then he kissed me...' and this rooted me to the spot.

I leant my ear as close as I could to the door, the light from the kitchen filling my peripheral vision.

'Ahh! Did you kiss him back? I would have,' Pamela gushed.

Then I heard another gasp from Pamela. Sammy must have nodded a yes.

I swallowed anxiously, heart drumming in my chest.

'Bet if he had the chance, he'd do more than that,' Pamela said.

'Ah, he's lovely, I just couldn't refuse.'

I started having difficulty hearing because of the music on the telly. But had I already heard enough?

I stared hard at the door again. Should I burst in and demand what the hell was going on? Maybe she was talking about someone else? Please say you were so I can relax, I thought.

From then on, I scarcely breathed, fearing I might miss something.

'... Wants me to give him a lift home on Thursday. Couldn't say no ... Invited ... to go out.' The rest became muffled again. Thursday ... lift home. It began to fit together.

Lately, she has been arriving home 30 to 40 minutes late, though she's been putting it down to the flexible hours of being a checkout supervisor. I believed her. Why should I have had any reasons to doubt her?

And while I'm thinking about it, what about all those weird phone calls we've been having lately? The ones where I pick up the receiver to answer, and the bloody line goes dead? I always thought they were just prank callers. Everybody has them, right?

Now I'd heard enough, and began to panic. The shock was causing my whole body to feel light as if it was going to levitate off the carpet at any second. Was I dreaming this? I hoped I was! If only I'd wake up now, everything would be just as it was.

But this was no dream! It was real, and so was my welling anger. What the hell was happening here? ... Was she really seeing someone else behind my back or what? ... Or was she referring to someone else? She could have been ... I may have just caught the back end of some silly story. No, it sounded too personal.

Shit, what happened now? Was she going to leave me? Why was she doing this? What the hell had I done wrong?

Whatever was going to happen, I didn't want to be caught standing there listening. I wasn't ready for a confrontation just yet. I had to get away from the house, have time to think this thing through.

Mouth cotton dry, I dived for the front door, and pulled it shut just a wee bit louder than I'd intended. In case Sammy saw me leave, I almost ran from our cul-de-sac, I didn't want her to know I was there at all. Luckily, I don't think she saw me.

As I trudged away from the estate, not really knowing where I was going, a plan was already beginning to form in my head. The only way I was going to find out for sure was to play dumb, and wait outside her work tomorrow night.

An icy breeze lashed at my exposed face, reminding me of the precious cosiness I'd left at home. Maybe I could go back to Mike's house to confide in him, which I had to admit was very tempting indeed. But I decided against it.

Instead, I chose to wander around the quiet, private residential areas where I was assured of greatly needed solitude. As I walked, my mind was so pricked full of stinging questions, my head felt like a pincushion. I could hardly think straight. I felt paranoid, as if the whole world was watching me.

A middle-aged man in a Berghaus navy blue rain jacket, walking his dog on a lead, approached me, and I put my head down. As we passed one another, I felt his inquisitive terrier nose the calf of my leg, and I flinched as if it could sense my disquiet.

I marched down the nearest street and heaved a weighty sigh, my head now cooling enough for me to at least gather my thoughts together.

Was I coming to the end of this relationship? . . . Was this it? . . . What was going to happen to me now? That was the question that most frightened me. And I think it was something I wasn't quite ready to address at that time. It was like being on board a sinking ship, but delaying the panic of going down until you actually saw the water lapping at your feet.

After all, it may have only been a one-night stand, it may have only been a quick kiss. Though she did say it was Thursday, but did that mean every Thursday? And a lift home in *my* car, I might add.

But how long had this been going on? Long enough for a full-blown torrid affair, it appeared. An affair that could be growing stronger week by week, draining the very life out of our own relationship? Was there still time to save ours? Or had finding out merely brought forward the inevitable?

I would have to confront her tomorrow. Even though doing it sooner, would be so much better. But no! If I challenged her about it tonight, it might anger her into dumping me before I even had the chance to try and make amends. Sometimes, when people have been caught out like that, they immediately resort to drastic measures. They do that because they feel that their escape route to a happier relationship is being threatened.

Or if it was only a meaningless fling she had had, she might actually convince me that there was nothing going on in the first place. '... It's just your silly imagination running away with you again, John! How many times do I have to tell you! ...'

Then I'd start believing her, yes ... what I'd done was take one piece of a jigsaw and let my panic-stricken imagination make up the rest. That was a relief!

On the other hand, if I made her aware before tomorrow night, she would have a chance to warn off this person, whoever he was. And I would never find out the truth.

No way! ... I was not putting myself through that kind of mental torture thank you very much!

No, this was definitely the way it was going to be! Just play dumb until tomorrow night, let Sammy think she was still safe, and pick up this mystery guy from work, then I'd know for certain. I just hoped that everything went to plan, and it wasn't foiled by irritating little inconveniences like the chap being ill. Or Sammy had to work a bit later and missed him. Anything that might thwart their cosy little Thursday night meeting. They had to be there for me to catch them.

The remainder of my thinking walk became a blur. I can't really remember where I went or how I arrived back at our estate. The only bits I do recall after finalising my intentions were fleeting glimpses inside people's cosy homes on my way past.

Families, couples, innocently performing their daily routines, completely ignorant of the fact that their rounded, blissful lifestyles hang on by a mere thread. Little do they know all it takes is a random act of fate to snap off that golden thread and they'll plummet back to earth with a terrific thud.

Thoughts of envy and self-pity maybe!

Eventually, when I arrived home, I was disappointed to find Pamela's car had gone. Can you believe the irony of it?

This now meant that Sammy and I would be alone, and I wouldn't be able to avoid facing her. Apprehensively, I slipped the key into the front door lock, feeling every groove on its serrated edge.

I honestly didn't want to even think of seeing Sammy at this time. If it was at all possible, I would have sold my soul to swap places with anyone until tomorrow night. I just hoped I wouldn't lose my temper, and blow my cover for tomorrow night.

I stood in the hallway. The living room was empty, with the door wide open. She had to be either in the kitchen or upstairs.

Suspecting she might be in the kitchen, I slipped into the living room, and was ambushed by the heavy scent of perfume and cigarettes. On the television, two young couples were living it up on some sun-baked island in the Caribbean or wherever. Their overflow of cheer and camaraderie made me want to put my foot through the TV screen.

Upstairs, I heard the lavatory flush, and I braced myself ready for her to come down. I just hoped she wouldn't be able to pick up any of my bad vibes, because if she did, I knew she'd pester and pester me to tell her until I gave in. Then it would all come out, and that'd be it.

Sammy is definitely one of those people with a very stubborn, inquisitive nature. If she senses something slightly amiss, she's like a bulldog with a bit between its teeth, she won't let go.

I'm sure women have a built-in radar that detects the presence of lies, or strange behavioural patterns in a man. For instance, whenever I'm secretly watching something a bit saucy on the TV, you can be sure whichever part of the house Sammy is in, she'll march right in just when I don't want her to and I have to turn over quick. Then subconsciously she'll find any kind of excuse to stay long enough so that programme on the other side has finished.

Once it has, and there's nothing left to watch, she'll disappear again for another hour or so. Women definitely belong to the strange and unusual.

Sammy appeared in the living room doorway, but I refused to look at her. 'You're a bit late, aren't you? Didn't even hear you come in,' she mumbled, walking through to the kitchen.

I had to say to myself, don't blow it, just keep calm, remember just be nice until tomorrow.

'Just got chatting a bit too long. Did your mate turn up?'

'Yeah, she left about an hour ago . . . Wanna mug of tea?' she shouted through.

I felt like telling her to shove it where the sun doesn't shine. 'No, I'm all right, had one just before I left Mike's.'

I strolled through into the kitchen and stood observing the apparently innocent way she pottered about making her tea. The leisurely way she hooked a hank of liquorice hair behind her ear.

You wouldn't think butter could melt in her mouth!

Never had it been so difficult to restrain myself from speaking my mind to her at that second. Never had I felt so lost and alone there in my own home. Never had she seemed so much like a stranger to me.

I just wanted to ask her why was she doing this to me. Why she was doing this to us. Look at what we'd achieved over the years.

'What's wrong with you?' Sammy woke me up. 'You haven't even taken off your jacket yet.'

'Got a bit of a stomach ache,' I blurted without even thinking.

'Just waiting for it to ease a bit, that's all.'

'There's some settlers in the cupboard there.' She took a sip of her steaming mug of tea as she left the kitchen. I stood there alone, thinking to myself, how can she be so cool about it?

Luckily for me, the rest of the evening passed fairly quickly, although Sammy retiring to bed early probably helped a bit too. Needless to say, I decided to stay downstairs to brood in front of the television and wrestle with my own demons. Little did I realise bedtime itself would be another portent of doom I had to contend with.

All night, I lay on a bed of brambles, and probably slept about an hour or so at the most. The rest of the time, I lay awake, fretting over our future. The way I felt that night I wouldn't wish on my worst enemy. I can only describe it as like being a prisoner with terminal cancer, in a prison perched on a rock somewhere in the middle of the Atlantic, in a bad storm. There's simply no escape, and no salvation.

It's hard to believe that in a situation like that, lying so close to someone, you can be so far away from them. I couldn't even bear the possibility of any part of her body touching mine, and I had to crouch as far away as possible on my side of the bed. Pathetic isn't it?

The following day at work was bad enough as well! Several times, Mike, my workmate (who incidentally felt much better than he did the night before), had to tell me to wake up. I just couldn't stop drifting off in a trance. All I can say is, it's a good job it was his turn to drive the lorry. And as for the actual unloading of the kegs themselves, at one particular pub I nearly crushed him in the cellar with a 70-kilo keg of Guinness. Perhaps I should have taken the day off.

But fair play, Mike didn't fly off the handle about it. The amount of times he's nearly killed me in the beer cellars because of the run-ins he's had with his missus, it's a miracle I'm still here. So I suppose he did what I always do with him, let the thing blow itself out, and be ready to listen if I wanted to talk.

Thinking about it now, I wish I had confided in him a little. With all his experience in these matters, he might have told me it was nothing to worry about, and I was just being a bit neurotic. If only that was true!

3

So now you know why I'm standing here, waiting to find out if my girlfriend of six years is really cheating on me.

But what am I expecting to see? Well, I know I'm not going to actually see her snogging with someone right outside her work. Perhaps they'll just walk out together and go off in the car somewhere for a while. Perhaps they might stop off down a quiet country lane, or even go up the Great Orme. Great Orme ... Yes, ideal secluded place for clandestine couples who want to go for a shag without being seen.

Shag!! She'd better bloody not! Christ, the thought of someone else touching my girlfriend with his thing. Bastard! Makes me want to rush down there and wait for him with a golf club.

No! ... Calm it down, you'll ruin everything. She could easily turn around and say she was just innocently walking out with a colleague. And I was behaving like an over-possessive, neurotic jerk. Then I would never know the truth.

It is now 9.05; any time now. Shit! The suspense is killing me. My mouth feels like the inside of a dustbin, my heart's pounding so hard, I have to hold onto this stone wall to stop myself from losing my balance. At least it's stopped raining.

At last, someone has emerged from the staff entrance gates, a woman with clacking high heels . . . No, definitely not Sammy, she's too heavily built.

Another throng of marching bodies appear. Is she amongst them? Looks like two women and three fellas . . . No, she's not there.

Where is she? Where is she? Come on! Come on! If all this proves to be the result of my overactive imagination, I promise I'll never react like this again. From now on, I'll take complete stock of the way I treat her, and I'll never take her for granted again.

Wait . . . Is this? . . . I can see her. It's the red padded jacket I bought her last Christmas. But who is that tall lanky chap walking with her? Is that him?

Got to be patient now, can't come this far and ruin it . . .

I watched intensely as they strolled along the orange-lit walkway, 50 yards away from my darkened hideout. At first, they seemed innocent enough, just chatting like normal work colleagues. Sammy's face glowing like a copper penny under the orange lights. Does she look very happy, or is it just me? I wondered.

They both stopped, exchanged a few more words, then went their separate ways, Sammy to the main car park, and the lad crossed over the road in my direction. Even though he probably wouldn't have known who I was anyway, I quickly slunk back to the coach shelter to hide. Furtively, I watched his wiry frame prance by, but I couldn't seem to get a good look at him. Bugger! All I caught was his head disappearing behind the stone wall guarding the block of tenements.

As he turned down Tudor Road towards the swimming baths, my suspicions begin to wane somewhat. Maybe I was wrong after all!

If I see Sammy's Fiesta boom past me on her way home now, I'll rest in peace and begin to put an end to this whole sorry nightmare. Phew! here she comes thrashing the poor car in third gear again, and for once it doesn't bother me. Just carry on going home, Sammy, and you can thrash the damn thing for the rest of your life.

But to my horror, she turned left down Tudor Road where that chap had just gone. Not wasting a second, I raced as fast as I could, and stopped dead at the corner. Chest heaving, I hunkered down and peered over the stone wall, my vision blurred with tears of exertion.

Sammy's Fiesta stood like a panting beast in wait, its rear lights like glaring red eyes, and the plumes of exhaust fumes like steaming breaths. As if out of nowhere, the chap jumped straight in, and off they sped, in the opposite direction, turning right at the junction and onto the promenade road.

Shocked and devastated, I sank back against the wall. My calves had turned to liquid and the balls of my feet were trembling. You'd have thought I'd just run a marathon. I leant over hands on knees for support.

What now? I seethed ... The anger began to swell up inside as if someone was pumping air into a tyre. God only knows what Sammy is going to get up to, and whatever it is, I'm totally powerless to prevent it. 'The fucking bitch!' I hissed. 'Thanks a fucking lot!'

Where on earth was the person I'd met and fallen for all those years ago? Who was this stranger that now shared my bed at night?

If only this was one of those terrible nightmares I could awaken from. Like the ones you have every now and again when you're feeling a bit insecure about your partner. The ones so real, that in the morning you still feel like kicking your innocent partner out of bed.

No! There was definitely no waking up to save me from this one!

Before long, I became aware of the traffic zooming by and the flashes of ghostly faces glaring at me from inside the cars. So fucking what! What's the point in trying to protect my dignity now? Sod them all, let them have their pennyworth. I just want to go home . . . or do I? If I do, I'll have to confront her for sure, there's no avoiding it now. That's it! All over . . . Six years down the pan.

I hauled myself up from the wall and began my wretched walk back home, then stopped, and changed my mind. No, bugger it! I'll go for a drink first. Under the circumstances, I think I deserve it!

After that, I seemed to drift through the town centre as if I was gliding on a very long conveyor belt, like the kind they have at airport lobbies. I don't quite know why, but I appeared to be gravitating towards a place that was an old haunt in my youth, an old pub on the other side of town that cuts into the foot of the Great Orme, just above the Victorian tram station. A pub reported to be some 300 years old and the longest-standing public house in Llandudno, the King's Head.

I entered through the narrow doorway, to the gruff cackle of laughter coming from a table of men whose ages varied roughly from 20 to 50. A few more customers were scattered around the bar area. I approached the bar, and felt the warmth radiating from the crackling log fire in the stone hearth.

The leathery-skinned barwoman with earrings like doughnuts smiled professionally, and I asked for a pint of Guinness.

While she pulled the pint from the shiny brass pump, I leant on the polished counter and gazed at the weird clock staring back at me between shelves of glasses and bottles of spirits. That's been there for quite a while now, I thought, and every time I come it always interests me. It was one of those novelty clocks where the numbers are back to front and the hands move anti clockwise. Or it was like looking at it through the reflection of a mirror.

My pint in hand and paid for, I sought a quiet and secluded corner in which to sit and brood with my drink.

The bar room itself stood somewhat polygonal in shape: with the main bar area occupying the centre, and giving the customers an almost all-round serving facility.

I found a suitable spot round the corner at the back of the room, and plonked myself behind a table. In front of me was a wall with two large framed maps of the Great Orme's head and Llandudno. Surrounding these were dozens of old photographs of the town's treasured heritage, dating back to the turn of the century. And above them, stacked on single shelves, were collections of various antique bottles.

By now I was beginning to feel a bit sorry for myself, and tried to block out the sounds of good old chum talk coming from the main bar area. The last thing I wanted to hear was other people having a good time. Even the sight of a shapely young waitress with a pigtail of flaxen fair hair failed to lift my spirits. No, Christ, don't want to be thinking of women now. That'll make me feel worse.

I sighed lightly and took a sip of my Guinness. Bit sour, could have done with a top-up of lemonade. I began to feel as if I was sinking further and further into a kind of delirium. Almost like sleeping while you're awake. Pupils back in school in a double physics lesson will know exactly what I'm talking about.

In the meantime, I'm sure the odd person or two drifted through my field of vision, although my optical sensory input didn't pick them up.

That, for the time being, was switched off, until one particularly strange object proceeded to eclipse my muddled view. A pale object that began to make a familiar sound. And when it called my name, I was snapped back from that vacuous outer space.

'John, you awake or not?'

It took a moment or two for all the marbles in my head to regroup.

The face that stared down at me at once burst open the locks off my memory banks. 'Pete!' I cried, and the person standing next to him clutching a bottle of Budweiser in his hand was none other than Simon. My two long-lost best friends.

'Shit, John . . . you're not on downers, are yer?'

'No, Christ, no!' I tried to make light of the situation, and gave myself another second to compose myself.

Christ! I hadn't seen either of them for years. We all grew up together on the Great Orme, until they moved away. Since then we'd sort of lost touch with one another. That must have been ten or fifteen years ago.

'You're not still a regular here, are you?' Pete asked, as they both joined me at my table.

Out of the three of us, Pete is the oldest, and tallest. Nowadays he is quite a strapping lad of about six foot two, with shaved bald head (nice to see someone else with even less hair than me) and a bit of a parrot nose.

We used to say that when he was a baby, his mum picked him up by his nose because she couldn't be arsed to reach down under him in the cot. On the plus side, he's always had those sobering cool mint-blue eyes to make up for it, which have never failed to pull the birds.

I'd always looked up to Pete like a big brother; he looked after us and made sure we never got into any serious trouble. Mind you, he was the only one out of us three who had a two-parent upbringing, so I guess the discipline his parents instilled in him kind of rubbed off on us.

And the bastard was bright too, academically. He could have done quite well in school if he had truly committed himself.

I think his parents had very high hopes for him when he was young, and often pressured him to do well. But the more they pushed the further Pete pulled away from all that. I suppose he just didn't like the way his life was being mapped out for him. Pete the revolutionary.

Yet in class, he was the one who never listened but was always the first to finish the assignment. Then he would just sit there gazing out of the window, waiting for everyone else to catch up.

Simon and I thanked our lucky stars we were able to sit by him and copy. But every now and again the teacher would shuffle us around a bit, especially if there was a Friday afternoon written exam.

As a reward, those who passed the test, were allowed to go early, but those who failed had to stay behind. And guess who she'd put as far away from Pete as you could get? Yes me! Typical.

Oh yes, there was nothing worse than seeing mnemonic Pete sitting at the far end of the classroom breezing through the written tests as if he'd actually written the sodding thing himself. Bastard! I hated him for that! Sometimes Simon and I used to get a bit suspicious and accuse him of shagging Miss Roberts for the answers to these tests. Just a case of sour grapes, I suppose.

I imagined Pete was the type who would grow up to be manager of a big firm, or owner of a small company somewhere. Instead he ended up working for some kind of insurance company. Still a fairly well paid job though.

As for Simon, he's just a little shorter than me. He's neither ugly nor good-looking, and at times has a tendency to be a little impulsive. In fact, he's always been a bit of a dark horse. But you need never doubt his loyalty. Often he would swear and cuss at you, but if you were in any serious strife, he'd be the first one there to help.

His most striking feature is undoubtedly his cold staring black eyes, which in moments of stress glisten like black marbles. A little unnerving for people who don't know him personally.

Nowadays, he has a mane of stringy, jet-black hair dribbling down his shoulders (which he didn't have when we were young) and looks a cross between a heavy metal rocker and a gothic – I think that's what they call them.

Unlike Pete, he was never really a brain box, which was something we both had in common. Except for his somewhat exotic sexual tastes, that is. (Wonder if he's still into lesbians?) Nevertheless, he's a sound guy in my books.

Still overcoming the shock of seeing them both again, I had to pinch myself they were actually there sitting with me. 'No! No! h-hardly come here now,' I stuttered like a buffoon. 'What are you two doing here anyhow?'

Pete first: 'Moved back to Colwyn Bay now, got a bit fed up of Bristol.'

'Yeah, I live in Rhos-on-sea now,' Simon joined in. 'Back from Manchester with me bird. Pete and I ran into each other in Llandudno the other week by pure chance. We got chatting and then you came into the conversation. We were going to arrange a get-together here for all of us. Last we knew, you were still living with your mum up the Orme. So that's where we tried, but we got no answer. But here we are, and here you are.'

'Is that fate or what?' Pete said, his favourite childhood saying, which was like turning a key to the door that has locked away all our best-kept secrets and memories for the past 20 years.

'Bloody hell, Pete, it's been a long time since I heard you say that!' And I felt myself squint a little as I used to do in my youth when I wore glasses.

'So what about you, John? Where do you live now?' Simon asked.

'Got a flat in town for a while, then met Sammy, got a house in Llandudno where the old gasworks used to be. Been with her about six years now,' I said, almost forgetting why I was sitting here in the first place.

'Not married yet then?' Pete asked, then dived into his pint of Stella.

'No . . . No!' I began fidgeting anxiously with the edge of the wax-polished table. 'Was thinking about doing it next year perhaps, then I, ur?' I felt myself backing awkwardly into a corner, so I quickly sought an escape. 'Anyway, what's brought you both back to Llandudno?'

Simon and Pete shared a look of derision. 'Woman trouble!' they said almost in unison.

I jerked back in surprise. 'What do you mean?'

Pete gulped down another mouthful of lager. 'Well, the wife left me about a month ago . . . I left her actually, and came back down here to cool off.'

'Wife?' I cried. 'How long have you been married?'

'About six years now . . . Got a kid now as well. I go down quite regularly to see him. The wife and I are going through a *trial* separation at the moment.' He rolled his eyes in torment.

I nodded with a mixture of wonder and admiration.

'What about you?' I asked Simon.

'I'm engaged at the moment, but for how long is the big question. Things are a bit rocky between us.' He flexed his eyebrows dubiously. 'She's originally a local lass, you might even know her ... Joanne Riley?' he asked, and I shook my head. 'Anyway, I've only been with her about ten months now, and she's always harked on about wanting to move back home. So I brought her back here just over a month ago, in the hope it would make her happier and perhaps help ease things between us.'

I didn't know what to say, and shook my head.

'So what's going wrong with your relationship?' Pete asked, and gulped another mouthful of lager.

'What do you mean?' I replied.

'Well, if you were happy with yours, you'd probably be sitting here with her now.'

I nodded in submission. 'I've just found out tonight that she's cheating on me.' I sank into my pint of Guinness before the sadness caught back up with me.

'You're joking!' Simon said in a way that wasn't sympathetic but calmly supportive. Obviously, he knew what I was going through.

'Join the club!' Pete raised his pint glass.

'Are you absolutely sure, though?' Simon questioned. 'I mean, if my memory serves me right, remember when we were young and how neurotic and suspicious you could get about certain things.'

I shook my head resolutely. 'Last night, I overheard her talking to her mate about this chap she kissed or something, and I caught her picking him up outside her work tonight.'

'Still listening behind closed doors?' Pete wagged his finger.

'Did she see you?' Simon asked.

I shook my head. 'No! I've got all that to look forward to when I get home.'

'What are you gonna do?' Simon asked the 64,000 dollar question.

'I honestly don't know, Si, I honestly don't know,' was all I could say.

'Could be just a fling to get your attention,' Pete suggested.

'Doesn't really matter what angle you look at it, she's still cheating. Fuck!' I banged my fist on the table, and they looked up at me. 'Just to think what she's probably doing at this minute, it's ripping me apart.' I saw the look on their faces then felt embarrassed at my outburst.

Pete continued to study me for a second, then asked Simon to get in another round. Simon got up immediately as if he sensed that Pete wanted to chat to me in private.

Pete leaned over to me. 'Look John, I know what you're feeling, it's only been about six weeks since I found out that my Jan was cheating on me!'

I looked up at him from my empty glass.

'I know it's very hard, but don't waste your time kicking yourself in the arse. I tried all that and it doesn't do you any good. If you want to get rid of some of that anger, go to the gym, or go run a few miles. Do it that way. Burn it up before it burns you!'

I smiled wryly, thinking it was a lot easier to say than to do.

Pete took in a lungful of air, and let it puff back out. I suppose he felt I was ready to hear his story. 'Do you want to hear why I left Jan?'

'Yeah, course I do, mate. Sorry I was being a bit selfish for a second.'

'Don't be silly!' He flicked my arm with his fingers. 'Anyway, with my wife Jan, when we first met, she was a really shapely size twelve girl, a real head-turner. We used to go at it like rabbits . . . all the time. Then after having our son, she just seemed to give up on wanting to have sex with me. Wouldn't let me anywhere near her. She had a bit of a rough Caesarean birth, you see, and the doctor reckoned that had something to do with it.'

I looked at him puzzled. 'Really?'

'Well, that's about the only feasible excuse she could give us. Apparently, because she had such a traumatic time, she associates all that pain with me and has in effect put up this kind of psychological barrier against me. Oh, she'll let me cuddle her and that. That's when I get around to cuddling her – I suppose I'm a bit guilty in that department, but I've never really been the affectionate kind. Maybe if I had been more affectionate and understanding in the first place we wouldn't be in this situation now . . . I don't know! At first, the doctor said it was just post-natal depression, and gave her some tablets. Didn't do anything though. Then you know what she did?'

I shook my head.

'She went out with another bloke just for the sake of trying sex with another man. Then she had the cheek to come back to me and tell me she fucking enjoyed it, so it must just be me she has the problem with.'

My eyes blazed with surprise.

'I mean, what a fucking insult. What the hell did I do wrong? It's like her shitting on my side of the bed and then rubbing my nose in it for good measure.' Pete gulped his lager as if to cool the tempest inside. 'Of course she says she loves me and doesn't want us to break up. She wants us to work it out, says it's breaking her heart. But what about what it's done to me? How the hell can you forget that? I mean, when she finally lets me make love to her, if she ever does again, how the hell am I going to get all that off my mind?'

At that moment, Simon reappeared with a tray of drinks and sat down.

'It's a wonder you didn't leave her for someone else,' I remarked.

'Well, when she told me that she'd done it with someone else and said that she felt fine, that just completely broke me.'

Simon spoke up as he began rolling a cigarette. 'Yeah, and I bet if it was you that had gone off shagging some other bird because you weren't getting it at home, you'd be called a typical male chauvinist pig. You can't win!'

I nodded in agreement and felt my eyes squint once more. 'What did you do after you found out?' I asked.

Pete made a face. 'Went ballistic, packed up my stuff, and moved back here. If it wasn't for Jeremy, I'd have put the house up for sale straight away. I had a few weeks off, and luckily got a transfer to work down here. I'm staying at my mum and dad's house now while I sort myself out. I need time to think about the future of our marriage and what not.'

I shook my head with concern, then turned to Simon, who was licking the sticky seal on his cigarette paper. 'What's your story then?'

Simon turned his black marble eyes to me. 'Well, we're still together at the moment, trying to make another go of it. But if she fucks up one more time, that's it, she's out the fucking door.'

'What's she been up to then?'

Simon tried to brave it out, but by the way he began

fidgeting with his rolled cigarette, you could see the deep hurt it was causing him.

'She's been putting it about, so to speak. She's done it to me twice now, cheated on me! One more chance I'm giving her, and that's it.'

'Like I said to you before, Si,' Pete piped in, 'after she'd done it to you once, you should have fucked her off.'

'It's a lot easier said than done though, isn't it?' Simon shrugged.

'Why does she keep doing it?' I asked.

'She's quite a bit younger than me, twenty-two actually, and she's a university student. And you know what they're like . . . She just gets a bit carried away sometimes.'

Pete and I flicked a dubious glance at one another.

'And from what you've already told me, Si, she sounds a bit of a feminist as well,' Pete added.

'Why, what do you mean?' I asked.

Simon seemed to be getting a bit flustered. I think he was running out of excuses to cover his girlfriend and didn't want to face the brutal truth.

'She just hung out with all the wrong friends at university, that's all!' he concluded.

Pete turned into Germaine Greer, the feminist. 'Basically, she thinks women of today have suffered long enough from that debilitating world of male domination and oppression. It's now time for them to rise up from those man-made shackles and endeavour to become the supreme goddesses they were always destined to be.'

'Come again?' I asked.

'She's not that bad!' Simon protested.

'No, she just expects the man to work a full day, come home, feed the kids, tidy the house, then take her out bungee-jumping or get bladdered at a rock festival for a few days.'

Simon shook his head.

'You know what excuse she gave each time she cheated on Simon? If he can't allow her to go out and explore her sexuality and help discover her true identity, then he can't truly love her. What a crock of shit, Si!'

'Did she honestly say that?' I asked incredulously.

Simon stared into his cloudy pint and nodded regretfully.

'So why don't you just go out and shag some women to find your own true identity, and see how she likes it?' I suggested.

'You want to get that sorted out, mate!' Pete, holding his glass, pointed a chunky finger at him. 'If you let her get away with that, not only will she fuck you up on the outside, she'll turn you inside out and fuck you all up in there an' all.'

'No, I've told you, if she does it again, that's it, she's down the road,' Simon snapped back.

Pete snorted contempt as he took another swig.

Listening to all of this suddenly made me realise something.

'Hang on a minute! Just what is going on here?' I announced, and both of them eyed me as if I'd just told them I was a closet transvestite. 'OK, if just one of us was having relationship troubles, that'd satisfy the norm on a statistics scale of heterosexual couples. Two of us having relationship problems, that'd be a bit of a coincidence, but all three of us at the same time, don't you think that's a little bit odd?'

'Well, what are you trying to say?' Pete queried.

'What I'm trying to say is, can't you see a bit of a pattern forming here or what? Why are we all having woman trouble at the same time? It's as if we're all cursed!'

Pete and Simon took interested sips of their drinks.

'I mean, at first, I thought it was just our bad luck, but the more I think of it . . . I've never really been able to have a proper relationship with a woman. Even you, Pete, you said yourself you've never been able to show your wife enough affection, and I suspect you, Si, have been the same.'

'Yeah, so?'

'Well, maybe we're all so emotionally damaged from – ' I almost said it: that fateful night back in the summer of '82 when we were kids.

Then Simon spoke up. 'Don't even think about that, John! It was nothing but childhood hokum, remember?'

Yet, was it? None of us had honestly sat down and chatted about it, not since that night. Perhaps to pretend it never existed was the only way our traumatised minds could barricade us from the real terror.

Speaking for myself, it was something I had long-since buried in the dark recesses of my subconscious, along with all the other eventful memories of our childhood past. That was until tonight, of course.

For just over 20 years now, Pete, Simon and I have been running away from a certain summer night when we were only 14 years old. For 20-odd years now, we have been safe from that living nightmare. And had we not met up here tonight, we might have been safe for another 20 more years.

As if we didn't have enough on our plates to worry about already.

4

Was it the right time to talk about the past? To be frank, I didn't know if I was ready or not myself. We might indeed find out some home truths about why we were all sitting here tonight. But would that be such a good thing at this moment in time?

Simon huffed out white cigarette smoke, and broke the silence.

'Let's just enjoy our little reunion, shall we?'

Thank God for Simon, I thought.

'I mean, we haven't really seen each other for near on fifteen-to-twenty years. Leave the wolf at the door just for tonight, and let's get drunk.'

Pete broke into a grin, and I joined him. 'Yeah, why not?'

We must have sat there for another hour or so. I had another pint, so did Pete. Simon, however, probably had about two or three more. As I recall, he never used to be such a heavy drinker.

We did, however, go over some of our more pleasant and sentimental childhood experiences, who wouldn't? Although we were extremely careful about which particular event in time we chose.

I, for one, really enjoyed myself, and even, for a short while, forgot about my problems with Sammy. What a laugh it turned out. I felt so relaxed and free from all that black misery. Being reunited with two of my best school chums was the best possible tonic I could have had at that time. They were my real friends, my second family.

These were people who had already seen me at my lowest. They'd seen me piss in my pants with fear, and not told anyone. They'd stood by me, no matter how bad a situation had become. My problems were always their problems, and vice versa. And no matter how badly we argued, it was never long before we made up.

In those days, life was so simple. Why does becoming an adult mean these people have to leave you? Why is it you can only stay together when you're kids? It's such a shame you have to grow out of that wonderful playground, that seemingly incessantly sunny magical kingdom where you never have to experience the hardship of earning a living. It's a place where your young inexperienced innocent minds are spared all the pain and suffering of being an adult.

Adolescence is a decade-long playtime when anyone can sow the seeds of their fantasies and dreams. There is no such thing as failure, pressure, poverty, depression. At that age you can be anybody you want, and do almost anything you wish, without having to actually go out and strive for it.

Life even gives you a memento of those excellent times in the form of little mental Polaroids that nobody can take away from you. And they never get lost.

However, every now and again, someone inadvertently leaves the safety gate hanging open to that sacred playground, allowing an uninvited guest to slip through. Someone much too old to play your silly little games, someone who wants to play different, scary, real games.

Someone who tarnishes our innocence with filthy promises and malicious lies, and spreads consternation throughout the group.

But no! I already said I wasn't going to go on to that ... Not yet!

Let's just talk about the rest of the evening.

To be perfectly honest, I could have stayed in the warm company of my good friends all night. It was like another little den for grown-ups, away from daily responsibilities, away from the henpecking women, away from the common rules of decency.

Don't be silly ... Act your age ... Oh, you pervert, there's something wrong with you if you think that. No, there'll be none of that tonight. In the lads' room you can be your true self, act the way you really want, say what you really want.

Go on, get it off your chest, we don't shock easily. Do you know, I like to put my wife's knickers on my head and chase her around the bedroom. Really! Well, you see that barmaid over there, I'd love to throw her over my knee and play the bongos with her arse, she's given me a right hard-on. Fine, go ahead that's quite acceptable. Is there anything else you want to tell us? Yeah, I think I'm starting to get a bit drunk.

Well, there's absolutely nothing wrong with that. Why don't you have another drink? Yes ... No! perhaps not, I can hear that voice telling me 'No more! Time to go home.'

'Arh, shit, you going home already, are you?' Pete grumbled.

'Got to, I'm afraid ... Things to sort out,' I sighed.

'G'luck mate!' Simon stretched out his sweaty hand, and I took it. He was well and truly plastered, and those black eyes of his were treading water in their sockets. Meanwhile, Pete was busy trying to scribble down something on one of the dog-eared beer mats, his bowed sweaty bald crown like a glistening pink egg.

'Listen, John me ol' mate, here's my number. Give us a ring, we'll do it again sometime next week, all right?'

I took the beer mat and stuffed it in my pocket. I was too drunk to copy it onto my mobile phone, I would do it tomorrow.

'Yeah, I'd like that!' I shook hands with him, and feeling as if I had to almost tear myself away, like a kid from a funfair, I staggered my way out.

Outside, I felt the cold night air bite, but I was lucky to have a warm blanket of drink wrapped around me, so I couldn't feel it. I burped, and shook my fuzzy head to try to wake up all the little soldiers in there; they had much work to do.

Passing the Great Orme tram station, I almost saluted the grand old Victorian tramcar inside, which under the illuminations, looked proud and majestic.

On my way down to the taxi-stand on Gloddaeth Avenue, thoughts of Sammy and what I was going to do about her began to sober me up somewhat. Shit, what am I going to say to her? Why do I have to go through all this tonight? Why does this have to spoil such a good evening, seeing friends I hadn't seen for years?

There were plenty of taxis to choose from, and soon I was on my way home. The ride was so warm and soothing, I could have easily told the driver, don't turn at the Links Hotel roundabout, but keep going in the opposite direction, and don't stop until you see the sunrise. Maybe in the morning I'll be ready to go back home and try to sort things out.

It was very tempting, but I said nothing and was dropped off at the entrance to our estate, where I began the long and brooding walk up to our close.

Before inserting the front door key, I took a second to brace myself, then scoffed at the absurdity of being so afraid of entering my own home.

The front door shut behind me so loudly, you'd have thought it was wired up to a pair of stereo speakers. I knew she was in the living room because the door stood slightly ajar, as if she'd pushed it to, to keep in the warmth. I felt uncomfortable about going in there, and went through to the kitchen instead. I wanted her to come to me and ask where I'd been.

I slunk clumsily into one of the kitchen chairs, which scraped the vinyl floor. While I waited for Sammy to come through, I pretended to read the front cover of our local weekly newspaper. Despite having taken plenty of Dutch courage, I stil felt as if I was going to give birth to a double-decker bus. Tonight all would be revealed.

In all, I had to wait about two or three minutes before Sammy's inquisitiveness finally got the better of her. The moment I saw her, my whole body reacted like petals of a flower withering at the breath of some contaminated evil.

'You're home late! Where've you been?'

'Out!' I grumbled, turning back to the newspaper.

While Sammy went to the fridge to find something to eat, I peeked at her slyly.

'Oh, I forgot to tell you last week that we were invited to Tracy's birthday party tonight.' She grimaced as she sniffed inside a tub of coleslaw that was on the turn. 'I didn't fancy going though, and I know you wouldn't have wanted to go anyway, so that's why I probably forgot to mention it. Her boyfriend Danny has got her a really nice ring,' she said.

I snorted to myself, saying in my head, You should have said to me that you wanted to go, that would have given you the perfect excuse to fuck around with that prick, and I never would have found out.

'Saw Harold again today.' She tried to make conversation. 'Guess what he did this week when I helped him with his shopping?' She was referring to that old man customer who comes in shopping every week, but I wasn't in the mood to listen, and rattled the paper miserably.

Irritated by the silent treatment, she turned. 'You've been a bit quiet since you came in. Still got that stomach upset?'

'Nope!' I retorted, determined not even to look at her.

Sammy flicked the fridge closed, and I heard her knee crack as she stood up. Then she unplugged the jug-kettle and began to fill it with water.

'Where've you been then?'

Every question she asked was like a pickaxe blow on my skull, and I couldn't take it much longer.

'What do you care?' I snapped.

Her face immediately dropped. 'What's that supposed to mean?'

I turned to her as she stood waiting for the kettle to boil. 'You know full well what I mean!'

'No I don't!' She threw me a filthy look and turned back to the simmering kettle. It looked as if she was so guilty she couldn't bear to look me in the face. This only infuriated me even more. All I could see in my mind now was this red vision of her getting humped in the back of my car down some dark back road. I stormed over to her.

'Why did you do it, Sam? Why did you fucking do it?'

I pinned her in the corner between the sink and the microwave. She had such a fright, she dropped the mug, which smashed to pieces by our feet.

'Why, Sam? Why, why, why?' I gripped her warm fragile shoulders and screamed into her face.

Fear and confusion blazed from her popping blue eyes, and for one sobering moment, I could imagine how a woman must look when she is being raped. That was when I tried to apply the brakes, but it was too late. There was no way to stem the raging torrent that had been unleashed.

'What are you doing? Stop it! Stop it!' she cried.

'You've been fucking about behind my back, haven't you? Haven't you?'

'No! Course I haven't! What's the matter with you? You've been drinking, haven't you?'

'Don't fucking lie to me, Sam, I saw you!'

'Saw me what? Saw me *what*?'

She started pulling away, so I gripped her tighter. No way was she going to run away from this one.

'You're hurting me . . . Stop it!' she cried.

'Tell me, Sam! Tell me why you're doing this to me?'

'I'm not doing anything?'

I fisted the wall cabinet, rattling the crockery inside, and Sammy cowered down in fright. 'You're . . . a . . . fucking . . . liar!' I blasted in her face, her eyes flinching at every seething word, and my spittle showering her cheeks.

By the look on her face, she must have thought I'd lost control. All of a sudden, I wasn't the person she thought she knew. This was not the gentle John she had had playful fights with in the past. Not the John who would only use minimum force against her, because he was scared to death he might hurt her. Not the John who would always let go of her the second she gave in. And this was certainly not the John she thought she could trust to father her children.

Christ, even I didn't recognise this raging monster inside me. This was the first time I had ever become so physically violent with her.

In a split second, I turned from being her soulmate, her soul-protector, into her nemesis, her arch enemy, even her executioner. I saw it in her eyes, that blind, terror-stricken panic to hold onto her precious life. Surely to God she didn't think I was going to kill her?

All I wanted to do was show how much she had hurt me. Show her that she had no right to do this to me, and show her that I meant it. But I guess I had gone too far.

She panicked, and tore away from my vicelike grip, but tripped over my right leg and slapped onto the hard vinyl floor. I just caught the sickening sound of her knee cap cracking like a hollow piece of wood.

Immediately, she grabbed her knee and gasped for breath, the shocking pain taking away her breath. It was as if someone had thrown a bucket of ice-cold water over me, quashing all the boiling anger and hate inside me. The old John woke up with a start.

'Are you all right?' I asked guiltily.

She didn't answer, she was too busy floundering in a sea of pain to care about anything else. I'd probably get it later. Boy, would I get it later!

I knelt down beside her, placing a sorrowful hand on her leg. 'Sammy, I didn't mean for that to happen, honestly.'

Indignantly, she snatched her leg away. 'Get away from me! Get away from me!' she sobbed, so I kept my distance.

In the meantime, all I could do was wait for her to compose herself, and hope things weren't too bad.

Carefully, she climbed back to her feet, and again I asked her if she was all right. Totally ignoring me, she pulled up the leg of her tracksuit bottoms, revealing a bloodied knee the size of cricket ball. The cut was just below the kneecap and reminded me of a jam doughnut.

'Shit!'

'Look what you've done.' She glared at me. 'You pushed me.'

'I didn't push you!' I retorted. 'You tripped over me trying to get away.'

Sammy hopped to the sink, tore off a sheet of kitchen roll, and began to dab it gently. I have to admit the gash did look pretty deep and gruesome.

'I think it may need a few stitches,' I suggested.

She wet another sheet of kitchen tissue, and began to hobble out of the kitchen.

'Do you want me to take you to the hospital?' I asked.

She stopped dead and gave me a real fetid glare. 'From now on I don't want you anywhere near me, understand?' Then she hobbled away.

I leant back against the sink and eyed the mess on the floor in front of me. I felt like a naughty schoolboy told to stand outside the headmaster's office. Don't just stand there looking at it, boy, clear it up, the resounding voice shouted inside, so I did.

Briskly, I collected up all the large, sharp pieces, and dropped them in the plastic bin with a loud clink. Next I thought about what I should say to Sammy when she'd calmed down.

Suddenly, I heard the front door slam shut. What the hell, I muttered, and dashed out, just catching Sam, pulling the driver's door shut on the Fiesta.

'Where are you going?' I asked, but she completely ignored me, fired up the Fiesta, and reversed away.

I stood there waiting for some kind of explanation, but all I got was the car's brake lights winking goodbye to me as it disappeared round the corner. And that was that!

But before slinking back indoors, I glanced discreetly about the close, to make sure there weren't any prying neighbours peeping from behind their curtains.

Later, as I sat in front of the TV I felt so frustrated, I wanted to slam my head into the living room wall. Alternatively, there was an empty mug at my feet, which nearly became part of the wallpaper, but I just managed to stop myself. I couldn't believe it, things were even worse now than they were before, and now it was me who had become the bloody bad guy. How the hell did that happen?

Why did she have to trip and gash her knee? Why did it have to happen at that moment? Why did I feel as if I'd pushed her?

Doesn't matter what she's done now, does it? Oh yes, I heard the voice of my conscience speak. She might have cheated on you, but there was no call for all that, was there? You're no better than all those other cowardly thugs out there who beat their women . . . Oh come on, I'm not that bad, I didn't hit her! . . . That's not the point though, is it? As a result of what happened, you might as well say you had. Why couldn't you have sat her down like a responsible adult, and just used words to express how you felt? Why did you have to resort to violence? There's no excuse for that, no matter what she's done.

So now I'm labelled as a woman beater, am I? All those years I've prided myself on never laying a finger on a woman. Unlike all those psychotic bastards out there who can only hit women because they know women aren't tough enough to hit them back.

True, I did go over the top losing my temper, which I regret. And when I saw her smash her knee, I felt like shit. But, remember, that was an accidental trip, I didn't push her, or bounce her off my fists. I'd never hurt her like that – never have done, never will do! . . . Unless she attacked me with a knife or something, but that'd be a completely different situation.

Oh yeah? Is that what Sammy's thinking right now, sitting in the casualty department with a suspected broken knee?

Well, whether I'm right or not, I bet she'll use what's happened tonight as a golden excuse to end our relationship and go off with that prick . . . Serves you right if she does!

Suddenly, the phone rang, braking me from my quarrel with my conscience.

'Hello?' I sighed, expecting it to be one of Sammy's friends or something.

'It's me!' Sammy replied.

I sat up alert. 'How's your knee?'

'It's all right! It's not broken, and didn't need stitching.'

'Good! That's something at least. So where are you?'

'At my mother's! I've decided to stay here for a while.'

'Why are you staying there? We've still got to talk this thing out. It's no good running away from it.'

Sammy sighed tediously. 'Running away from what?'

'Christ, Sam, you're not still denying it, are you?'

'Look, John, I'm not going to have a slanging match over the phone at my mother's. All I wanted to say was that after your behaviour tonight I think it's best I don't come home. You really frightened me tonight.'

'Yeah, I know, and I'm sorry that happened, but it was an accident, remember? If you'd hadn't struggled to get away you wouldn't have tripped would you?'

'I shouldn't have had any reason to struggle away from you in the first place, John!'

I sighed in admission. 'Yes I know, but it wasn't as if I was going to belt you one or anything, I just wanted you to see how much you hurt me. Christ, you should know me well enough to know that by now. I mean, how would you react if you thought I was cheating on you?' Once again, I felt I was having to defend myself.

'Look, John, I'm going OK? I'm sick and tired of you accusing me. It's you that needs to sort yourself out, not me. I'm going. Goodbye.' The line went dead, and that was it.

Well, if that's your attitude after me trying to apologise for tonight, then sod you! I chucked the cordless receiver on the couch beside me. You're the one that's been screwing about, not me. And just because you tripped and gashed your knee, that doesn't pardon you either.

That's it then! I slumped miserably into my armchair, trying to focus on the film on telly and block out all this turmoil around me. But it was no use.

That night in bed, I don't think I slept a wink, it was like trying to sleep on a gorse bush. All I kept seeing in my mind was the terrified look in Sammy's eyes that she might get her head smashed in. And the pitiful sight of her crumpled on the kitchen floor clutching her injured knee. In actual fact, that hurt me just as much as finding out she'd cheated.

5

At 6 a.m. the following morning, the alarm clock wailed at me like a banshee, and I sat bolt upright. Then someone took a run at me from behind with a cricket bat to the head . . . Hello hangover.

Reluctantly, I opened my eyes to total darkness and despair, and no Sammy. Such a forlorn place as this was surely a glimpse of what hell would be like if I was unfortunate enough to go down when my time came.

I rose, washed and breakfasted with the heaviest of hearts, then at about 6.45, in the coldest of blue dawns, I walked to the entrance of the estate to await my lift to work.

The depression I felt at that particular time, I could honestly understand how all those desperate lost souls in the world must feel when suicide is the only way out.

Mike picked me up, and the journey to work seemingly passed in a deep haze; all I did was just sit there. Poor Mike must have found making conversation with me very hard work indeed.

Over the last three years, Mike and I have got to know each other pretty well and disclosed a fair bit to one another about our personal lives. Which, I guess, is quite understandable when you share a cab with someone eight hours a day, five days of the week.

But I was so cabbaged about what had happened with Sammy last night, I couldn't have talked about it, even if I'd wanted to. The other morning was bad enough, this was even worse.

In the end I had to lie that I had a hangover to explain my miserable black mood, although I don't know whether he believed me or not.

From then on, I couldn't even remember going to the depot to clock on. Or picking up our load, getting the paperwork for the day, and having a last-minute mug of tea in the canteen with the other lads.

The only respite came on our first call for the day, when Mike and I were treated to a full breakfast by one of the more hospitable landlords on our route.

Finally, I saw light at the end of the tunnel, the end of an extremely long and draining day, we were on our way back home. Inside, my stomach began to warm with the hope of Sammy coming back home tonight after work. Even though we'd still probably end up with another debacle. But I didn't care about that at the moment; at least she'd be there, and that alone would be worth the trouble.

I bet myself that while I'd been at work, she'd already been home to sort out a few things and what not. Wish I could have been a fly on the wall to see what kind of a mood she was in.

Mike dropped me off, and I began preparing myself for what promised to be quite an eventful evening. I already knew Sammy would be at work, so that eased the pressure somewhat.

When I went in, I was greeted by the few pots I'd left in the draining rack this morning. Contrary to what I'd thought, Sammy hadn't been back. If she had, she would have tidied the pots – I know her. And she'd have left a note to say she'd been home.

For a second, I stood there still holding my small canvas backpack, trying to work out what her game plan was.

Either, she had gone straight to work from her mother's and planned to come back home later on. Or she'd taken all this much further than I'd anticipated. Maybe she'd already moved in with her new lover. I'd just have to wait and see.

No! She'd just decided to stay at her mother's a bit longer, that's all. If things were any different, she would have told me last night.

With that, I went about doing my usual after-work chores.

In fact, so sure was I that Sammy was coming back home later, I began treating the day like any other. I even made her tea for when she finished work.

At about 9 p.m. that evening, quarter of an hour before she usually arrived home, I began imagining what it'd be like actually losing Sammy. Up until now, I was more concerned whether or not I would take her back after she cheated on me. But what I hadn't taken into consideration was, what if she'd decided to go off with this person for good?

What if it didn't even matter whether I forgave her or not? Where would that leave me? First, I'd have no Sammy to come home to at the end of the day. And second, I'd be plunged back into the lonely, sad life of a single person again that nobody wants. No! I had to admit, the bare idea turned me cold with dread.

Then there was the house to take care of, shopping, cleaning – everything. Christ, I shuddered, which was I more afraid of, the breakdown of my relationship, or the breakdown of my home?

Answer ... both, yet until now I hadn't given much thought to the latter.

Incidentally, just in case you were wondering, with regards to the actual domestic chores and the basic running of the house, Sammy takes care of the shopping and washing. My job is to keep the place looking tidy, and make most of the meals. Occasionally, I do handle some of the shopping and the washing chores. (Aren't I a good boy?)

As for paying the bills, direct debit from my account takes care of that, so that's something I wouldn't have to worry about.

Needless to say, home wouldn't be the same without Sammy. I just couldn't imagine what it'd be like without her in it.

However, when, or if she does come back home tonight, how should I treat her? I wondered. Do I wait for her to have her tea, settle down, ask her about her knee, then ask straight out for the truth? Or do I jump straight down her throat the second she steps in, and get it sorted right away?

Perhaps it'd be better just to wait for her to speak and hear what she says.

... Yeah make sure you don't lose it this time! I heard the voice of my conscience speak. Whatever she says, try to keep your cool, don't screw it up like last night...

I glanced at the time, which read 9.24. One thing's for sure, by tomorrow morning, I'll know whether or not I'm going to be a single tenant in this house. There's no way I'm going back to work in the morning like a headless chicken again, not knowing what the hell I'm doing, or where I'm going.

Thank God we don't have any children at this period in our lives.

She should be here soon – have I time to make a quick cuppa before she arrives? Naw, don't think I'll bother. Probably end up throwing it at her and break another mug. (Just joking – about throwing the mug at her that is.)

The last time I felt this nervous about seeing Sammy was our first night out together.

Outside I heard a car pulling into the close and my heart yo-yo'd up and down my body. I just sat tight, and waited.

A minute ticked by, two. Obviously it wasn't Sammy at all. I dared to peek out from behind the curtains, and found the neighbour's car had just been parked in his driveway. Huffing a sigh of frustration, I plonked back into the easy chair.

'Where the hell is she?'

By 9.41 I knew for certain she wasn't coming home, even if she had been working late. So the question again was what the hell was she doing, and why didn't she at least let me know?

Whatever the outcome, I needed to know what was happening, so I phoned her workplace.

Not surprisingly, I was told she'd left about half an hour ago. OK, I thought, so she has to be either at her mother's or . . . at someone else's.

I phoned her mother's and lo and behold, guess who answered?

'Sammy, what the hell's going on? Are we going to sort this out or what?' I hammered down the receiver.

But judging by the lengthy time it took her to reply, it was clear she didn't want to talk to me.

'John . . . I think it's best we don't see each other for a

while.' She sighed. 'I'm going to stay here at my mother's to think things through.'

'Think things through? Should be me thinking things through. You're the one . . .'

'John, I've told you I'm not going to have a slanging match over the phone.'

'Then come over here so we can sort it out!'

'What? So you can stand there shouting and bawling at me for – '

'Look, Sam! You're gonna have to face up to it sometime, you can't just run away from it forever . . .'

'I'm not running away from anything, it's you that's – '

'Bloody hell!' I cut her off. 'should be me going off with the hump not – '

'You see? That's why I didn't come home tonight. In the whole six years I've known you, all you've done is accuse me of seeing people behind your back.'

'Oh, so that's your excuse is it? I've been accusing you for so'long now, you might as well go out and do it?'

Sammy groaned helplessly as she was being drawn into the showdown she'd been trying to avoid. And even though I had promised myself not to go at her like a bull in a china shop, I just couldn't help myself tearing into her again!

I could hear my conscience screaming at me, For Christ's sakes, you're doing it again, you're gonna blow it . . . But it was useless trying to fight it. I felt like a jet-fighter pilot spiralling down to earth, out of control, facing certain death, and too late to eject to safety. There was no escape, and nothing to stop me from crashing. It was hopeless!

'Come on, Sam, just admit it to me now, put me out of my misery, you're seeing someone else, aren't you? I know you are!'

'You're just never going to change, are you?' she droned on.

'Come on then, admit it.' I squeezed the plastic handset so hard it began to crack.

'John I'm putting the phone down now. By the way, I've already been home to get enough stuff to last while I'm here.'

So she had been home, after all! She could have at least done the pots while she was here. 'So while I'm at work you're gonna start sneaking back here until you've got everything?'

'No! It's not like that at all! Last night was the final straw, enough is enough!'

'Christ! Talk about overreacting. What about some of the times you've accused me of cheating?' In truth this probably only amounted to maybe once or twice in our relationship; as opposed to the dozens of times I had actually accused her, but who's counting? And anyway, when you're pointing an empty gun at someone, they don't know the chamber is empty, do they? Metaphorically speaking, of course.

'Oh come on, John, I've hardly ever accused you!'

I cringed to myself, knowing this was true, but I had to keep her talking somehow. 'Yes, you have quite a few times, and I didn't pack my stuff and leave, did I?'

But Sammy had already given up fighting this futile argument.

'John, I've got to go now.' Which really meant, I can't be arsed to talk to you any more, so bugger off.

That second I wanted to say, So that's it then, is it? We're finished? Call her bluff. But in the mood she was in, she might agree, and the whole thing would backfire. Case closed.

Nevertheless I had to show her I was just as strong. I certainly wasn't going to beg her to come home; remember, she was the one that left me. 'Yeah, I've got to go too,' I said finally. 'Ta ra.' And put the phone down.

You stubborn git! My conscience slapped me in the face. Have you already forgotten how you felt last night? What did I tell you before? Oh, you've really fucked it up now! . . . Yes I know, I replied, and here comes another tidal wave of depression ready to devour me. Here we go again! *Whoosh*!

Back I slumped into the easy chair and just shook my head. What else was there to do? With both hands gripping the arms of the chair, I held on for dear life and let that furious wave ride itself out.

Why is it when women do something wrong, they try to turn us into the bad guys? Christ, if it had been me that had done the dirty, Sammy would have already kicked me out of the house. And I would have accepted that as part of my punishment.

I bet now, whenever her friends want to know what happened between us, she'd tell them I drove her to it. It was my fault for being so insecure and over-possessive.

And they'd probably reply, 'Oh, in that case, Sammy, you're probably better off without him.'

Or if the shoe was on the other foot and I'd cheated on her, it'd be, 'Oh he's not worth it then, he's just a rat like all the others. You're probably better off without him.' You can't win!

Why couldn't she just come out and say it? OK, John, yes, I've been seeing someone behind your back. I'm so sorry. Can you ever forgive me? Or, I'm not sorry, in fact I'm leaving you for . . . whoever that person was?

At least then I'd know where I stood, instead of having

to run around in bloody circles with my head up my arse. Maybe it's true what they say, 'Women are the best and worst of God's creations'.

Don't think I'll ever bother with relationships after this . . .

6

Summer '82

'Fucking girls!' I hissed as I clung to the flaky branch of a pine tree some 30 feet above the ground. There I was, a 14-year-old boy in his tee shirt and jeans, seeking a solitary spot to deal with the pain and humiliation of being teased about his dolphin-like forehead.

It was the first day of the summer holidays, late July 1982. The Argentine forces had surrendered at Port Stanley, ending the Falklands War, Italy had won the World Cup, and Martina Navratilova had won her third successive Wimbledon title. The main box office hits in the cinema at that time were *ET* and *Rocky 3*.

In the music charts, the new romantic pop groups like Bow, Wow, Wow, Duran Duran, and Depeche Mode were clambering over each other to get to the number one slot.

It was the year of some pretty weird haircuts too, like the mullet (short and spiky on top, and long at the back, sometimes dyed), Gerry curls, wet looks, and Sunsilk hair sprays. And last but not least, on the TV we had the brilliantly funny sitcom called *The Young Ones*. Fantastic!

As I gazed out from the tree, the crisp morning sun, a

white molten eye, beamed down from a mint-blue sky, making dappled patterns through the dense woodlands on the Great Orme.

That's where Pete, Simon and I spent most of our growing-up years, 679 feet above the marshy land of the Creuddyn peninsula, better known as the Victorian seaside resort of Llandudno.

Coming to the woods? we used to say to one another, and we'd all trundle down to acres of forestry running down the north side of the great mountain. It was our own vast back garden, where we lived out all our childhood adventures.

How fortunate we three innocent young kids were to have such a place to hang out! But as fate would have it, how unfortunate we were that particular summer. And by the time it ended we had lost both our innocence and our youth.

'John! . . . John!' My name echoed in the clearing around the miniature golf course

I hoped they wouldn't have found me so soon, and I hurriedly swiped a tear from my cheek.

'Where the fuck is he?' Pete and Simon cried in their bray-like voices that had only just broken.

I thumbed my glasses back up and turned to see how far away they were. As they descended the footpath towards me, I just caught sight of Simon's short dark hair in between the green leaves of a nearby birch tree.

Should I give myself a few more moments to compose myself, or just give myself away? I thought. Might as well let them know.

'I'm up here!' I wailed down to them like a little girl (my voice hadn't quite broken yet).

Simon and Pete looked up at me, their faces like two

white ping-pong balls. 'What the fuck are you doing up there?' Pete cried.

'Nothing!' I muttered down at them miserably.

'You comin' down, or are we comin' up?'

'Come up!' I said, and within a few seconds, I could feel the mighty tree totter as they scrambled up the ladder of branches like two spider monkeys.

Out of the three of us, Pete was definitely the best climber, and when it came to heights he had nerves of steel. Once I foolishly dared him to hang upside down from a branch 20 feet above the ground. That was nothing! He even dangled by one arm, and then had to pull himself back up to safety. Mad bastard!

Simon was also a fairly good climber, and any tree Pete conquered, he would have to do it too. I, on the other hand, had a bit of a fear of heights (acrophobia, I think it's called) and would usually freeze halfway up.

Yet today, I didn't seem to be doing too badly.

Pete reached me first, and clambered around to get a good sitting position, shaking the tree top even more. I tightened my hold on the branch, and closed my eyes to steel myself against feeling dizzy.

As Simon appeared, his arm brushed my leg, and I could smell Hubba-Bubba strawberry bubblegum on his breath.

'Give us one!' I ordered.

'Haven't got any more, Pete had my last.'

Pete blew a big bubblegum smile down at me, then asked, 'Why did you shoot off before? Was it because of that stupid Karen?'

Before I replied, he dropped a blob of spit to see if it would reach the ground without hitting any branches.

'She's just a stupid bitch!' I hissed.

Pete scoffed at my wimpishness. 'If she takes the piss out of you, give it her back!'

I could feel a cry well up inside me, but quickly stifled it.

Meanwhile, Simon snapped off some dry twigs beside me. 'You're not miffed 'cause of that, are you? Fuck it, she's not worth it!'

'No! . . . I'm not!' I lied.

'Anyway, she's got tits like a sparrow, so I don't know what she's talking about.' Pete spat again.

I coughed a little laugh. 'Yeah, fuck it!' I squinted, thumbing the bridge of my Ronnie Corbett-type glasses back up again.

'Hey, you've climbed quite high today, John.' Pete bounced a twig off Simon's head to get his attention. 'Fancy tackling the squirrel tree today? Could be fate or what?' He had that challenging gleam in his eye.

'Fuck that!' I said straight away. 'I've already told you I'm not ready to die just yet.'

'Come on, John, up until now, you're the only one who hasn't conquered it. It's becoming embarrassing!' Simon added. 'Just think, in about ten minutes' time you could have already done it and that'd be it.'

But I shook my head steadfastly.

'Wimp!' Pete tutted.

The infamous 'squirrel tree' they were both referring to was the tallest known tree on the Great Orme, a grand old pine about 60 or 70 feet in height. Until now, only the gallant handful of 'Ormies' (the nickname for the Great Orme kids) had succeeded in scaling right up to the very pinnacle.

Pete and Simon, incidentally, were among those honoured few, and already had their names proudly etched into its scaly bark. To them, I was letting the side down, and that summer, they constantly badgered me about it, hoping I would give in.

Yet I was in no particular hurry to risk my scrawny little neck falling from the top of that wooden death trap, thank you very much. Especially as there were a line of spiked railings at the bottom, that looked like a voodoo chief's tooth necklace.

'I'm going to the top!' Pete said, and off he climbed.

'You comin?' Simon asked, hot on his heels.

Not when the whole tree began to shake dizzily again with all their clambering about. Even looking up at them made it feel as if I was looping the loop on a roller-coaster ride.

The basic shape of a tree always reminds me of a wrist and hand sticking out of the earth, with the gnarled fingers reaching for the sky. Each one of these claw-like fingers makes an ideal hummock on which to recline. If you had the nerve, that is. Even seeing Pete and Simon casually lying there some 30 feet above the ground as if they were in their own back gardens, it was completely beyond me.

Bastard! I wish I had the courage to join them, I thought. Why don't I just do it? It can't be that bad, surely. Then I suddenly got angry with myself. I thought of Karen the bitch and her friends laughing at me just because my forehead stuck out a bit more than usual.

Kids can be really cruel, they're like monsters, they have no conscience, show no remorse, and if they discover your weaknesses, you're in big trouble.

OK, so I do have a bit of a big forehead. I know I've got a big forehead, I can see it every morning when I look in the bathroom mirror. But I've learnt to live with it, so why can't they?

And in any case there's nothing I can do about it, so

why don't I show them all by stopping snivelling and climb up this fucking tree? At least it's not the squirrel tree. Bugger it! If I fall, I fall! At least I'll die fighting.

Aggressively, I reached for a higher branch and pulled myself up. I stepped up another and kept going. Am I there yet? No, you've only gone two feet. Shit! Keep going.

Cautiously, I increased my ascent, face almost grating the rough bark, and the pungent smell of lime-sap burning into my brain. Soon I had reached Simon's foot.

'Fuck in hell! Look who's here,' he sang.

I mustered a nervous smile, my face squinting erratically and my glasses had steamed up. I now stood below them, straddling two branches the width of telegraph poles, my hands and legs trembling with fear.

'Here, John. There's a space here we've always reserved for this occasion. Glad you could join us!'

Acting while I still had the adrenaline rush, I scrambled up a bit further and wedged myself in between two branches that looked like a crab's claw. I looked down for one fleeting second, and saw an image of me flip-flopping down through a spiral of branches that seemingly went on forever. A vision I didn't particularly need right now.

I pinned my head against the coarse bark, and tried to think of something else. Simon watched me with derision. 'Don't worry, John, you won't fall . . . Look!' He seized two branches and began swaying the tree top again.

'Stop it, Si, or I'm going down!' I cried.

'Yeah don't, Si. If you shit him up now, he'll never do the squirrel,' Pete barked at him.

Simon stopped, and blew me a big bubblegum smile.

'See, it's not so bad up here, is it?' Pete wriggled comfortably.

'Yeah, it's great!' I replied sardonically.

'Have a look around, get used to it a bit.'

'Yeah, perhaps when I've done this about another fifty times I will!' I huffed. Soon, however, I began to relax a bit more, and even enjoyed a laugh until Pete ruined it by climbing up to the very last few shoots of the tree.

Why did he have to do that? Why couldn't he have just stayed put?

Simon nudged me to follow, and despite hearing that warning voice in my head saying, You're pushing your luck now, mate, I followed them.

As I emerged from the pine needles, warm yellow sunlight hit my head and shoulders. From there, I could see the top of Haulfrie mountain in all its colourful splendour, I could see some of the roof tops of the houses on Llwynon Road. And when I turned the other way I could see an ocean of chipping-sized buildings some four hundred feet down in the town below.

I had conquered my first tree, and it felt terrific.

Pete joyously broke into song. 'Nice one, Cyril, nice one son . . .' And so on.

'See? Karen and her shitty friends don't bother us, do they?' Simon shot a two-fingered salute at them.

Then we all whooped and yowled at the tops of our voices, like a troop of howler monkeys. I turned to Pete and asked him, 'I don't have a forehead like a dolphin, do I?'

And he curtly replied, 'Naw, course you don't, but you're as ugly as fuck.'

'Gangly turd!' I retorted.

So, basically, that was how we spent the first day of our school holidays, and as I think back now, it couldn't have been any better.

7

Some 20 years later, back in the safe confines of my easy chair, I padded my forehead with my fingers and was satisfied to find it wasn't like a dolphin's head any more. One of the benefits of adulthood.

Once again, Simon's 14-year-old voice echoed inside my head: *Karen and her shitty friends don't bother us, do they?* And I remembered his two-fingered salute to them. I wished it was that simple right now.

What I'd give to hear my two mates knocking at my front door this moment. I felt like shit, I honestly did! And almost gave Pete a ring on his mobile for a chat. Had I not remembered he had domestic problems of his own to sort out, I probably would have done so.

Strange they should turn up like that in the King's Head last night. 'Fate or what?' Pete would say.

Speaking of which, what about Pete's situation? Imagine your wife going off sex with you, and then having sex with another man just to find out if she's normal. That itself would be bad enough, without having her turn round and say she enjoyed it as well. Now if that isn't the ultimate insult!

Pete himself always struck me as a one-woman man. In my mind, I knew that if he ever settled down with someone, it'd probably be for keeps. During our teens he never went out with that many girls, he was definitely more fastidious than Simon and me.

Meanwhile Simon's relationship with his margarine-legged girlfriend (she spreads her legs very easily) seems to be hanging on by a thread. One more hard tug of infidelity, and that'll be it. Or so he told us. I wonder why he's gone for someone so young.

With Simon, I get the feeling, it'll always be a case of 'this is definitely her last chance'. To be honest, he's always been a bit on the gullible side when it came to the opposite sex. I don't know whether or not it was because we were only kids, but he never took any of them that seriously. I'm sure he thought girls were like pets, just give them their daily dose of attention, and let them have whatever they need.

When we were young, Pete and I used to go mad at him for giving things away to girls, anything he had in is pocket from chewies to money. They all knew he'd just give it them if they asked.

Secretly, I think he was getting something in return, probably a flash of their knickers or a promise of a feel in the woods later on. Can't imagine why else he'd do it. Don't get me wrong, he was always a sound guy, just a bit of a perve, and I mean that in the best possible way. I just hope that the woman he's with now doesn't take advantage of him too much.

As for me, with my Ronnie Corbett glasses and my slightly protruding forehead, I had to take whatever girl came along.

Thankfully, nowadays I no longer need those ridiculous-looking goggles, and the calcium deposits in my skull have evened out that ugly-looking swelling. But back then, my slight physical anomaly did prove to be a bit of hindrance for me, especially when it came to girls. Which was why during my late teens and early twenties, I tended to keep away from the dating scene.

My family background wasn't what you'd actually call the norm either. I was brought up as an only child by my mother. My father died in a mototcycle accident when I was four, so I don't recall that much about him. Hence there wasn't much to miss.

Just for the record, he was riding his Triumph Bonneville on his way home from work one winter evening, when two stupid bastards were racing two-abreast round a bend. One hit my father head-on, and that was it! He was killed instantly.

These days, I suppose those so-called child psychologists would label that as a dysfunctional family life. But if that was the case, then many of the kids on the Orme also suffered from the same fate, although most of them seemed to turn out fairly normal.

Understandably, it was hard for us both at first, particularly my mother. But we coped, I was never left wanting for anything, and in hindsight, we had a very happy home life. However, in the intervening years, when there were other men in my mother's life, I used to get a bit edgy and worry that one of these strange men was going to take my place. At night, I often used to eavesdrop behind the living room door, a habit that became hard to break, and one that even followed me into adult life.

But none of these men turned out to be a serious threat, and my mum remained a widow. Once I remember asking her why she didn't settle down with anyone else, and she just said she wasn't ready.

For her sake, I hope in her twilight years she does find someone to grow old with. I wouldn't like to see her lonely for the rest of her life. She deserves much better than that!

As I've already explained, Pete was the only one who grew up having two parents (his mother worked as a receptionist – his father was a mechanic), although sometimes when they argued, he often wished he didn't have any parents at all.

That was one of a few advantages of having only one parent – there were never any unpleasant domestic fights going on. And on the whole, home life didn't seem to be as strict.

On the other hand, Simon's situation was similar to my own, except he was brought up by his grandmother, while his mother went off to London to pursue a career with a singing troupe of some kind. Although in all fairness, she never forgot his birthdays and always came home for Christmas.

Like me, Simon never knew his father, who apparently is still alive somewhere in this big, wide world, and probably doesn't even know he has a son. Yet Simon hasn't ended up insecure (unlike me).

I suppose it boils down to your own self-esteem, and just how much you value yourself. The world is like a mirror: if you scowl bitterly into it, it'll scowl right back at you.

Growing up on the Orme itself, Pete and I lived two blocks away from each other on the Llwynon council estate, while Simon lived only a stone's throw away in a semi-detached cottage on Tyn-y-coed Road just above the estate.

Looming over this well-populated residential area was a mountain that to me always resembled the size and shape of the RMS *Titanic* without the funnels. Especially if you stood from a west point, just below Anglesey Road and looked at it lengthwise.

And on the other side, blocking our view of the

splendid town and bay, was a large football pitch and an 18-hole miniature golf course (as I have already mentioned). The pitch-and-putt itself meandered down into Haulfire Gardens, which was where we all mainly hung out – a catacomb of footpaths, mysterious passage ways and secret dens buried within dense woodlands that sloped down the face of the Orme.

I don't want to get all mystical and superstitious here but I do believe the Orme emanates a strange kind of power. After all, she has been there since before the Bronze Age. That's thousands of generations of life she's absorbed. By now, she must be like a 679 carboniferous limestone battery.

An old wives' tale goes that the Orme is like a mother who never lets go of her children. Whosoever leaves is destined to return.

Well, if there's any truth to that, Pete and Simon must have been summoned back, for what reason I don't as yet know. But since our little surprise reunion the other day, I can't stop thinking about that certain summer of '82. I get the oddest feeling that it has something to do with the way our lives have turned out.

Haven't even told Sammy about all that . . . Yet!

Ring . . . went the phone beside me, jolting me back to the world of the living. It was like waking up after a deep sleep.

Maybe it was Sammy on the phone.

'Hello?' I answered tentatively.

'John, mate!' It was Pete.

'Pete! Christ, I was just thinking about you, Si and me on the Orme when we were kids.' Then we both said in unison, 'Fate or what!'

'I know it's pretty strange,' Pete remarked, 'I can't seem to get all that out of my head either. It's probably us coming back here that's set off that nostalgia. Anyhow, the reason why I called was to set a day for another get-together, maybe this coming Thursday again? What do you think?'

This I didn't need to think about, my mind was already made up.

'Yeah, definitely. Listen! Why don't you and Si come around to my house, Sammy won't be here.'

'Oh shit, yeah ... How did it go the other night? I forgot to ask.'

'It's a long story, mate. I'll tell you all about it Thursday. But basically, she ended up denying it, then fucked off to her mother's for a while.'

'Sounds a bit of a pisser.'

'Tell me about it! Anyway, is that all right? My house, for Thursday?'

'Yeah fine!'

'I'll send you a text message with the directions to where I live. By the way, how's your love life? Heard from your missus?'

'Nothing! And that's the way I want it for the time being.'

'What about Si?'

'Nothing to report, but you know him, he'll just put up with it. Anyways, I'll be seeing him at the weekend and tell him about Thursday. What happens if Sammy does come back home? Will she mind?'

'Don't worry! She's got no reason to mind, I have to put up with her friends coming round once a week. So if you both want to pop around anytime for a chat, I'll be here on my tod all weekend.'

'Yeah, might do that. If not, though, see you Thursday

night, about eight-ish. Keep your pecker up mate, taa-raa.'

The line clicked dead, the sound so abrupt and final, it was as if I was in a space shuttle somewhere in outer space and I'd just lost radio contact with Earth. I felt a wave of loneliness wash over me.

Yessir, it was going to be a very bleak weekend.

For a while, I tried to lose myself in a film on one of the Sky channels, but couldn't. So early on a Friday night, I ended up going to bed ... Friday night, for God's sake.

But could I sleep? No way. As I lay there, waiting, praying for sleep to relieve me of this living misery, I wondered if Sammy had gone out with her friends. And if so, would she meet up with that so-called chap from work?

The mere thought of her having a full-on snogging session with another man while I lay here suffering, made me grip and twist the duvet in frustration. Especially now that she wouldn't have to hide any more.

Something may have to be done about that bastard she's with. Can't let him get off that easily. If he wants her that badly, he's going to have to pay the price. That, I'll have to give a little bit more thought to.

Breaking my little trance, a car pulled into our close, its blazing headlights spilling through the cracks of the curtains. And as it reversed, it made two blocks of yellow light move up and across the ceiling of my bedroom.

I glanced at the illuminated time on the digital alarm clock. It was only 11.01, and a truly fed-up sigh escaped from my body.

I wished I had some extra-strong sleeping tablets to take. Or a crate of lagers to drown out this all-devouring, cancerous despair.

Perhaps I should go out myself and try to cop off with a shapely young filly. Yeah, right, like I'm simply going to click my fingers and one will come running to me. Doesn't happen like that though, does it? I find it's irritatingly easier to pull a bird when you know you're not allowed to, but different when you're available to shag anything that moves. When you're single and gagging for it, you have about as much sex appeal as a breath of dog shit.

As a matter of fact, if it did come down to being single again, could I actually find a woman to replace Sammy? Am I capable of finding someone who will put up with me? And more to the point, do I really want to start off from scratch all over again?

Christ, I wish there was a tablet that could cure heartaches. Imagine how much of a relief that'd be. Pop in a tablet, and in five minutes, bingo, no more pain, no more stress, no more bitterness. Just think of all those mental breakdowns and suicides it'd prevent.

Remember how Lois Lane felt when she fell in love with Superman, then discovered she couldn't have him? With one brief kiss from those dynamic lips of his, he erased all the feelings she had for him. You could actually see the anguish and torment drain from her body. Only in the movies!

At last, I think I'm falling asleep, what a relief to leave all my troubles behind for a while. Problem is they'll all be waiting there for me again when I wake up, won't they? Bummer!

28th July 1982

Pete, Simon and I made our way down to number nine

green to have a kick-about while we waited for the others to join us. This was the flattest part of the miniature golf course, opposite the school garden, and level with the houses on Llwynon Road. To us, it made a great little soccer pitch.

Mr Golf, as we called him (a short, stumpy old man, with neatly combed peppermint-coloured hair and lime-green body warmer), had already shot off home for the day, so we knew we were safe for the rest of the evening. And it was a glorious summer evening, the bright copper sun was still burning the back of our red necks. It was so warm people were still sunbathing in their back gardens.

As we passed the bunkers on number eight green, Simon began counting how many times he could tap the ball on the end of his foot. Deviously, I footed a mound of grass cuttings at him to try to put him off. Grass and pollen exploded in the air.

'Ar . . . yer fucking idiot!' Simon struggled, but managed to keep going.

'John, yer turd! You know I get hay fever,' Pete protested.

'Oh yeah sos (sorry) I forgot!' I cringed.

Pete and I skidded down the hill, and Evel Knievelled off the bunker at the bottom, sound effects included. But my scrawny little legs couldn't handle the impact of landing, and I went into a forward roll. Pete saw his chance and dived on top of me, trying to give me a dead leg. I yelled out loud in submission, so he let me go.

'Yer bastard yer!' I taunted him.

Pete showed me a 'V' salute, and waited for Simon to reach us with the ball. 'Come on, Si, yer not gonna do that all night, are yer?'

'. . . Twenty-one . . . twenty-two!' He shouted so he

wouldn't lose count, then messed it up halfway down the hill. 'Yer fucker.' He spat. '. . . Twenty-five taps, I got twenty-five taps.'

While Pete and Simon begun passing the ball between them, I wiped a skid mark off the thigh of my jeans. Fearing my mum would kill me for dirtying them. I don't know why, but I suddenly thought about Sharon Roberts, the girl I secretly fancied. She was 14, the same age as me, but the trouble was she just happened to be the cousin of one of the Orme's most notorious trouble-makers, Jonno Edwards. A real pain in the arse.

One of the reasons I liked Sharon was because she didn't swan around thinking she was something special, like most of the girls her age. She dressed basic, and didn't wear very much make-up. Mind you, to look at her, she didn't honestly have that much worth making up for. It was fair to say Sharon wasn't a babe . . . well, to everyone else she wasn't. She had a bit of a crater face, and although I wasn't actually Prince Charming myself, acne on a girl's face in her early teens was like having leprosy and the plague all in one.

You see, in teen world, you're only as good as the bird you can get. So if you pull a cracker of a bird, you earn a few nudges and winks of respect from all your mates, plus make them jealous at the same time. Not only that, all the other girls would see you with a babe, and remark, 'Oh there must be something special about him if she can go out with him.'

In spite of that, you never really got much more than a quick feel behind the bunkers at the top of the golfie or in Haulfrie Gardens anyway. You very rarely got lucky. If you did, it was a lottery win.

So you see, back then, unless you could get a smart-looking girlfriend, there wasn't really much point in going out with a plain girl. I know it seems extremely insensitive, politically incorrect and typically male chauvinistic to us nowadays, but hey ... we were only kids. And let's not forget how brutally fastidious girls could be when choosing a boyfriend themselves. As I can remember, if you didn't happen to look like Simon Le Bon, Nick Rhodes or Gary Newman, you had no chance.

So why was I wasting my time thinking of Sharon?

Well ... call it a hobby interest. There was definitely something special about her, but at 14 years old, you don't know what the hell that is, and God knows, I tried my best to fathom it out.

But it wasn't until later on in adulthood, when I had developed a better insight into these things, that I could put my finger on it. Looking back now, I thought I could see an exceptional-looking woman waiting to be born in her. Remember that saying, 'ugly in the cradle, pretty at the table'?

Sometimes, when she walked she would drop her head, letting that river of long vanilla-blonde hair wash over her plain, spot-infested face. Then she would brush it all back, with the panache of a Hollywood starlet, seemingly rolling waves and waves of butter-shiny hair over her head, and when she looked up, that's when that beautiful woman would appear. If you looked closely, an emerald-eyed lady would take a furtive peep around, and you became hypnotised. Well, I did anyway.

And if you ever got to talk to her close up, she would let you stare into those warm gemstone eyes for as long as you wanted, without making you feel uncomfortable. Ordinarily, you would never gaze too long into a girl's eyes unless you were waving an enormous banner in front of her with the slogan 'I fancy you!' written all over it.

But with Sharon's they were the entrance to a special den where everyone was invited. She would be willing to share all her prized possessions and best-kept secrets with anyone, boy or girl. So you see, it didn't matter if you fancied her or not, whoever you were, you were her friend.

But even though I did have a bit of a crush on her, I knew that at that time in our lives it couldn't make any difference. It wasn't the right time. Yet I always knew that one day, she would awaken and blossom like the butterfly from the chrysalis. And she'd certainly be quite a catch then.

I thought, I hoped, I was the only one to have noticed this. And it kind of made me feel like the only shopper sleeping outside a Debanhams store, waiting for the fantastic sale on in the morning.

Sharon was my very secret darling! All five foot five of her, with a taut bouncy little arse that could crack walnuts if she clenched it, and two inquisitive-looking nipples rising from her chest like two tent poles holding up the fly sheet.

But she never knew that I was watching! And looking back now, I'm glad she didn't. You know how sickly and irritating it can be to the unfortunate victim of a persistent lovestruck kid who would go through fire and water to find out if he or she will be their sweetheart.

Yet if I had pursued her in such a way, my best mates would have probably stoned me to death for cramping their style. Not only that, her cousin (who will be introduced very shortly) Jonno would have had the perfect excuse to single me out and run my face up and down the bark of the nearest tree trunk like cheese on a grater.

*

Whack! A numbing white flash and the football just tried to take away my face.

'Wake up, yer dick!' Pete cackled.

Simon doubled over in hysterics.

'What are you doing, you arsehole?' I barked at Pete as I adjusted my glasses, which clung on valiantly to my lower jaw. And my cheek had gone numb.

'Wasn't me, it was 'im!' Pete pointed towards the hiccuping culprit.

'Sorry, mate . . . I just passed it to you. I didn't know you were just gonna stand there and stop it with your face.'

Then Pete broke into a fit of giggles.

I shook my head, feeling angry and a bit embarrassed. How about if I kicked his shitting football into the woods? I wonder how funny he'd find that, I thought, which made me feel a little bit better.

As the evening progressed, about another seven or eight lads turned up for our five-a-side soccer match, Terry, Mike, Alan, Rich, to name but a few. And to my delight, Sharon and a handful of girls turned up to watch, as they sometimes did.

Normally, the girls would sit in this old hawthorn tree behind the bunker. It was a strangely shaped shrub tree that twisted up at an angle, with the branch arms splaying out to provide an excellent stadium seat view, wooden handrail included. And it was so easy to climb, even pet dogs used to scramble up and back down again with no trouble.

Playing football 'on the back of the golfie', as we used to call it, was one of our favourite summer evening pastimes, especially if the girls were there watching. Everyone would play just that little bit harder to try to impress them. Yes, me included! And knowing that

Sharon in particular was there always gave me an added kick of adrenaline.

Of course, they'd hadn't really come to enjoy the game, it was all merely a way of swanning themselves in front of us.

Where are all the boys tonight? . . . Oh they're playing football at the back of the golfie again . . . Well, they can't see how nice our hairdos are, or how cool our new leg warmers are, standing here in our bedrooms, can they? . . . Let's go and hang out there for a while . . . Might see Timmy, I know he likes me.

That's how they liked to flirt with the boys. Every girl in her best togs, and wearing their mothers' make-up, some with wet-looks, some with mullet hairstyles, each one trying to outshine the other to get noticed, as if it was some high-profile fashion show. And every now and again, you'd catch one of them taking a sly peek to check we were watching them. You've gotta love them!

Although Sharon's presence inspired me to play better, you could guarantee I would always play absolutely crap and end up looking like a right pillock. Either I would trip on the football, miss an important goal, and have all my team mates cuss at me, or I'd simply get out-tackled by every player on the field. I suppose I was just trying too hard to impress.

About three-quarters of an hour into our game, we were three–one up with ten more minutes before we packed it in. Even though the burning sun had long disappeared behind the quarry mountain, the sweat was still pouring off me, and I had to wipe down my glasses every five minutes. My tee shirt was so wet, my back was starting to feel prickly. I longed for a drink of sweet Ribena and some jam butties.

I hope Sharon stays long enough to see us win.

Out of the corner of my eye I noticed some lads clambering over the rusty tractor's gate, the whole metal frame wobbling and clanging against the latch. My heart sank with dread, it was Jonno Edwards and his clan.

Jonno Edwards, a 14-year-old degenerate from our estate, was a short, thin piece of wasted gristle. To me, it seemed he walked with a slouch, the way a giant conscious of his height would walk. And those sunken cold blobs for eyes were like hidden landmines just waiting to detonate on anyone willing to cross his path.

Although Jonno Edwards was notorious as the Orme's trouble-maker, he wasn't actually known as hard knock, as we used to call them – someone who could actually talk the talk and walk the walk, so to speak. He wasn't that tough! Nor for that matter were any of his so-called mates, who always followed him around like lapdogs. But collectively, as a gang, they were Jonno's muscle, and quite a formidable force to be reckoned with. Their reign of terror knew no limits.

Jonno was indeed an evil sort, and at the best of times he liked inflicting pain on anything that breathed, man or beast. One of his favourite leisurely pastimes was to take his scrawny mongrel dog (shit-face, I used to call it, because it had a shade of brown all over its snout) over the Orme hunting for rabbits, just for the pure pleasure of seeing it rip the poor mammals to bits.

Yet if you were unlucky enough to cross young Jonno, he'd make you feel like a shrew caught in the claws of a cat. He wouldn't go straight for the kill, no, that'd be too easy, too quick. He'd toy with you for days, maybe weeks, then just when you thought he'd forgotten about you, he'd pounce when you least expected it.

It was as if he got more pleasure from terrorising his victims than the actual violence itself. To him, the torture was just a formality, something that needed to be done, like flushing the toilet after taking a crap.

But what enhanced his reputation even more was the fact that he frequently hung around with many of the older lads, even some adults, the kind of depraved scum that could only impress the younger, much more naive generation, because people their own age wouldn't bother with them. When you're young, and you know of someone who hangs around with an adult, you think they must be pretty cool to have a grown-up as a mate. You are impressed! So the last thing you want to do is get on the wrong side of them, especially with such an arsenal of friends.

But before I make him sound like Ron and Reggie Kray rolled into one, everybody on the Orme, at some point in their time, had had a bit of a run-in with him, but nothing serious.

In other words, he was happy to swagger around as king of the mannor, just as long as everyone accepted that, which meant no heads got smashed.

Where was I? Oh yes . . .

Jonno and his mates marched across the fairway like an army of rats, shit-face the dog, hot on their heels, marking his territory every few yards or so. Pete instinctively fished up the football, and the game automatically halted.

Jonno, as he passed, eyed everyone in the hope of catching someone foolish enough to stare back.

'Oh look who it is!' the girls sitting in the hawthorn tree hissed at him. (Don't you just hate it when girls can say anything they want to bullies, and get away with it.)

Jonno kept walking, but turned his head coolly towards the tree.

'Hey Sharon yer tart, what are you doing hanging around with those whores?'

'Piss off, you! We're not whores.' They spat back, and Sharon pulled tongues.

'Hey, give us a kick.' One of Jonno's mates nodded to Pete, and Pete, knowing the hassle he'd probably get if he didn't, reluctantly tossed him the ball. The lad, a long streak of paralysed piss, took the ball and blasted it over the school garden wall.

'Ah for fuck's sake!' Simon barked, and everyone sighed in contempt.

This seemed to please Jonno, who smirked like a proud father seeing his son score a goal in a school soccer match.

Pete eyed the lad for a second, then trotted off to fetch the ball.

Pete, being as big as he was, could easily have sorted out that prick if he'd really wanted. But he knew, like the rest of us, if he had, Jonno's lot would have been on him quicker than a pack of hounds on a joint of meat. It wasn't worth it!

Satisfied with their little fix, the gang marched off towards Haulfrie Gardens. Relieved, I glanced over at Sharon in the tree. Her troubled expression made me look twice. Somehow she couldn't seem to take her eyes off the gang until they were well out of sight. It was as if she was watching them walking down into the gates of hell or something, then she woke up . . . Weird!

Pete lobbed the ball back over the school wall. It thumped on the ground a few feet away from me, and everyone dived for it as if it was a *Mayfair* porno magazine. I walked over to Simon, who also seemed interested in where Jonno and his gang were going.

'Why do they all go into Haulfrie this time of night?' he asked.

'Dunno!' I shrugged my bony shoulders.

'Bunch of fucking wankers, aren't they?' he snarled. 'I'd just like to see how hard they really are when you get 'em by themselves.'

'They never are by themselves though, are they?' I told him.

'Come on!' Pete shouted. 'Let's not let those tossers spoil our game.' So we picked up where we left off, and held our score for a three–one win.

Afterwards, we relaxed on the warm grass, giving our tired, sweaty bodies the chance to cool off and dry out. It was time for chatting up the girls, who had now come down from the tree to sit on the bunker.

Every now and again I would steal a look at Sharon, who always seemed to be looking towards the darkening woods. At least it gave me the chance to perve at her without getting copped.

Meanwhile, Simon and Dave began having a bit of a play-fight, probably to impress the girls, yet nobody really paid much attention.

What a great feeling it was, all of us here together on the back of the golfie on such a wonderful summer evening. There's definitely something magical about these type of nights, especially if you're in the right company. It's like a euphoric high, more powerful than any stimulant. It makes you want to stay with these people for life, and never have them leave you.

And I remember thinking to myself at that time, Whatever this lot end up doing with their lives, whatever careers they choose, whichever part of the world they may end up in, I have them here with me now, to share this particular moment. Nothing can take that away from me. Fantastic feeling!

Soon the golden daylight faded to a smooth pink, then to blue, then navy blue. The grass beneath us became moist with dew, bringing out that raw pithy scent you get inside a tent at night. And it was starting to get cold.

I know most of us would have happily stayed there till morning, but we had to say goodnight sometime. Finally, when we did all go home, I craved for just one look-back off Sharon. A little something to top up that high and see me through those lonely twilight hours. But it wasn't to be. Never mind.

8

Smothered in the darkness, flickering flames, dancing shapes, painted faces glaring over me. Do they want to scare me or hurt me? Who are they? What the hell's going on?

That's how my 35-year-old body woke up back in my bedroom in the middle of the night. The duvet was wringing wet from perspiration and icy cold against my warm skin.

I looked at the time on the digital clock, it read 3.41 a.m., still roughly four hours or so before dawn. Thank God it was the weekend and I could have a lie-in.

Outside, I could hear the soft mellifluous rain saturating the close. It made me feel even more lonely. Then I looked at the empty space beside me.

Sammy, my latter-day Sharon, I missed her terribly, and although she had betrayed me, my heart and soul still cried out for her. I needed her right here, right now . . . especially at this desperate moment. Nothing else mattered.

I got up to go to the toilet and stumbled around in the dark like a typical Saturday-night drunk, despite not having touched a drop. After emptying my bladder and towelling down the sweat off my body, I settled back in bed, pulling the damp duvet over me. I lay back against the pillow with a weary sigh.

I wondered, is Sammy wide awake like me at this moment, and if so, does she feel the same? Or is she basking in the warm embrace of her new lover? Don't want to be thinking about that right now! Nobody should be alone at this ungodly hour of the morning. Now I feel sorry for myself, and I can't help it!

My body needs a good cry to release some of the pent-up tension, but I cannot. The tears are there but won't fall. I must try to get back to sleep. Will someone please take me back to some of those wonderful times we had on the Orme? I miss all my friends. Don't ever want to wake alone at this time of the night again!

How dare fate pull the plug on me when I was having such a pleasant dream! Take me back!

Eventually, I did get back to sleep, but this time a dreamless sleep that released me at about 9.30 that morning. At least daylight made me feel a bit better.

Later that day, I decided to do a bit of shopping and remembered Sammy had the car. Oh well, perhaps I could do with the exercise. Yeah right ... On my way back home I only had two bags of shopping and I felt as weak as a 90-year-old. Every 50 yards or so, I kept stopping to tie my shoelaces up so I could have a sly breather. It was embarrassing.

Sunday. I even managed to get some washing done. Yes, I know how to use the damn washing machine. Don't forget I used to do all my own shopping and washing before I met Sammy, so I'm not a complete imbecile.

Come Monday, I had a touch of the miseries again and didn't fancy facing a full day at work, so I called in a 'sicky'. I'm not usually prone to skiving off work, but as I hadn't had any days off for two or three months, I decided under the circumstances, it was justified.

After giving the house a once-over (it didn't require

much of a tidy as I'm not a messy person) I found myself sitting with a mug of tea, watching one of those morning chat shows on the television. Normally, I'm not interested in that sort of thing, but as the topic being covered was 'cheating spouses' I had to endure it.

Sitting on the stage, this chap who looked like a grown-up Harry Potter was giving the audience the run-down on the seedy exploits of his cheating wife. Shit that's me, I cringed . . .

He explained that his wife, whom he'd been married to for about ten years spent most of her time going out nightclubbing with her pals. This he didn't mind, he even gave her money to go out and enjoy herself. But in giving her all that freedom, he'd now discovered she'd been putting it about with at least one man a week. The crowd went 'Ohhhh.'

Next, the presenter suggested she may have done it because there was something missing in the relationship. Kick him while he's down, why don't you!

So out came the wife to rapturous applause. A petite portly blonde with her nose stuck in the air, and looking like Ken Barlow in a miniskirt.

'Well . . .? Are you indeed guilty of having all these affairs?' she was asked.

'No! Not true at all!' she replied solemnly.

Her husband swung round in astonishment and asked her about the explicit text messages she'd forgotten to erase.

Just a harmless joke that's all, she retorted and shouldn't be going through any of my private stuff anyway.

Finally, however, he did manage to corner her into admitting one casual affair, and the audience again went 'Ohhhh.'

'Hang on a minute!' she protested. 'He doesn't talk to me, he doesn't tell me how nice I look, and he never takes me anywhere.'

As the camera switched back and forth between the disputing couple, you could see the veins in her husband's neck sticking out like cords, the more frustrated he became. In the end, he erupted. He told the riveted audience that whenever he tried to talk to her she told him to be quiet because she was watching the television. He'd always reassured her that she didn't look fat, and as for going out, whenever he suggested it, she told him she couldn't as she'd already promised her mates.

Oh my God! I shouted at the screen, and I think I've got problems.

But what really infuriated me was the type of comments the mostly female audience made to the husband.

Maybe if you'd have taken more interest in your wife from the beginning, she wouldn't be like she is now . . . Maybe if you'd showed her a bit more trust, and not accused her of being unfaithful so much . . .

I shook my head at this disgraceful one-sided show of male-bashing.

Yet that wasn't the end of it. The next guest, a man, admitted to having a one-night stand, but did he receive the same kind of open-minded consideration as the woman in the last segment? No he did not! They fried the poor bloke alive, spitting lava-hot criticisms at him.

You bunch of hypocritical, two-faced stupid bitches, I screamed at the television. What the hell is going on here? I think the producers of this programme need to examine their own moral standards just a teensie-weensie bit. What message are they sending out to all those young impressionable people out there? Are they trying to say that when men cheat on women, it proves they're nothing but lowlife, two-timing cheats? But when women cheat on men, it's only because the men didn't treat them right in the first place?

I wondered if the majority of the production team were women who had themselves had bad experiences with men, and this was their way of getting back at them. Hell hath no fury like a woman scorned, and all that.

I think I'll switch over to the kids' channels and chill out with a rerun of *The Magic Roundabout*. Phew!

Tuesday, I returned to work. I couldn't stay at home moping about all the time. The thought of Sammy was still fresh in my mind, like a deep laceration that hasn't yet formed a scab.

And to rub salt in the wound, at work I was met with another debate about the possibility of cutbacks at our depot. That's all I needed at this time.

Wednesday afternoon, as I arrived home from work, I found a white-enveloped letter amongst a batch of brown ones. A letter with my name and address written by hand – it could only be from one person.

Funnily, during the day I'd wondered how long it would be before I heard from her.

I stared down at Sammy's neat forward-slanting handwriting, and snorted at what might be inside. Was I holding a classic Dear John before me? Dear John in literal terms.

I ran my tongue across my lips in anticipation. Should I open it now or later? I took in a large breath, and let it out gently. I'll open it now, I decided.

In the kitchen, I pulled out a chair and tore open the

seal, my mind dithering between the alternatives I might find: 'John, I'm so sorry, please forgive me, I'll never do it again.' *Or* 'John, I think it would be best if we just finished it now!'

My heart ascended to a jogging pace as I unfolded the lined note-paper, probably off one of those 80-leaf pads that cost about 60p. Did she buy one especially for this occasion, or did she nick a few sheets off her mother? Stupid questions!

I smoothed out the four creases, and took another deep breath. Was that the whiff of Givenchy perfume I could smell?

Dear John,
I thought it would be better to write to you instead of us ending up shouting at one another over the phone. Basically I think we should split up for a while. (My skin turned icy cold ... Hey, wait a minute, shouldn't it be me saying all this not her?)

What happened between us the other night was the boil in our lives that finally broke. (What did she mean?)

It is obvious to me now that you don't trust me, never have, and probably never will. It is this that led me to do what I did.

(Here we go ... at last the confession.)

When I first met you I saw that you were a very insecure person, but thought that would dissolve away as you grew more confident with age. Unfortunately, that wasn't the case! In all honesty, I think you have got much worse. You definitely need to sort yourself out! (I found myself thinking of that damn talk show the other morning ... If a woman cheats on her man, it's due to something he has done wrong – I shook my head at the irony.)

I have often thought why on earth is he such an insecure person, and why has he never confided in me. I'm sure it stems from something in your past, other than that you wore glasses and had a big forehead. (Yes . . . I'd already told her that much.)

Which brings me to another aspect of our crumbling relationship . . . Communication! Being completely open with one another. Perhaps I might have been able to help if you'd have let me.

(No! I really don't think so, Sammy.)

By the way, I'm staying at my mother's until I can get a flat somewhere in town. (Is she though? Or is that just a cover-up for 'I'll soon be moving into my new lover's home'? Why doesn't she just come out and say it?)

I've left quite a bit of stuff there with you, which I will come to collect in time. (I felt an eerie calmness creep over me, probably the stone-cold realisation that it was now over between us.)

By the way, I appreciate you letting me have the car for a while, and I will bring it back to you very soon. (Oh yeah she's quite happy to take that, isn't she?) Please don't ring me for a chat just yet, give yourself time to calm down and have a good think. I'll be happy to chat to you after we've both had a bit more time to ourselves.

Perhaps I'll ring you in a few days to let you know about picking up the rest of my things, and to give you your car back.

Samantha X

PS. I feel just as bad as you do!

I sat for what seemed an eternity, reading and rereading the letter in case I had missed something vital. Eventually, I sat back and chewed my nails with intense deliberation. My concluding thought: What will be, will be!

9

Thursday evening, an hour before Simon and Pete were due to arrive, my mother phoned me to let me know it was my grandmother's birthday the following week. She's going on eighty-seven, she cried.

Funny how these birthdays suddenly creep up on you, isn't it? Then she asked about Sammy.

That, however, was something I had wanted to put off for as long as I possibly could, or until I had a better idea of what was going to happen between the two of us.

My main concern about telling my mother was that I knew she liked Sammy quite a lot, and think she saw her as the daughter she never had. I suppose having an only son, she missed out on that typical mother-daughter bonding thing.

She loved it when Sammy and I used to go up to her house for a visit. As soon as we'd arrive, the two of them would start gabbing, and I'd usually end up either watching the TV or merely pottering about the place.

In a way, I was lucky they did hit it off so well, as at time my mother can be a bit too straightforward, especially if she meets someone she doesn't like. And there's nothing worse than having hostilities between the two women in your life, as all those unfortunate men out there stuck in that kind of situation will know.

'Yeah, mum, everything's more or less fine! Yeah, I know you've asked about Sammy, I'm going to tell you now . . . Well, that's the only thing that doesn't seem to be fine at the moment . . .' I bit my lip anxiously. 'We've . . . urm . . . split up for a while.'

A downpour of whys? what happened? and whose fault was it? flooded through the phone. Of course, I didn't want to ruin the impeccable friendship they had by mentioning betrayal, treachery, lies, so I merely explained that it was an amicable parting. We just needed a bit of time to ourselves, that's all, I told her. And to cushion the blow even more, I said we'd probably sort ourselves out in a week or two.

Hopefully, by that time Mum will have got used to the thought of Sammy and me not being together. And when the final blow does come, she'll be better equipped to deal with it. That was my quick-thinking plan anyway. I only hope Mum doesn't put a spanner in the works by ringing Sammy herself to try and talk some sense into her.

Finally, I promised my mum I would drop over in a few days for a chat. But in truth, I'd probably leave it a bit longer. I honestly didn't fancy an hour-long dissection of our six-year-old relationship to try to find out where we went wrong.

I replaced the phone with a weary sigh. The time on my imitation Tag watch said 7.12. Three-quarters of an hour before Pete and Simon were due to arrive. In the fridge I had about a dozen cans of Carlsberg export, which should be enough, I thought. Might as well vegetate in front of the telly while I wait.

It was about 8.05 when their knock sounded at my front door. They'd arrived in a taxi. Pete did have a car, but obviously wasn't going to risk drinking and driving back home. Quite right too!

Pete strolled into my living room carrying a plastic bag almost splitting apart with lager cans. 'Very nice, me old mate!' he remarked, looking around the interior of my home as he parked his arse onto the couch.

'Planning to stay the whole week?' I nodded at the laden Asda carrier bag.

'Just a few provisions!' He winked, laying it down, and making the lager cans clank together inside.

Simon eased himself down beside him, and gave the room the once-over. 'Tis a nice little place you've got here!' he said in one of his funny voices.

'Cheers!' I said. 'By the way, I've got plenty of cans in the fridge, you know.'

'Don't worry!' Simon held up his hand. 'We always like to travel well prepared.'

So once that was sorted, there was only one more thing to ask. 'In glasses or in cans?' Cans, we all agreed.

I had to admit, after losing touch with my two best friends for so long, I never imagined that one day I'd have them back here, sitting in my living room, in my own home. The feeling was strange, but extremely warming.

After we popped open the first cans, the conversation began to flow effortlessly. Soon all the pain and worry over Sammy began to dissolve away, and to be completely blunt, the more it did the better I felt.

But once I'd downed a few more cans, my mind felt like a shingly beach that up until now had been littered with all sorts of washed-up debris, all sorts of crap nobody would ever want. Now this wonderful golden liquid called lager came like an incoming tide rolling, washing over all that rubbish so I couldn't see it any more. Very shortly, I wouldn't be aware it even existed.

And on that very beach where the sand was like white sherbet, Pete, Simon and I languored as we gazed out into the blue yonder. Call it our own little lager-land island.

Fed up with your mundane existences? . . . Wife left you for someone else? . . . Lost your job? . . . Escape from all that anxiety, let us handle the weight of your luggage, leave it all behind you.

Come to lager-land beach, where the mere price of your drink covers the entire cost of your trip. We're waiting to greet you!

'Go on, Pete! give us another can of I don't give a shit!'

Two or three more of those, and I'd be on my way to becoming plastered.

'Ah shit . . . look at that!' Simon drawled at the TV screen as he cracked open his third can. It was the Latin-American singer Jennifer Lopez cavorting on a sun-drenched beach in skimpy gold swimwear as she belted out her latest single.

'Shit, imagine that sitting on yer face after ten pints of lager and a chicken vindaloo.' Pete shook his head.

'Fucking devil's candy!' Simon growled.

I just lounged back in my chair sipping my can of tranquillity.

The more alcohol we drank, the more our tongues loosened, and the more we began to talk openly about our own personal problems.

First, I gave them the quick run-down on my current situation with Sammy, then it was Pete's turn.

'She phoned me yesterday,' he began, 'telling me we need to talk and sort something out, we can't go on like this forever . . . and all that shit!'

'What are you going to do?' I asked.

Pete shifted to the edge of the couch and let his can swing between his fingers. 'I'm not ready to make that decision yet! As odd as it may seem, I'm still reeling from the blow.'

I studied him for a moment, wondering how he coped when he was all alone at night. Was he suffering the same as I was? And if so, how did he get himself through that seemingly impossible labyrinth of despair? So I asked him.

Yet, by the way his shiny bald crown swung up at me, I thought he was going to say, none of your business. Or was I just getting drunk?

'The thing is . . . right!' He downed another mouthful of Dutch courage. 'Thing is, I honestly don't think I can face the prospect of ever making love to her again!'

Simon and I both took meditative swigs from our cans.

'Now she's racked with guilt, and wants to start afresh. She says she loves me and doesn't want to lose me . . . But still, she can't bear the thought of me touching her, not yet. What the fuck can you do?' He flung up his arms.

'Yeah, after she's had her free shag, she wants to start again!' Simon muttered as he fiddled with something.

'That's exactly what I'm talking about! OK, if the problem with her is just something psychological, I can accept that. And with the proper medical therapy there's an excellent chance we'd sort it out, great! I can accept that too. But . . .' Pete struggled with a dose of hiccups. '. . . What I can't accept is what she's done to me now by going with someone else just to see if she can still enjoy herself. To me that's like a trainee nurse stabbing some poor bloke in the stomach just to find out whether or not she can stand the sight of blood. If she can, great!

That's her future secured, but what about the poor sod she's just killed? I honestly don't think I'm capable of forgiving and forgetting that!'

Simon and I nodded in agreement.

'You see, even if she did eventually let me make love to her again, how the hell am I going to feel inside? I'm going to be thinking all sorts of shit, aren't I? I'm going to think, Christ I've had to go through all this just to be able to have normal sex with my wife. And yet she can quite easily go off and do it with a stranger just like that. The most precious, and intimate expression between a couple is the act of lovemaking . . . agreed?'

We both nodded our support.

'When a woman allows you to be inside her, for that short time, you are her god, her king, her whole world. Just for that one sweet moment, you know you are the most important thing to her. You are the only man she wants! That's why most men after they have been cheated on find it difficult to take their women back. It's not just the fact that it hurts their male ego, and it makes them feel anything less than a man. It's much more than that! Deep down they know that someone else has been allowed into that sacred place, beneath the surface. A place that can only hold one person at a time, a special person, only the most privileged of all. And for a husband, he knows that he can no longer wear the prestigious crown that says your woman loves you more than anyone else in the entire world; nobody means as much to her as you do; and while she's with you, she would never allow the seed from another man's loins be nurtured by the loving warmth of her womb. How the hell can I ever look into my wife's eyes again and feel like a real husband?'

A stunned silence befell. That was an extremely articulate outburst, I thought, even if Pete was half soused. And it also made me realise just how trivial my circumstances were compared to his. Fuck! If he could go through that, surely I could put up with my lot.

Pete popped open another lager and flopped back in the couch, mentally exhausted. I didn't quite know what to say after all that, I suppose he had answered all the questions we could possibly ask.

In the meantime, Simon managed to roll up a joint from some hard-baked skunk he'd bought. 'Don't mind if we have a bit of a blow, do yer?'

'No,' I said. 'As long as it's nothing major.'

'Don't worry!' Simon scoffed. 'It's not going to blow your head off or anything.' So I trusted him.

Not that I was really worried. I'd had a spliff or two in my youth, so I knew what to expect. Or at least I thought I did.

Simon asked me for a dish or something to drop the ash into, so I went off to the kitchen to get one. When I returned, Simon had lit up, taken a puff, and handed it over to Pete, who took hold of it as if it was some magic pill to cure all his emotional ills. He inhaled deeply, and let the thick white smoke crawl lazily out of his mouth.

On that exotic beach of ours, I saw him drift out to sea on a floating lilo. It was a moment he needed to himself, a moment of complete weightless bliss. And after a few more puffs, he became so free that he was no longer somebody's father, somebody's husband, or somebody's friend.

He looked like someone who'd just died and gone to heaven. Then he leant over and offered me the limp-looking dog-end. I hawked my throat somewhat hesitantly, and took it.

'Don't duck-arse it!' Simon said, patiently awaiting

his turn. (Meaning, don't wet the end and make it all soggy.)

I poised before my tug, and glanced at him wearily. 'Haven't done one of these for a long time.'

'It's all right! Just don't take too much of it, or you'll get a whitey.'

I looked at him oddly. 'A what?'

'A whitey's what you get when you overdo it with a blow. Makes you feel like shit. You'll feel so ill that you'll be making deals with God, just to get better.'

I gave him a goggle-eyed look.

'No! . . . It's all right!' Simon nodded assuredly. 'You have to take quite a lot for a whitey.'

So I indulged, and almost choked on the pepper-like smoke burning the back of my throat. I exhaled, but not much came out. Obviously, I was out of practice.

Soon, the joint had done a few laps around us, but still I didn't feel anything. This ain't so bad, I thought. Pete asked how I was doing, and I told him, Fine! Then he turned to Simon.

'So how's things with you, Si?' he asked.

Simon made a face, and took another drag. 'No better, no worse, I suppose!'

I turned to him curiously. How come he was so sober? 'Hey Si, after a few cans and a tug or two of blow, everybody has something to say about their personal life.'

'Come on!' Pete tapped the ash into the cereal bowl. 'Talk to us!'

Simon just shrugged. 'Well, she seems to have settled down a bit since her friend came over to stay.'

'What friend is that?' I asked.

'Just a girlfriend from her university. I don't mind her going around with her. At least it keeps her occupied and free from doing something else out of boredom. If you know what I mean?'

'Yeah, that's why a lot of these women end up going off. They're just bored, aren't they?'

'But have you noticed, or is it just me?' I questioned. 'These days women seem to be so much more demanding don't they? They want this, they want that. I mean, OK, I believe in equal rights, the Equal Opportunities Commission, and all that. If women are doing the same jobs, and the same hours as men, then they deserve the same pay. Fair enough! ... But it's not enough, is it? These days, they're not happy enough with equal rights, they want more ... Look at all that political correctness rubbish going on now. Any job title these days that has any masculine connotation to it, like a "manager", they want to change, just because it's demeaning to women.

'And if you make the mistake of wolf-whistling at a woman at work, she'll take you to fucking court. Talk about petty or what? I mean, if someone whistles at you, so what? It's just a compliment, for Christ's sake! And if they do or say something more sexually suggestive, then tell them to piss off and just ignore it! You can't just keep on wasting the taxpayers' money suing someone every time they whistle at you or make some kind of untoward remark. Pretty soon, a man will get sued for even looking at a woman the wrong way ... Then they'll start suing because they think someone's thinking obscene things about them.'

Pete joined in with me. 'What about that advert on the telly, when that guy drinking a can of Coke passes outside the window of that office block, and you see all those women drooling and wetting their knickers over him. What if that guy decided to sue all of them for sexual harassment? I know it's only an advert but it's what would happen if it was the other way round!'

'It's not just in jobs either.' Simon chimneyed white smoke towards the ceiling. 'They're starting to get too fussy in relationships as well. Did you read that article in the paper a while ago about that book written by a leading female lawyer?'

'Oh . . . yeah . . . Something to do with divorce is all the fault of the women,' Pete remembered.

'Yeah, she says that it's women's behaviour that is causing the breakdown of many relationships today. They're too aggressive and demanding . . .'

'That sounds like your girlfriend!' I joked.

'She says that they're always arguing with their husbands and complaining too much about things which really don't matter. And they seem to be very critical about their men. She reckons that when they don't get what they want, they scream and complain. Women are nowadays behaving very badly, and the men have taken quite enough from them.'

'Yeah, but is she talking about the SASSY women, or is she referring to those ladettes?' I asked.

'What do you mean, SASSY?' Pete enquired.

'Single, affluent, successful, sensual and young.' I struggled to stay focused after all the alcohol and blow I'd taken.

'The typical yuppie women, you mean?'

'Yeah! The kind that chooses a man the same way a fastidious employer chooses someone to work for their company.'

'Or those irritating ladettes,' Pete growled. 'Have you seen them? That's another example of sexual equality that has gone wrong: girls trying to compete with the men to try and prove they are just as good. I'm not talking about the ones who compete in work or in sport. I mean the ones that dress like men, drink like men, fart and burp, and even talk like men.'

'Yeah! I have to admit,' Simon put in, 'my girl's a bit like that, but she doesn't go that far, and she'd better not go any further.'

'Well, with all due respect, Si . . .' Pete slapped him warmly on the shoulder '. . . Just speaking about it in general, I wouldn't like to have a woman who'd try to drink me under the table, not because it'd hurt my male ego or anything. I just don't think women should do those kind of things. It's not very ladylike, is it? I tell you that's part of the problem with them these days, they seem to be losing so much of their femininity.' Pete looked at me for support, and I gave it.

'A man wants a woman, right? A real woman! I don't mean a Stepford wife with a frilly dress and apron standing there with his slippers in her hand, waiting for him to get home. And then ready to strap on the suspenders when they go to bed. A man loves his woman to look nice, not every minute of every day, granted. But at least to remind him from time to time just what it was that attracted him to her in the first place. And likewise for the woman too, she likes her man to make an effort now and again.

'What I'm trying to say is that men want their women to look and act like women. They don't want someone who resembles one of their mates down at the pub. They appreciate women for all those wonderful traits Mother nature gave them . . . things like grace and beauty. They don't want some short spiky-haired tearaway dressed like a fourteen-year-old boy, who farts and gobs in the street. Is that what women think is appealing nowadays? Or are they deliberately trying to be different?

'How would these ladettes feel if their men suddenly started prancing about in women's clothes, putting on fancy make-up and skipping through the fields? Bet they'd have something to say about that!'

I took my turn with the joint, and had another quick blast.

'Anyway!' Simon tapped some ash into the cereal bowl. 'The way things are going, men will eventually become redundant.'

'Do you reckon?' I winced as if I'd just swallowed something too hot.

'Well, yeah! We're all being blamed for not being able to please these women in bed, so they're inventing all these mechanical devices to stimulate themselves.'

'Maybe if they didn't expect us all to be bloody mind-readers and let us all in on their little secrets now and again, we might be able to do something about it,' Pete snorted.

'True! . . . True! . . .' I nodded appreciatively.

'What was that thing I read in the papers a while back?' Simon pinched his head. 'Oh yeah! In Germany, I think, they've invented this device which works by implanting a generator into the women's buttocks which is connected to electrodes in the spine. Then you've got this TV-style remote control that you press, and it apparently triggers off sexual ecstasy equivalent to an orgasm.'

'You're joking?' I choked.

'They're fucking welcome to it then!' Pete huffed. 'Just as long as they leave open the brothels, and we have a quick wank every now and again, we should be all right.'

'I don't think we need worry about that at the moment, though!' Simon smirked. 'The fucking thing costs around five grand to buy!'

'Yeah! . . . But I bet it only costs about a couple of quid to make,' I added.

Simon asked me where the loo was, and after I'd told him, off he staggered.

'Wouldn't it be great to be able to smoke this stuff all the time?' Pete remarked. 'You'd never need to worry about anything, would you? Women, children, money problems, health . . . you'd be so free from all that unnecessary burden.'

'Yeah, but it'd probably scramble your brains in the end, and you'd wind up in a wheelchair, sucking pea soup through a straw.'

'Hey, are you sure Sammy isn't going to make an unexpected appearance tonight?'

'Naw! She'll be too busy enjoying herself with that prick she's with!' Suddenly I began to feel as if someone had a spoon inside my head and was stirring my brains around. Was the skunk I'd smoked finally taking effect?

'You all right?' Pete asked, noticing.

'Yeah . . . Just feeling a bit strange, that's all.'

'Probably comin' up. It's all right, it's normal.'

But inside my head it certainly didn't feel normal. In the past when I'd done this, it was only a very mild stimulant, and definitely not as strong in comparison with today's drugs. Foolishly, I hadn't taken that into consideration.

Simon breezed passed and flopped back onto the couch. 'What's happening?'

'John's having a bit of a trip,' Pete told him.

'It's all right, John mate, you're just going through a bit of turbulence.'

I remember nodding my head that I understood, but sensed the fuzziness was getting worse. It was like being the passenger on the back of a Suzuki Haybusa motorcycle and going from 0 to 100 m.p.h. in about three seconds. My heart began to pound in my chest, as if it was banging to get out before its muscle-and-bone home was about to explode.

I leant forward in my seat, and saw Pete looking at me through snake eyes as he took another drag. 'Yer all right?' he asked again.

The psychedelic motorcycle increased its speed, and I tightened my grip to hold on. Faster and faster we went, the wind screaming in my ears, and now the Devil himself was riding up front. Christ, when are we going to stop? This isn't normal!

I began to panic, and I remember thinking of all those students and teenagers who have died through misuse of drugs. Although in truth I don't recall reading anything about any deaths related to taking joints, but that didn't matter. I could still end up a name on that short list. I was becoming psychotic.

Oh shit! Is this what happens . . . am I going to shoot over the edge out of control, straight into oblivion? It made me think back to all the things I did with Sammy, all those simple mundane things we did together . . . My turn to make a cuppa or yours? Ah, bloody hell, Sam, you've put suger in mine again, haven't you?

Having her sitting beside me, innocently reading her magazine while I watch the telly. Both of us there again together after another hard-working day, cosy as fuck! Who cares about anything else as long as we've got this? Watching her sip her tea, listening for the click in her throat as she swallows. Hearing her stomach pop and gurgle as the liquid pools with her gastric juices . . . The pitiful look on her face when she cracked her knee on the kitchen floor. Will she ever forgive me?

I wish I could see her one last time!'

(Shit, if Pete and Si could hear me now, they'd be pissing themselves laughing, but I don't care, this is my life.)

All those safe earthly memories were falling away from me as I slipped further and further away from my life. It was like falling down a black tunnel, watching the mouth of light above me grow smaller and smaller.

My head felt as heavy as a cannon ball, and dropped into my hands. Finally, a wave of nausea washed over my whole body, leaving me in a cold sweat. I opened my eyes to a shivery awakening. At last my white-knuckle ride was over, and I jumped off while I had the chance.

'He's back with us again!' Pete rejoiced.

'Enjoy that?' Simon grinned devilishly, as if he had been my dreaded demon rider.

'No! Did I fuck?' I blew with shock. 'Don't want any of that shit again, that's for sure.'

'Did you make any deals with God?' Pete asked.

'More like deals with the Devil.' I shook my head.

Simon slapped me on the back. 'You probably took a bit too much skunk and had a bit of a whitey, that's all.'

'No shit?' I muttered, and flopped back in my chair.

As I sat there recovering, Pete turned up the volume on the music channel, and the both of them turkey-necked to the beat.

At around 11.40, Pete and Simon's taxi hooted outside, and before they bundled out of the door, they promised they'd contact me in a few days.

Once again, I was alone for the night, and facing one more day at work before another soul-destroying week-end. I hoped I would cope with that one a bit better.

10

Summer '82

Goat's Path halfway up Wyddfyd mountain was quite a popular spot for sunbathing for us when we were kids. But most of all it boasted an excellent view of the tram tracks, the black gate newsagents, and the old brick and mortar homes cascading down the Great Orme. Beyond that was the splendid bay of Llandudno's north shore.

'Tell yer what, shall we all meet up at midnight tonight and watch the fireworks from heaven?' Simon suggested to Pete and me as we sprawled in the hay-grass on this our second week of the school summer holidays.

'Fireworks from heaven?' Pete lifted his head with a stalk of grass dangling from his mouth.

'Yeah! Me gran said that in the early hours of tomorrow morning we're gonna have a shower of tiny meteorites failing from the sky.'

Although I was all for it, Pete grimaced at the idea. 'Dunno if I can wangle that one, Dad's already grounded me for putting one of those cigarette exploders in me granny's fags and nearly giving her a heart attack.'

'Should have given it to my gran!' Simon sat up with

his arm across his face to block off the blinding sun. 'Told yer, yer wouldn't get away with it, especially with your old man. My gran wouldn't have minded, she'd have probably just laughed. That's if she'd have survived.'

'Miserable old bastard just hasn't got a sense of humour, that's all!' Pete spat out a bit of grass, then mimicked his father's voice. '"You silly boy, don't you know how dangerous it is to frighten an old age pensioner like that? Tomorrow night, you're in at eight thirty, no later!"'

'Come on, Pete lad! Just sneak out for half an hour, they're not gonna know, are they?' I tried to coax him.

'Dunno . . . I'll get really shitted on if they catch me.'

'Hey!' Simon yapped. 'Look down there . . . Karen, Lisa, Sharon, and those two smart ones from town.'

We all sat bolt upright, Pete and Simon peering for a look of the girls from town, while I tried to catch a glimpse of Sharon. From our vantage point, they all looked like a handful of walking Quality Street sweets in their multi-coloured skimpy summer wear. But which one was Sharon?

Pete and Simon craned their necks like two inquisitive meercats.

'Where are the ones we like?' Pete squawked.

'I think they're the ones at the back!'

We didn't take our eyes off the girls until they vanished behind the houses sloping down Llwynon Road. Then we flopped back onto the warm yellow grass, our sweaty tee shirts now gone cold on our backs, and listened to the crickets ticking in the grass. Far down below, I could hear the whirring of the trams' cables rolling over their pulleys as they began another run.

'I'd love to shag that ginger one!' Pete drawled. 'That's if it was her lucky day.'

'She's not as nice as the blonde with the big wobbly arse,' Simon argued.

' 'Course she is! Yours is like a fucking horse in a miniskirt!'

'It's better than having a hairy ginger arse.'

Pete and Simon loved to disagree about girls, so I let them get on with it. I closed my eyes and listened to the rumble of the trams, and wondered where Sharon was going on such a searingly hot day. And, man, it was definitely a hot one! The sun was a cauldron of white heat pouring down on us.

Lying there with my arm over my eyes to shield them from the glare, it felt like I was being slowly cooked in an oven. Not only that, it was difficult to breathe; the heat from the sun was sucking away all the oxygen in the air. It must have been way up in the nineties that day.

'Yer comin or what?' Pete tapped my shoulder with the toe of his trainer. He was now standing over me. 'We're going down to the shop to get some eats and drinks, and then we're going to Lovers' Green in Haulfrie to eat 'em.'

Tardily climbing to my feet, I asked why we were going there.

'It's too hot here!' Simon began making his way down.

'He only wants to go there for a perve at the mags after seeing that heifer with a big arse.' Pete shoved him forward.

'Oh yeah! How do you know the mags are still there then?' Simon retorted.

' 'Cause you're always going on about them.' Pete shoved him again, nearly causing him to tumble down the steep grassy slope.

Simon turned on him, but Pete was already on the run.

The side of the mountain itself was about a 70 or 80

degree incline, and with the long common scurvy grass, it was like trying to walk down a cashmere rug.

Deciding to take my time, I let them bustle ahead. I certainly wasn't going to race, not in this heat anyway.

Later, as we strolled through the woods towards our den, Simon again mentioned coming out late tonight.

'Course he's coming,' I answered for him, and Pete finally relented.

'If I get caught though, I'm going to fucking crucify you both.' He twanged a thin branch back to hit Simon in the chest, which just missed.

'Nice try, arsehole!' Simon flicked a twig back at him.

After crunching through the thick foliage past the bend from Lovers' Green, we arrived at our secret den buried deep in the heart of the woods. In fact, it was just a formation of tree creepers and bush shrubbery that had grown into a kind of small dome similar to tent. All we had done to make it into a den was clear out some offending thistles and leaves. The rest was ready-made by Mother Nature.

Inside, Simon immediately unearthed his plastic bag full of *Mayfairs* and *Penthouses*, which he'd hidden beneath the soil and ferns.

'Hah . . . my babies.' He rustled his hand inside the bag, and began handing them around.

Sitting cross-legged in the dirt, in the shade, we flicked zealously through our glossy issues, each one of us wondering if any of the girls in the mags resembled anyone we might know.

'Hey!' Pete alerted us, finding two pages stuck together. 'Who's been having themselves away at home with this one then?'

More or less knowing but not saying, I sniggered into my mag.

'It's probably 'cos it's a bit damp down here!' Simon said, somewhat sheepishly.

'Yeah! Yeah! Yeah!' Pete sneered, then turned his magazine to look at it from different angles. 'Fuckin' hell, look at that. Looks like a ham sandwich, doesn't it?'

'I think it looks like a cut that hasn't healed,' I remarked.

'Just looks like a twat to me!' Simon said bluntly.

'Well, it takes one to know one!' Pete nudged him with his knee, and got the finger salute in return.

'John . . .' Pete turned to me. 'Out of the ones walking up the road before, which one did you like?'

Stumped for a second, and not wanting to reveal my secret fascination for Sharon, I blurted out, 'None of them.'

'None of them? Really?'

'You must be interested in someone.' Simon looked up from his magazine.

'Oh yeah!' I replied, hoping they didn't think I was queer or something.

'But just none of them, that's all!'

'I bet that Sharon Roberts is gonna have a nice arse when she's older!' Simon muttered into his mag.

Shit, I thought, why is he mentioning her? Have they found out that I like her or something? Are they trying to trap me into admitting it?

'Bet he's got a secret thing for that titless Karen,' Pete smirked guilefully.

'You must be joking.' I kept my head down, hoping they wouldn't ask me any more questions. Thankfully, they didn't. Instead, Pete began pestering Simon to swap mags over.

For a short while, we carried on reading our magazines and enjoyed the shade from our den. When we got a bit bored with that, we decided to head down to the Golden Goose arcade at the entrance to the pier.

During the summer holidays, that was another one of our favourite haunts. Or perhaps I should say one of Pete and Simon's. They were crazy about those hi-tech video games, especially the one called Pole Position. As soon as we got there, they'd make a beeline for it, and that's where we'd be all afternoon.

I myself hated the fucking thing, and only went along to be sociable. As a matter of fact, the whole place used to make me feel like throwing up. Maybe it was the whiff of seaweed and algae drifting off the shore. Or the smell of suntan lotion, baking doughnuts and candy floss from the abundant refreshment stalls.

And who could forget those bored-to-shitless young serving girls in their ice-cream huts, leaning head on hand, gazing out into the great blue yonder. The only thing they had to take their languid minds off their shitty jobs just to pay for their college fees was the odd cute lad with a wet-look or Gerry curl passing by.

Then you had the swarms of screaming, sunburnt kids with their stupid cone-shaped hats and melting Cornettos dribbling down their chins. Not forgetting the incessant flocks of seagulls who had, over the years, become quite adept at knowing when to swoop down and snatch food from the unsuspecting tourist.

Last but not least, you had the dreaded arcade itself, or the greed demon, as I used to call it. All you could hear when you walked past were the high-pitched wailings and mewing sounds coming from all those starving machines inside, machines repeatedly crammed so full with loose copper and silver, it made you sick. I want your money! I want your money! is what they cried.

At night, the place stood out like a giant naked prostitute decked in colourful neon lights, the ultimate lure to those who wished to enter the house of sin and gamble away their hard-earned cash.

Take all that surplus away, and yes! I do honestly love the seaside.

Pete shifted into gear and yanked the plastic steering wheel left and right. The game was, yes, Pole Position, and Simon, by his side, banked with each turn as if he was actually riding as a passenger.

Bored shitless, I wondered how long we would have to spend in this dump this time. At least it was cool in here. Somewhere in the background, I heard the clatter of coins pumping out from one of the machines. Although it sounded quite a lot, I bet it was probably only a few quid in coppers; and however much it was, I guessed that to win it, someone had to put in twice as much.

To take my mind off the place, I scanned round for totty.

Suddenly, I spotted three smart-looking girls, all about our age, on one of the pinball machines by the window. Two of them had long, dyed mullet hairdos, the third had an ocean of blonde hair. All of them were wearing tit-busting tops and arse-hugging cut-down shorts ... Serious eye-candy. I was just about to nudge the other two, when the blonde girl glanced my way. Perhaps she was bored too?

Our eyes locked for a few seconds, then she turned away. Was she looking at me or what?

She looked again, and when she shone those pretty daisy eyes at me, it felt as if someone had touched the back of my neck with a hot spoon. Christ! ... I'm being eyed up here. I turned nervously back to the Pole Position game.

I gave it a moment, and had another look, and so did

she. She didn't smile or anything, just stared like someone looking through a two-way mirror, unaware they were being watched on the other side. That struck me as odd.

A battle of trying to stare each other out ensued, but which one of us had the more bottle? Who was the more wilful?

She was! I turned away, blowing as if I'd just pressed about 150 pounds above my head.

Revelling in this precious attention I seemed to be getting, I decided to keep it to myself for a while. After all, Pete and Simon had their own interests, and now I had mine. Plus I wanted to make sure it was me the girl was looking at.

When I turned for another peek, she had her back to me, playing pinball. Alas, this gave me a good opportunity to view her arse. And what a succulent, well-rounded arse it was. It looked as if she'd stuck two ripe grapefruits down the back of her shorts. Wouldn't I just love to get my hands on them!

I couldn't contain my excitement any more. 'Hey, you two ... Seen those girls over there on the pinball machine?'

Pete hissed at being interrupted, but still had a quick glance over.

'Yeah great!' he humoured me, and carried on playing.

However, Simon took a good long look over.

'What do ya think?' I asked.

'Blonde one playing pinball's got a nice arse!' (That was the one I'd been eyeing-up.) 'Heh! She keeps looking over here!'

'Really?' I played dumb, not wanting them to know I had already done most of the donkey work. I looked again, and just caught her flick her head towards me. A bolt of excitement shot through my body. It was true, she was flirting with me. Can you believe that?

'Bastard!' Pete thwacked the side of the video game. 'Fuck it! Come on, let's go. I'm not wasting another penny on this piece of shit!'

No! No! I cried inside. Not now! The only time I've ever wanted to actually stay in this despicable place, Pete has to have a bad day on the Pole Position. 'Have a go at something else,' I suggested desperately.

'Fuck it! I'm not in the mood, it's just not my day, that's all.' And he marched off towards the exit, Simon shrugged helplessly, and followed.

Shoulders slumped, I plodded after them, trying to delay my departure as much as I could. Unfortunately, the girl was still playing pinball and didn't notice me leave.

If only she'd have turned as I passed, something might have happened. Something might have been said, the ice would have broken, and I'd have ended up getting off with my first proper bird. Miracles do happen!

As I left the arcade, I hurried to catch up to the other two, and had one final look back. There she was, standing in the doorway with the biggest come-on smile I'd ever seen in my life. She'd just missed me . . . Bastard! I had to wrench myself away from the place.

Pete and Simon were waiting impatiently by the clump of oak trees on Lovers' Walk, and I had to cook up some silly excuse to explain my delay. But that didn't matter! I was on such a high, I felt as proud as a peacock and nothing could ruffle my feathers.

For the rest of that afternoon, all I could think about was that damn girl in the Golden Goose, and how I could get to see her again. She was obviously a holidaymaker, as the amount of times I have been dragged to that cursed arcade, I would surely have seen her before. However, being a holidaymaker meant she could go back home anytime, so if there was any chance at all of me copping off, I had to get back down there as soon as possible.

I decided it would have to be tonight – tomorrow might be too late. Although if she was there again, I'd have to go straight up to her, no doodling about. Someone like her wouldn't be left standing by herself for too long, especially with some of the oily weasels that hung around that dive at night!

Please God just let her be there tonight, and I promise I won't mess up my chance. To show my appreciation, I'll even say a prayer every night until I go back to school. All I need now is a good excuse to get Pete and Simon to go back down later on.

By the time we'd got back up the Orme, the good news was I managed to convince them to go, the bad news was it turned out costing me three quid. I bet Pete that he couldn't break his top score record on the Pole Position by the end of the day. A bit of an easy gauntlet for him, as he more or less beats it every time he goes there. But at such short notice, it was the best I could think of.

'After I take that three quid, I'll chuck you in the fucking sea for daring to challenge my genius.' Pete held a sporting fist to my face.

'Go on, lad!' Simon spurred him on even more.

Great! They'd fallen for it, the scene had been set and now it was all down to me.

But before I go tonight, I decided, I think I'll have a bit of a wash, and a gargle of Listermint mouthwash, just to be on the safe side. And what are my chances of getting hold of a condom? Only joking!

At about 7.30 that evening, we were back at the Golden

Goose arcade, hogging the Pole Position game once again. There I stood with one eye on the score counter, checking to see if I was about to lose my bet, and the other nervously looking out for that girl.

I wished I had some chewies to take that strange coppery taste out of my mouth. All around was the chorus of wailing sirens, bleeps and the clatter of loose change. But even these became drowned out by the booming thunder coming from the cockpit of the Missile Launch game nearby.

Pete slapped the side of the video game again, waking me up. On his first lap, he had just frustratingly missed beating his record by two seconds. But that only spurred him on ready for his next lap. I knew it was just a matter of time before he succeeded, but as long as that girl turned up it would be money well spent.

Three-quarters of the way through Pete's second lap, I scanned around for the girls once more, and spotted them sitting on the stone wall outside. My heart nearly exploded in my chest.

'Ha ha, yer fucker!' Pete cheered. 'I've done it! You owe me three fucking quid.' As expected, he had beaten his record, and without any hesitation I handed over his reward.

Simon burst a bubble of chewing gum in my face as if to say 'serves you right'. But all I was interested in was the girl outside. Quickly, I had to coax Pete and Simon out of the arcade. 'Come on, let's get some fresh air, I can't breathe in here.' I marched off, hoping they'd follow.

Still gloating, Pete was hot on my heels. 'Ah, that's fucked you up, hasn't it? That'll teach you to mess with the Pole Position king.'

'Yeah! Yeah!' I humoured him as we got outside and

into the cooling night air that stank of rotting seaweed from the shore.

We sat about ten yards away from the girls, and while I stole furtive looks at them, Pete and Simon carried on crowing about the Pole Position victory.

The girls were now wearing thigh-hugging short skirts and fruit coloured cami-tops. Their sunburnt arms glowed like rhubarb sticks in the soft dusk light. Yet each time I looked over, my girl didn't seem to smile back as much as she did earlier. Was this because she'd suddenly lost interest, or was she simply playing hard to get?

Naturally, this didn't do much for my confidence, and I started getting second thoughts. Perhaps this task was going to be more difficult than I had imagined. But I had to do something before she got fed up waiting for me and left. Then that'd be it! Over! Shit, this was tough!

I was so glad I'd kept Pete and Simon in the dark. By now they'd have put so much peer pressure on me, it would've been unbearable.

Go on, talk to her, you idiot . . . She wants you to . . . Look, if you don't do it now, you'll blow it! . . . This is your last chance, matey boy. What's the matter with you? She's only a girl, don't be a big poof.

No thanks, lads! I can do without that kind of encouragement, if you don't mind.

Finally, at last, something happened . . . One of the girl's mates, the one with a dyed red streak in her mullet hairdo, strolled toward us, her high heels clacking like horse's hooves, and baby-boobs jiggling merrily with each step.

She stopped beside me, quite a pretty girl as it happens, with a lovely caramel tanned face. Then she turned to Pete and said in a broad Northern accent, 'Me mate fancies you, will you go out with her?'

Wait a minute . . . She's asking Pete. Is this some kind of sick joke? Why the hell is she asking Pete? Up until now he wasn't even aware these girls existed. My bubble was burst . . . It wasn't me, after all.

I was gutted, well and truly! I went so cold and numb that I could hardly move. It was as if someone had quietly scaled the wall behind me and tipped a whole bucket of ice-cold sea water over my head. I was absolutely soaked to the skin with shock and disappointment.

Now it felt as if the eyes of the whole world were watching.

Pete, however, just sat there looking stupid. He didn't know what the hell was going on.

'Well . . . will yer?' She flicked her head as if to say, She's over there.

Pete and Simon leaned forward to have a look at this so-called girl.

I just sat there thinking, Shit . . . what if he says yes to her? That'll be another kick in the stomach.

'Which one, the one in the red top?' Pete asked.

The girl looked back as if she'd forgotten herself, then nodded.

Taking it all very coolly, Pete sat back and draped his arms over the metal rail. 'Naw . . . Thanks!'

Yes! I secretly clenched my fist, at least I'd be able to see her suffer the pain of rejection too.

'I'll shag her!' Simon chipped in. God only knows if he was joking or not.

The girl's reproving eyes darted to Simon, then back to Pete. 'Are you sure?' she asked one last time.

'Maybe another time,' Pete replied so coolly.

There and then, he became my hero even though he was still a twat for being the chosen one.

The girl spun off as if she couldn't wait to tell her mate the bad news.

To cover myself, I blurted out, 'Jesus! It must be hard with all these girls wanting to hang off your dick!'

'It's a terrible burden, I tell ya!' Pete hammed it up.

'Should have taken her up to the Happy Valley and shagged her brains out. I would have.' Simon nudged him.

'You'd shag a fucking goldfish if you could get your dick in it,' Pete insulted him, and incited another playful scrap between them.

When we left the arcade, the three girls were still sitting on the wall, probably waiting to be chatted up by the next gang of lads to turn up. As we passed, Pete simply ignored them, as if it was a big joke. Simon, being Simon, couldn't resist flicking his tongue out to them, whereas I couldn't even bring myself to look at the girl.

As far as I was concerned, she was now just another loathsome addition to this place I despised. I just wished I knew why she'd done all that eye-flirting with me in the first place.

What I needed now to cheer me up was to get a bag of chips and gravy from the Orme chippy and eat them up one of the cedar trees beside the school wall. Question was, would Pete and Simon go for that? . . . You bet they would.

At home later on, after arranging to meet the lads for our little midnight rendezvous, I stood alone in front of my bathroom mirror. Now, in the privacy of my own home, I could bear the full brunt of my disappointment earlier.

Staring right back at me, was this short, bespectacled, godforsaken freak with a forehead sticking out like a sideboard cabinet. Tonight, for some reason, it seemed to look even larger than ever!

'Bastard! Why couldn't I have been born a bit better looking?' I seethed, trying to push my forehead back in with the palm of my hand.

Needless to say, the rest of the night wasn't a total despair, thanks to an episode of *The Young Ones* on TV. That cheered me up a bit.

And by the time I was due to meet Pete and Simon later on, I had more or less got over that damn girl.

About five minutes to midnight, I listened at the bottom of the stairs to make sure mum was asleep. Lucky she's on an early shift, I thought. If I was her, I would hate having to get up that early to go and work in an old people's convalescent home, but there you go.

Strictly speaking, Mum wasn't all that keen about leaving me down-stairs this late. I knew if it wasn't for the school holidays, I'd have been in bed already. Yet she knew how much of a fanatic I was about unplugging all the appliances before I went out, so it was not as if I was going to burn the house down. More often than not, it was me that had a go at her, especially when she left the plug in the kettle before she went to work.

Yet, staying up late is one thing, going out with your mates in the early hours of the morning is something else. Christ! If she had any inkling at all, I'd be grounded for life. You know what mothers are like about their kids wandering off by themselves. Especially with my mum having only me left after losing her husband all those years ago.

I remembered little six-year-old Garry Bainbridge from number 46 going missing once. For hours, all the estate were out looking for him, until he was found fast asleep in his garden shed. That's when my mother warned me that if I was ever caught wandering off without telling her, she'd have the police lock me up for the night as punishment.

Would she honestly do that, though? Or was she just trying to scare me? Anyway, I'd cross that bridge when I had to.

Time to go. I pulled the front door closed behind me, and cringed at the noise of the latch fastening; which at that time of night sounded like two cannon balls being shot.

As I made my way to Pete's house, which was just around the block, I did feel a chilly vulnerability at being out at this time of night. The sky, a yawning mouth of consuming darkness, whispered to me, 'What are you doing out at this time of the night then?'

In the daytime, we'd think nothing about gallivanting off to the most treacherous parts of the Orme without telling a soul. Places that if our parents ever found out about, they would have a fit.

But even though we did it time and time again, we always felt safe in the knowledge that if we ever did get into strife, our great mummies and daddies would send out the search party to rescue us. And when they did, we'd still be home in time for supper and a good film on the box.

However, sneaking out behind our parents' back at this time of night, we didn't have that kind of insurance. If anything was to happen to any of us, nobody would know! It sort of felt like risking a rock climb without any safety ropes or harnesses. If we fell now, there'd be no one at the bottom to catch us.

Reaching Pete's back garden, I waited patiently for him to appear out of his bedroom window and hang-jump down onto the lawn.

Question: How was he supposed to climb back up to his bedroom window later on? Well, he'd have to stand on the fence, reach up to the veranda, and scramble back up outside his bedroom, SAS-style, of course, and trying not to kick off too many pebble-dashings off the wall.

Oh yes, his house-proud parents would notice if any chippings went missing, and that would lead to a full Spanish inquisition. Even Simon and I would be in the path of their fury, if they found out we were involved.

Hah! . . . Here he is now. For one sobering moment, I thought he'd fallen asleep on me. That of course would mean I'd have the extremely perilous task of chucking chippings at his window to wake up the lazy bastard.

Pete landed feet first on the lawn with a heavy thud, then stayed down for a few seconds to make sure no one had heard him. Seeing this whole pathetic scene almost made me burst out laughing.

'Come on!' I hissed. 'You look much more fucking suspicious squatting down there than you would just walking out.'

'It's all right for you!' he growled, clambering over his back fence. 'If I get caught, I'll be fuckin' crucified.'

'Come on, let's go!' I hurried us away before someone saw us and raised the alarm.

'These fireworks from heaven better be fucking worth it,' Pete warned, then we headed for Simon's.

Simon's grandmother's house was part of an old semi-detached terrace on Tyn-y-Coed Road, one of the few remaining housing developments originally built for the copper miners who worked down the shafts of the Great Orme during the nineteenth century. Over the years, these dwellings had been modernised to keep up with the standards of progress. Yet despite the passing of a century, they still managed to retain their quaint, time-worn appearance. Nowadays they made perfect homes for retired folk, and the young first-time buyers.

As we climbed the grass embankment onto Tyn-y-Coed Road, Simon's downstairs living room light was on, and we feared his grandmother was still up. 'Shit! What if we knock and she answers? What do we say?' Pete tutted.

Fortunately, by the time we'd reached his front garden, the door creaked open and Simon cautiously crept out, straining not to make too much noise.

'Quick, before she gets up and realises I'm not there. She's only just gone up. Thought she was never going to fucking go.'

So off we walked on the balls of our feet, until we got out of earshot. It wasn't like living in some urban area where there are always people walking around, or the odd car booming up and down the street. On our Orme at night, there was hardly a soul about. The only sounds you were likely to hear, apart from the deathly silence, were the odd hoot of an owl or the clicking call of a fox in the distance.

Still, we'd got away with it, and off we went in the middle of the night, to gaze at the supposedly wonderful heavenly spectacle waiting to dazzle us.

11

At the top of the golf course, we leant over number 4 bunker to gaze at the spectacular view of the town lit at night. Cautiously, I tapped my jeans pocket just to make sure I still had my front door key. I certainly didn't want to lose that here. Imagine having to try and find it in this pitch darkness. Talk about needle in a haystack, and how would I explain that to my mum when I had to wake her up to let me in?

Simon shook his head in wonder. 'I love looking at Llandudno when it's all lit up like that!'

I had to agree, it did look very pretty dotted with all those thousands of white and orange lights. I also noticed there was a strange incandescent rusty glow hovering over the town, like an errie phantom mist. I think they call it radiation fog.

One trick I liked to do at night was to look at the town from an upside-down angle. This I did by leaning backwards with my legs hanging over the bunker. Thinking about it, it resembled the magnificent mother spaceship from the film *Close Encounters of the Third Kind.*

As we lay waiting for these so-called fireworks from heaven, we gazed up at the clusters of stars in the night sky. Tonight, the sky was crystal clear, no floating mist or vapour, no masses of clouds to obscure our view. It was like a wide-open window into the entire universe and all its constellations. You could see them all, the Great Bear, the Centaur, the Plough.

'Do you think there's anything out there?' Simon pondered philosophically.

' 'Course there is!' Pete retorted. 'All those stars and planets out there, and we should be the only one with life on it. I don't think so!'

For a moment or two, we all dreamed of the possibility, each one of us creating our own little alien fantasies. Then Pete added. 'I bet someone, or something, out there now is staring up at its own sky thinking the same thing.'

I snorted to myself incredulously.

'Just think . . .' Pete put his hands behind his head making himself comfortable. 'To travel to the Moon in a spaceship would take two and a half days . . . To go to the Sun would take three weeks!'

'Christ! Listen to Patrick Moore,' Simon jeered.

'Listen to this then,' Pete continued. 'To get to the nearest star would take five hundred thousand years!'

'No way!' I argued.

'And to get to the nearest galaxy would take twenty million years!'

'Fuck that!' Simon replied.

'Honestly!' Pete was enjoying our amazement.

'Jesus!' I blurted out. 'Imagine setting off on a journey like that. On a time scale, it'd be like going to Spain from here and dying before you'd even set off.'

'Even less than that!' Pete added.

'We said we'd all like to go to Spain when we were older, didn't we?' I recalled, but didn't get an answer.

'Where did you get all that shit from about the stars?' Simon asked.

'Got a space manual in the house. Got it from me grandparents a few Christmases ago. Quite interesting, actually!'

Simon huffed to himself, as if to say, Bloody swot . . .

'Maybe when you die, that's where you go!' I suggested. 'Out there somewhere on another planet.'

Both of them looked at me strangely.

'No, I mean, something's got to happen to you when you die. Don't tell me any of you haven't thought about it?'

None of them answered.

'OK, we're young now, and it seems a hundred years away before we even have to consider any of that. But one day, it's going to come, isn't it?'

'Well, you're a bundle of fucking joy, aren't you?' Pete retorted. 'No wonder we don't get invited to many parties.'

'No, but listen . . .' I tried to be serious. 'Sometimes I wake up in the middle of the night, and think, shit! One day I'm gonna die! . . . All this isn't gonna be forever, it's gonna end, we're gonna lose everything around us, and everything we've ever known and loved.'

Simon interjected, 'My gran reckons we reincarnate. She says that we're all part of nature's never-ending cycle. Just like the leaves are born in the spring, and die in the autumn, and then the whole thing is repeated again the following year. It just keeps on going, and so do we.'

'How come we don't remember all the other lives then?' Pete asked.

Simon shrugged, unsure. 'Maybe our memories die with our bodies, and when we have a new one, we have a new memory? I dunno!'

Pete then had his little say on the subject. 'Well, my mum reckons that when you die, your spirit progresses to a higher or lower level depending on how you've lived your life down here.'

'That's what most people think,' I replied.

'Yeah, but wouldn't it be good to know for sure.' Simon raised to his elbows.

'Well, I'm not in any immediate hurry to find out, thank you very much,' Pete groaned.

'Tell you what,' Simon said, inspired. 'Whichever one of us dies first has to make some sort of sign to the others to let them know.'

'OK! I'm in!' I added.

We both turned to Pete.

'If it means I can come back and haunt the fuck out of you two.'

'Hands on it!' Simon ordered, and we all put one hand on top of each other's. The pact was made.

'Hey!' I pointed excitedly as a shooting star fizzed out in the sky like a silent firework. 'Did you see it?'

'Yeah, I saw it,' Simon confessed.

'I just hope for your sake, Si, you haven't dragged us out here just for that little fucker!'

'No! That's just the beginning, there's got be lots more than that,' he said, fingers crossed.

'There'd better be!'

And soon enough, dozens of shooting stars began whizzing through our atmosphere. To me, it was like God had just lit a giant roman candle to go off in space. When all the good stuff came, Pete and Simon played one another, to try and spot the best one.

All this went on for about 30 to 40 minutes, a display worthy of a Guy Fawkes night. Towards the end, as I yawned quietly to myself and looked forward to my warm cosy bed, a sweet summer breeze swept past us. The scent was quite intoxicating, a kind of forbidden delicacy we kids shouldn't be allowed at this time of night. It made my head spin a touch, and caused my insides to ripple with excitement. Here we all were, out in the middle of the night, breaking our parents' rules, having our little adventure . . . right on!

Pete and Simon stood on top of the bunker and gazed into the heavens, their heads set against a backdrop of planets, milky ways and other faraway galaxies. In some surrealistic way, they looked like space travellers wondering which distant planet they'd like to explore next.

'Are you ready then?' I yawned again, and Pete dived on top of me, giving me a fright. I pushed him away, and we started off. But Simon didn't move.

'Come on, divvy!' Pete told him.

'Hang on a minute! What's that down in the woods over there?' he puzzled.

'What now?' we groaned and lumbered back to have a look. Simon pointed towards Lovers' Green, below Haulfrie mountain, where there was a shimmering red glow.

'Hey, what's going on over there then?' I wondered.

'Probably just some kids camping!' Pete proposed, which should have satisfied us enough to have left it at that and gone home.

When suddenly, we heard what sounded like a distant crowd cheer.

Did that sound like some serious partying going on? Something just a teensie-weensie bit too unruly to pass off as a simple camping night out? It did for Simon's depraved, hormonally imbalanced adolescent mind.

'Hey, I bet there's a bunch of naked girls doing things to each other down there!'

'Yeah, you would think of that you perve!' Pete shoved him.

'Yeah! And I bet they're all high on drugs or something!' I said, hoping to dissuade them from any wild ideas they might have.

'That's right near our den as well, isn't it?' Simon turned to us restlessly.

'No! Forget it. Let's just go home now, we don't wanna push our luck.' I could see what was coming.

'Yeah . . . come on, leave it!' Pete agreed, then there was another cheer.

Simon turned to us with a fascinated chuckle. 'What the hell are they doing? Let's just have a quick look.'

'No, Si, forget it! Let's go!' I walked away, but the other two stayed put.

'Come on, John!' Pete changed his tune. 'It won't hurt just to have a little look. We might as well make the most of it. It's not as if we can do this every night, is it?'

'Naw, fuck it!' I shook my head firmly. 'I'm going home. I remember those old rumours about what goes on in the woods at night.' I hoped they'd fall for my bluff, but they didn't.

'You go then! We'll see you tomorrow.' Simon waved me off sarcastically.

'Come on, John,' Pete pleaded as he backed away.

I knew only too well that if I did go back home, I'd spend the rest of the night fretting over whether or not they had made it back safely. And if I found out the next day that they hadn't, I'd have to live with it for the rest of my life. What could I do?

'All right! Wait there I'm comin' . . .' I marched back, pissed off at being made to do something I didn't want to do. 'If anything happens, I'm off, whether you two are behind or not.'

We trotted down the fairway, sinking deeper and

deeper into the dark woodlands. All the while, I was telling myself we shouldn't be doing this. We were pushing our luck, and what was it going to cost us?

In the past whenever I walked up Llwynon Road at night I'd cast a wary eye towards these dark creepy backwoods where we were heading. Everytime I would shudder at the thought of a hundred different eyes belonging to things that waited patiently in the darkness for me. The things that loved to try to seduce me as I passed.

'Come on, just take a few steps down this way, I dare you. Come on, we really really want you . . . Just come as far as the gate then? Half-way down then? . . . Just a few steps, we beg you. We always like to have visitors. We love visitors. We just want to be friends . . .'

Then I'd feel the hairs on the back of my head prick up. Was I actually considering this ridiculous and dangerous idea? Suddenly that mad, insane fool that resides in all of us would take over, the one that likes to flirt with death. See how many times you can pass your hand through the crocodile's open mouth. Sometimes it snaps shut, sometimes it doesn't . . . Come on, be brave, be a man, others have done it . . . Just do it once to prove you're not a wuss then . . . Just once?

Yet never did I take up that chilling invitation. Never did I end up walking into those dark woods alone, no matter what. No! I'd always walk on to live another day. Once again I'd foiled those demons, and mad with rage, they'd spit and hiss back at me.

'We can wait! We can wait! One day we'll get you, and then you'll find out why you're so afraid of the dark. And once we get you, we'll never let you go . . . We can wait! We can wait forever! Oh, the things we're going to do to you!'

Relieved, I used to pray to God that nothing would ever make me go down there alone at night.

Now I couldn't believe I was here! After all that worrying, all that praying. They were right! All they had to do was wait. Fate or what, as Pete would say. At least I was not alone though!

Down at the bottom of the golf course, the town's lights beaming through the copse of pine trees made me feel a bit better.

High above us a gentle breeze tousled the surrounding pine trees, making it sound as if they were grassing our presence to the forces of evil. I thought I could actually hear the trees whispering, They're here! They're here right under your noses. The long wait for these tasty little morsels is over!

. . . One day we'll get you, and then you'll find out why you're so afraid of the dark!

I was so wound up now that a bird flapping its wings would sound like a round of gunshots being fired. A tiny rodent rummaging through the undergrowth would be like King Kong stomping through the woods. I had to keep telling myself the place was exactly the same, except for the dark, that was all.

Simon's face in front of me was just a white blur in the dark.

'Go on, you first!' I pushed him on. 'It was your idea!' So off he went, blending into the night. Pete was second, and unfortunately I was at the rear. I was always either the one at the front or the one at the back, never safely in the middle.

We crept along the winding footpath towards Lovers' Green like a six-legged centipede. My eyes were like tiny infra-red lights trying to see through the blinding darkness in case anything jumped out on us from the bushes. In a way it felt crazy to be so afraid of a place I knew so well and had been to so many times in the daylight hours.

With my imagination beginning to run away with me, I didn't know which I was more afraid of, the dark woods at night, or what we might find when we reached Lovers' Green. Maybe we'll be safe there, I thought, maybe it's just a bunch of Orme lads having a good laugh. They may even walk us back home later.

Then again, what if we saw something we didn't want to see? Why else would people like the ones on the green have a party at a time when everyone else is supposed to be fast asleep? . . . Shit!

'Will you stop touching my arse!' Simon barked at Pete, who almost burst into hysterics.

'Shhhh!' I spat at them. 'Christ, you're gonna get us caught.'

'Anyway,' Pete retorted, 'it's my knee that keeps knocking you, not my hand, you queer! I can't help it if you're walking too fucking slow!'

'Well, you fucking lead the way then!' Simon snapped, and I had to hush him up again.

The trees and thickets began to rustle again, as if we were disturbing their slumber.

'Do you believe in the Orme beast that wanders through the forest at night?' Pete sniggered.

'Oh fuck off, Pete!' I said.

An enormous yowl from Lovers' Green stung us all with fright. In a way it served as a kind of warning siren to let us know how close we now were.

'Shit, I nearly pissed myself then!' Simon gasped.

We turned the corner into the glade. About 15 to 20 yards ahead, and branching off to the right was Lovers' Green. Already, we could hear their muffled voices and see the soft red tan from their campfire bathing the surrounding pine trees. We could even smell the kind of hickory smoke.

We tiptoed towards the entrance to the green, then had to duck into an ape-walk past a wall of hawthorn shrubs in case they spotted our heads over the top. Hunkering down, we tried to peer through the mesh of dense thorns.

'Shit, we'll have to get closer!' Simon whispered. 'Can't see anything through here but flickers of light from the fire.'

We crawled up to a narrow strip of light, marking the pathway that led onto the green itself. Being at the back, and unable to see, I whispered to the other two to tell me, but they just flapped their hands back for me to keep quiet. I shook my head with frustration, and took off my glasses to give them a bit of a wipe.

'What the fuck?' Simon uttered.

Without another word, both of them exploded back against me, almost knocking me and my glasses over. The message was loud and clear: 'Run', and we took off like panic-stricken chickens, me last as usual.

Back through the forest, we stampeded like a herd of buffaloes, Simon still leading, with his short terrier-like legs going all hell for leather, Pete taking his long giraffe-type strides, and me at the rear with my wiry legs pumping like pistons. With hearts thundering, adrenaline coursing through our bodies, and that sick feeling in our stomachs, it felt as if we were running for our lives. Maybe we were?

But for one terrifying moment as the others began to pull away from me, I thought I wasn't going to make it. They would, but I wouldn't, and whatever had scared them into this frenzied sprint was going to get me, and me alone.

Thankfully, my good cross-country running legs didn't let me down, and I soon caught up to them, spluttering, 'What did you see? What did you see?'

But all Pete could say was, 'Just keep fucking running! Run for fuck's sake!'

We ended up running nearly all the way back up the golfie. Only then did they feel it safe enough to stop. Now we all knew how one of those country foxes must feel when chased by a pack of bloodthirsty beagles.

Simon and I collapsed onto the wet grass, while Pete doubled over, hands on knees, looking as if he was going to puke his guts out.

Right there and then, if something had appeared, I would have just lain down ready to die. I was completely spent!

When we finally got our breaths back, I asked again, with a raw throat, what the hell had we just been running from.

Simon heaved one last sight of exhaustion and turned to Pete, who was now vertical again, but still blowing a bit. 'Did you see it?'

'See what?' I pressed him.

Simon swallowed to moisten his dry throat. 'Looking through that narrow gap I saw someone sitting by the campfire in a curly black wig and women's make-up. It looked like a transvestite or a very big ugly woman.'

'Oh . . . yeah!'

'Honestly!' Simon looked to Pete for support, and Pete's bowed head nodded.

'It was just sitting there, then it turned its head towards us like an owl, as if it knew we were there.'

Simon took over again. 'Once it saw us I was off! I wasn't gonna stay and ask for the time.'

'Bollocks!' I huffed, as Simon gobbed into the grass.

'You're both just trying to shit me up because you didn't get to see anything after all.'

'I wish we were.' Simon climbed wearily to his feet. 'Wanna come back down to find out?'

'No thanks!' I got up, ready to run if they tried to drag me back down there.

'Come on, we'd better be getting back home!' Pete sighed, which was definitely music to my ears. 'We've been out long enough, and I'd be lucky if one of my parents hadn't already popped their heads in my room on the way to the toilet, to check on me.'

Shakily, we trudged back home, departing in the same order we all met up. Simon slunk back to his grandmother's house, and Pete returned to his house, which to his relief remained dark and dormant. Evidently, his parents hadn't been to the toilet yet.

But before I went home, I just waited to see that Pete made it back up to his bedroom window, which he did. However, not without turning and sticking me the 'V's before he disappeared. Satisfied, I scuttled off round the block.

Although it only took me a few seconds to get home, those creepy midnight thoughts caught up with me again. I began to imagine having to go back down to the woods now, without my mates. Even as I slipped the key into my front door, I looked behind just to check that no one was behind me.

The following morning, early, about ten-ish, Pete and Simon rapped on my front door. Hair sticking up and eyes still puffed from sleep, I let them in. My mother was already at work, and had been since around 7.30, so I had the place to myself.

First things first, before anything, the customary toss-up to decide who was going to make the teas. As usual, I lost, and after making them, we went in the living room to watch TV and talk about last night in great detail.

On the telly *The Banana Splits* was just finishing on BBC1. Simon began singing along to the signature tune, much to Pete's disgust.

'You fucking kid liking *The Banana Splits*!'

'What do you mean? It's great, I always watch it!'

'Well come on then lads!' I clapped my hands with anticipation. 'Let's get last night off our chests.'

'Fucking hell of a night, wasn't it?' Simon let it all gush out, as if he'd been holding it all in his bladder all night.

Pete took a sip of his drink, then grimaced, as if he'd discovered a dead rat in it. 'Ahh, fucking hell, John, your tea's like piss. Bet you haven't put any sugar in it again, 'ave you?'

I couldn't help a snigger before admitting I hadn't. Then off he went to put some in. In his absence, I turned to ask Simon if his grandmother had found out about him going out last night.

'No, she was dead to the world when I got in, and farting like a drunk. As soon as she nods off that's it, I could go in there and piss all over her head, and she wouldn't smell the stink until the morning!'

'What about your parents, Pete?' I shouted through. 'Did they find out?'

'Didn't suspect a fucking thing!' he gloated, as he re-emerged and plonked himself into the couch.

From beginning to end, we went over the entire night, right up to the argument about what they said they saw.

Simon, the crazy bastard, even suggested we go again next week to find out for sure.

'No fucking way!' I said firmly.

'Why not? Just think, in about twenty years' time from now, John, you'll be asking yourself, Were they pissing about or not? Shit, I wish we'd gone back and found out for definite.'

'No, Si! In about twenty years' time, I'll be thanking fuck that we didn't risk our lives going back down there! Christ, I thought we were pushing our luck last night. Let's not be stupid! What if they're a bunch of fucking maniacs who drink blood or something, and they catch us sniffing around? What do you think they're likely to do to us?'

'What's the most they can do? Give us a bit of a smacking and tell us to fuck off home. Anyhow, we'll take some weapons just in case. I just want to see what they're doing, that's all, then I'll leave it.'

'Yeah, and remember what happened to the curious cat, Si?' I lectured.

'Well, Pete's coming with me!' He shrugged nonchalantly.

I looked at Pete, aghast. 'You're not, are you?'

Pete gave me his wisest look. 'It'll be a bit of a laugh. We'll go a different way next time, they won't catch us. And just think what stories we'll have to tell when we go back to school after the holidays.'

'I thought you'd have had more sense than to agree to that, Pete.' I shook my head in contempt.

'Come on! You can't go through life without taking a little risk every now and again ... Fate or what?' He raised his mug in a toast.

'Just think ...' Simon butted in enthusiastically. '... We might even end up being invited in, and have the time of our lives. Drunken birds will go with anyone.'

'Oh, thanks a lot!' I replied, offended.

'No! I mean, for all of us.'

'So that's what it's all about!' I wised up. 'Ah, I knew you were pissing about with seeing that thing in a wig.'

'No, honestly, I swear we did!' Simon crossed his heart and hoped to die.

'Well, I'm not gonna fucking mess with a bunch of trannies!'

'Of course we're not, yer freak!' Simon shook his head. 'If it turns out that it's a fucking queer party, we just chuck a load of stones and fuck off sharpish.'

'And what if we end up going and there's nobody even there?'

Pete and Simon looked at one another as if it'd already been discussed. 'End of story, we'll leave it at that! . . . So what do you say?'

I had to admit, it was one of those situations where I was caught between the devil and the deep blue sea. I was back in the same position I was last night, when they wanted me to go. If they went without me, and they never came back, or got seriously hurt, I'd always blame myself that I didn't try hard enough to discourage them.

Then on the other side, there was the possibility of missing out on what might turn out to be the best adventure we'd ever had. And should the latter be the case, I knew for certain that my two mates would lord it over me for an eternity. That, I'm afraid, I couldn't live with either. What should I do?

'Well?' My eager mates were waiting.

'If you both solemnly promise me that this will be the last time we go. That also means whether anybody's there or not.'

They gave each other a few dubious shrugs and grimaces, then agreed, Pete stressing once more that we had better take some weapons, just to be on the safe side. Did that make me feel any better? Absolutely not!

Looking back on it all now, if I'd had any idea what lay in wait for us the next time we went, I would've literally tied them both to the couch for a week, just to make sure we didn't go.

12

Again, I awoke with a start. It was the middle of the night . . . where the hell was I? In my head, it was like stirring up a glass of sandy water and having to wait for the grains to settle before it became clear.

It took me a few minutes before I realised where I was, what I was doing there and, more importantly, what year it was.

The recollections of my childhood playing back in my dreams appeared so real and so vivid, it felt as if I was actually living through them all over again.

My mind felt like a bush of dense thorns, just like the ones in my dream. Yet it wasn't really a dream, was it? Those things actually happened. I rubbed my face hard to sober myself up.

Christ, I think I'm going mad! Maybe all those intense memories were brought on by the ganja I'd smoked earlier. Yes, I bet that's what it was. I flopped back on the bed, and listened to the soothing pattering of the rain outside.

Early morning . . . Shit, what time was it? I shot a look at the red digits on the clock. It was 4.32. I still had another hour and a quarter before I had to get up for work. I sighed, relieved. Today would be the last day of the week, then another lonely weekend ahead. I wondered what Sammy would do with herself.

Friday work dragged and groaned like a migraine headache on a wet weekend in Rhyl.

When I finally arrived home, the sight of my car parked outside on the driveway made my heart feel like a lump of burning coal. Sammy was back! Could this be the light at the end of the tunnel? But when I entered, I found another letter wrapped around a set of car keys. Thanks for use of your car, dickhead, now fuck off!

I picked up the note and read that indeed, she was thanking me for the use of the car, but not in the manner I was expecting. However, in the postscript she said she was taking a fortnight's holiday abroad with a group of friends, to give herself a well-deserved little break. Well, boo-fucking-hoo!

Why was she bothering to tell me that? Probably to let me know she was capable of getting on with her life and enjoying herself without me. Also to get me jealous while I was suffering alone at home on these cold bitter winter evenings. Who said women were the weaker sex? You do something bad to them, they punish you. They do something bad to you, they punish you. I once read a great philosopher's description of women as being more bitter than death. Now I know why!

Well, I said with a conclusive sigh, if she sends me a fucking postcard, then I'll know she's taking the piss.

Saturday night, I popped into Llandudno for a few drinks with some of the lads from work. I tried my best to be as sociable as I could, and promised myself I would hold out until about 10.30. At least by then I would have stayed a good few hours, and my working mates wouldn't kick up too much of a fuss when I told them I was going home. Which they didn't, fair play.

Back at home, I hardly felt any effects from the three or four pints I'd downed. Either my body was becoming accustomed to the regular amounts of alcohol I was consuming (blame the return of my two mates for that), or the alcohol was simply stonewalled by the overpowering depression hanging over me. Hopefully the latter.

Still, I was cheered a tad by a text message gleefully bleeping on my mobile. It was from Pete, and read, 'Alright for next Thurs night? Wife wants to talk to me, tell u bout it nex week.'

Wife wants to talk, I said, feeling a bit sorry for myself. At least someone sounds like they're making progress.

Hard as I tried to ignore it, I simply couldn't get that accursed letter from Sammy out of my mind, especially the bit about her going on holiday with her mates. Mates yeah . . . sure!

In the end, I had to tell myself to get a grip . . . Listen, at a time like this, if she can go away on holiday and enjoy herself without me, she obviously doesn't give a shit about me. Sod her! If she's strong enough to do that, why bother? Remember, she's the one who two-timed you, she should be the one that's suffering, not you.

Next Thursday night, instead of staying in my house, perhaps Pete and Simon and I could go out on the town. Maybe even dust off the old dragnet and see what we can catch. After all, it appears that I'm more or less single now, doesn't it?

She's gone on holiday with that fucking prick, I know it! . . . Bastard! . . . Can't help brooding about it.

Why doesn't she put me out of my misery, and come clean about the whole thing? If she wants to start a new life with someone else, why doesn't she do the decent thing and finish it with me completely? Why is she keeping me hanging on? Why is she punishing me like this?

Something tells me she's just using me as a reserve, in case it doesn't work out with this new guy. I bet once she knows for sure that this guy is the one, she'll dump me for good. That's if I allow her to.

On the other hand, if it didn't work out, and she came crawling back to me, would those dark cumbersome clouds of doubt, jealousy and mistrust ever lift and allow the sun to shine back in our relationship?

I really don't know!

Shit! This is completely doing my head in. It's like a raging tempest that instead of gradually weakening, grows in strength the more I think about it.

I miss her to bits! And still can't bear the fact that I may lose her forever. That much I know is true!

It's like a typical episode of *The Twilight Zone*...

Before a man goes off on a business trip for a few days, he kisses his wife goodbye. However, when he returns, he discovers that his wife has had an attack of chronic amnesia during his absence. She now has no recollection of her husband's existence whatsoever. All the memories of their first meeting, their courting and subsequent marriage have now been erased. In the space of a few days, her husband means nothing more to her than a wrong-number caller on the telephone.

To me, that's how it feels for Sammy to suddenly go off like that. I might as well be a passing stranger in a crowd.

I mean, when you've known and lived with someone for so long, you've become so attached to them, it's like they're a part of your body. So imagine your legs all at once severing themselves to elope with a pair of someone else's arms. Only you can't find another pair to match your body because the ones you had were made to fit yours, and yours alone. Completely ridiculous, I know, but that's how crazy it makes you think.

And it's all right somebody saying to you after you've split up with someone, Just pick up the pieces and get on with your life. Where on earth do you find that strength?

Whatever emotional or physical tragedies we may suffer, time is supposed to be the great healer. *Don't worry, in time you'll look back on it all and laugh about it.*

Whenever I hear this, I always picture that peace of mind place they refer to as a palace of salvation, hidden somewhere in the desert. A kind of convalescent home for people who have survived their traumatic encounters. A place where they can now relax again, and begin adapting to their new environment. A place where they can start living once more.

Sounds wonderful, does it not?

But how many of these lost souls actually make it to that place? How many drop off by the wayside? How the hell are you supposed to find your way without specific guidance? How long does it take to get there?

As far as I'm concerned, I'm here now with my own pack of pain and eyeing up that palace on the other side of the Grand Canyon. How the hell do I get across there? Can anyone help me?

No, I'm afraid not! We can hold you and comfort you for a while, even point you to where you need to go, but soon we have to set you off, and you must make your own way there. We'll be waiting for you on the other side if you make it. Good luck.

Oh . . . thanks a lot!

*

Back to the world of the living (wish I could stay in dreamland a bit longer) another tough week has gone by, though I feel as if the worst is now over. Thank God!

Wednesday evening I phoned Pete up on my mobile to suggest we go out on the town instead of staying in my house.

'Yeah . . . why not?' Pete growled fervently down the phone.

I proposed we all meet up at the Fat Cat bar restaurant at the bottom end of town at around 7.30. It was set!

At least it was something different to look forward to, and far better than just wanting to lock myself away full of self-pity. Perhaps that palace of salvation wasn't as far away as I'd thought.

13

At 7.20 on Thursday night, another typical cold, wet, black as pitch winter evening, I walked into town to the Fat Cat.

Outside, I joined a small queue of lads being filtered through the entrance by a doorman, a short stalwart chap in a snot-green bomber jacket, looking as if he was herding cattle in a meat market.

Eventually, I got inside, which appeared busier than I'd expected. The music was pumping, and on the way to the bar, I threaded through the jostling crowd, hoping to catch sight of my mates. I didn't, so I ordered a pint and stood leaning against the bar, feeling like a complete lemon.

A slip of a young girl assistant wearing a black tee shirt and baseball cap placed my pint on the counter. While she waited for my money, the look on her face made me feel as though I was just another potential arrogant piss-head. Nevertheless, I smiled politely just to let her know that at least I was making the effort.

While I continued looking for my mates, herds of young girls spilling out of their skimpy outfits poured through the doors. But still no Pete and Simon!

Shit, where the hell are they? If they don't show up soon I'm going to drown in bodies saturated in exotic perfumes and aftershaves.

Just as I was thinking about that, the doughy arse cheeks of a young woman brushed over the back of my hand. I coughed awkwardly. It was an accident, I swear! Although she didn't even flinch. I suppose she's quite used to that happening, I thought. But, just to be safe, better keep my hands tucked in, in case it happens again. Next time I might get accused of trying to touch someone up, and that'd be a bit embarrassing in front of all these folks.

As I took another sip of lager, I felt a tap on my shoulder. Oh shit, it's the boyfriend of the girl whose arse I'd just touched. No, it was Pete and Simon at last.

'Where the hell did you two come from?' I had to shout above the clamour.

Pete leaned towards my ear. 'We were right at the back near the restaurant, it was Si that spotted you.'

Simon suggested we all grab an empty table near the window before someone else did.

Sitting down, we could at least hear what we were saying. I sat with my back to shelves of old moth-eaten books, which were just part of the decor.

'This is what it's all about!' Pete chicken-necked to the beat of some hip-hop music, then drooled at some blonde girl by the bar, whose bulbous arse was so tightly squeezed into her vanilla skirt, it looked like it was going to pop out at us any second.

'Grab her by the hair, and fucking give it to her, the dirty cow,' Simon growled.

I smiled with a mouthful of lager, the first sign I was beginning to relax and have a good time.

Yessir, it was time for another one of our lager vacations: leave the psychological baggage behind, and collect it on return. Let's get pissed!

Remembering the text message from Pete the other night, I asked about his wife. But by the look on his face she might as well have been in another universe for all he cared.

'Oh, I went down there to see my son, and she told me it was time I sorted my head out, and I'm not being very fair to Jeremy, who keeps asking where his daddy is.'

'What did you say to that?' I shouted.

Pete went a bit pensive, and rubbed his head with his thumb and forefinger. 'I just said to her that she was in no position to hurry me up, and what's more she had no right trying to use our son as an emotional weapon either.'

'Good for you!' Simon remarked, and dived into his pint.

'Then she tried putting the frighteners on me by saying that if I intended punishing her for the rest of our marriage, we might as well call it quits right now!'

I gave him a 'did she now' type expression, and Simon huffed in contempt.

'"Fine then!" I said. "We'll do that! I can start divorce proceedings first thing in the morning," and then the tears started again. So I said, "Well, it's either that or you'll just have to be patient. If I'm not ready and I come back just to please you, it's going to be a lot worse for you and poor Jeremy when the arguments start again. There is no easy way about it, but this at least is less stressful for everyone. If I decide to come back, it'll be because I've accepted what you've done, and am willing to give it another go. At the moment I'm still not ready to do that." "Well, how long is it gonna be? You can't expect me to wait forever," she blubbered. And I said, "One way or the other, you'll know pretty soon."'

'How long do you think that'll be?' I asked.

Pete made a face. 'I know I can't string it out too long, but a few more weeks at most, then I'll make a decision.'

I was tempted to ask what that decision might be, but

thought it best not to. Instead, I asked Simon how his relationship was going.

He shrugged happily. 'Haven't really seen that much of her since her mate from uni came down. So I suppose no news is good news.' And that was that.

I dug into my jacket pocket for my packet of Silk Cut and discovered I only had one fag left. I told them I was popping down to Londis for some more, and stood up from the table. Pete nodded, and off I went.

Londis store was only a few doors down, so I was only gonna about a quarter of a pint. Yet when I returned, I found Pete chatting up these three girls at our table. Simon had probably gone for some more drinks. So now where was I going to sit? They'd even brought over more chairs for the girls to sit on. Christ, I thought, that's got to be one of the quickest pulls I've ever known. What did they do, drug them? Pete was so busy flirting, I could have back-paced back out without being seen. (The thought had crossed my mind.)

To be honest, all I wanted tonight was the company of my two mates. I wasn't really in the mood for socialising with anyone else. Even a group of girls.

'Here he is.' Pete finally noticed me, and I dredged up the widest false smile I could.

All three faces flashed at me, and I could see that they were pleasant-looking young women: two blondes and a brunette, their ages ranging from about 20 to 25. Teeth like pearls, a little bit too much make-up, tidy figures, just below voluptuous, but deliciously girlish, you might say. Overall, not bad, which immediately made me wonder why on earth they would want to associate with the likes of us.

I don't know if it was just my imagination, but I sensed the women giving me the sly-eye like I was a stranger joining a group of roguish card players. One of them, the horsey-looking brunette named Jenny (must be the ringleader) took a long hard drag on her cigarette as she coolly looked me up and down.

That's when it began to dawn on me why they were at our table. They were just good-time girls – girls who target guys like us, just to get a free night out. They flirt and let us think we're in with a chance, so we will supply them with drinks. Yet at the end of the night, they dump us. I bet they're seasoned pros who know how to hook in fish-out-of-water chaps like us, I thought. Then again, maybe I'm just being pessimistic about the opposite sex. Can you blame me?

At last Simon was back on the scene, having surfaced through the throng of people while holding a tray of drinks. He handed out the pints and half-pints like Father Christmas giving prezzies to the kids.

Standing there with a fresh pint in my hand, and feeling like a gooseberry, I decided to try to have a private word with my two mates later on.

Fortunately, that opportunity came about ten minutes later, when I collared Pete in the loo.

'Hey Pete, what's the story with these girls then?'

Pete began unzipping his trousers. 'Oh, we met them while we were waiting for you to arrive. Then they came over when you went out to get the fags.' He let out a grunt of relief as he emptied in the urinal.

'They came over when I went? That says a lot for my charm,' I snorted. 'Anyway, was tonight the first time you met them?'

'Yeah . . . why?' He gave me a 'what's so strange about that' look.

I blew with contempt. 'They only want you to buy them drinks all night, and then they'll fuck you and Simon off.

Believe me . . . I remember it happened to one of my mates at work.'

Pete gave himself a quick shake, and turned to rinse his hands in the wash basin. 'Come on, John, live a little. We're only having a few drinks with them, we're not gonna buy them all fuckin' diamond rings. Christ, you might even get a shag out of them! I mean, if they're out to use as you say, we might as well use them too!' he shrugged.

'Tell you what then, just to test them, let's see if they buy the next round, and if they don't, we'll know.'

Pete tapped me warmly on the shoulder, and I could smell lager on his breath. 'John, come on, we're on a night out. I'm more or less single, you're more or less single, let's fucking enjoy ourselves while we're still young. No offence, mate, but for as long as I've known you, you've always been a bit of a wuss when it comes to taking a risk.'

It was true, and I couldn't help but smile at his drunken candour.

'See . . . It's only one night. Do ya think Sammy somewhere in the Bahamas or wherever she is, cares? No, she's too busy doing the same.'

'Oh, thanks a lot, mate. That makes me feel so much better.'

'No! Come on, you know what I'm saying . . . Life's too short! And besides, you have to admit they're not bad-looking girls, are they? Even Si's not turning his nose at them, and he's the only one out of us three who's still attached.'

'Well, he wouldn't would he? He's probably lining them all up for a lezzie display later.'

At that moment, Simon entered the toilet. 'What's going on? I thought you two had sneaked out of the window and left me alone with the three skirts.' He unzipped his jeans, and aimed into the urinal. 'Not that I'd mind, of course.'

'See, Simon doesn't mind.'

'Doesn't mind what?' He turned his head towards us.

'John's trying to warn us that those girls are only after us to buy them drinks all night.'

'Well, I've bought one round for everyone, and that's enough for me. If they want any more they're going to have to buy their own, so I guess we'll soon find out. What are you so worried for anyhow, John? You're single now, aren't you? It's not as if you're doing the dirty on Sammy, is it?'

But to me, in some odd way it did. Even sitting innocently with a group of girls felt as if I was doing something I wasn't supposed to.

'Anyway,' Simon said giving himself a few shakes, 'if you don't want yours, I'll have the both of them. Maybe they'll put on a bit of a display for me.'

'What did I tell you?' I turned to Pete and we chuckled to each other, leaving Simon looking a bit bemused.

'Come on!' Pete led us away. 'I bet they think we've done a runner on them.'

I pulled at Pete's shoulder. 'Well, if you do cop off with them, don't bring them back to my house, for God's sake.'

I certainly didn't mind the lads coming back, but I wasn't going to have the place turned into a doss-house.

'Listen, John, even if we did cop off with these girls, what the fuck have we got to worry about? I've stayed faithful to my wife for ten years. That's when I believed marriage wasn't worth risking for one stupid moment of selfishness. Then I find my wife has shagged another bloke behind my back. And now when I think back over the years, all the girls I could have had if I'd wanted to, it makes me feel sick . . . And don't forget your Sammy's done the same to you, and Simon's to him. So don't you dare feel guilty about it. Learn from my mistake, get it while you can. The days of monogamy are over.'

What could I say to that?

When we returned to the girls, I found they had brought over another chair from somewhere, so now at least I could sit down.

As the night wore on, I began to relax a bit better. That was until I noticed the blonde girl, Karen, whose fine hanks of hair hung over her face like long spider's legs, was beginning to take an interest in me.

While this was going on, Pete was winking devilishly at me from across the table.

Now, I was faced with a bit of a dilemma. Was this girl chatting me up for real, or was it all part of their whole game plan? In sensing my less than lukewarm reception towards them earlier they may have decided I would need a little working on. Perhaps when we went to the toilets, they elected Karen to come on to me, so I wouldn't put a spanner in the works and ruin it for them.

But whether they did or not, it didn't really matter. My defences were already becoming weaker and weaker with the endless flow of lager down my gullet.

That was when I suppose I had what alcoholics call a moment of clarity. I suffered a flashback of that time at the Golden Goose when I thought the girl at the pinball machine liked me, but it turned out it was Pete she was interested in. Oh yes, I remembered the humiliation very well, and that alone more less sobered me right up.

It ain't going to happen to me again! There's no way she could be genuinely interested in dolphin head. The only certain thing this girl wants from me at the end of the night is the taxi-fare back home.

I sucked in a lungful of fresh breath and glanced at my imitation Tag watch. it was nearly ten o'clock. OK, how do I get out of this fool's outfit? The only thing I could come up with was to say I had to go because I had to be up early in the morning for work. Yes, that should do it, and even if they did have portable lie-detectors on them, they'd be able to see I was telling the truth as it was completely true.

Just as I was about to open my mouth, Pete announced across the table that the girls were going to take us back to their flat just round the corner. And everyone rose out of their seats ready. What the hell was I going to do now?

Shit . . . I couldn't very well stand up and tell everyone that I had to go home to get my beauty sleep. I'd have to collar Pete outside to give me the diversion I needed.

Anyhow, why were these girls inviting us back to their pad? I thought they only wanted us for the drinks. Had Pete being saying he was a millionaire again? Maybe they wanted to get him paralytic so they could lift his wallet and credit cards. Just joking!

Outside the Fat Cat, the winter cold blew its icy breath in our faces. I tried to grab Pete but the girl called Susan had already linked arms with him and wasn't going to let go for anyone. I wasn't having much luck! Even Simon was almost halfway up the road, not surprisingly.

Most lads, I know, would surely give their right bollock to be in a situation like this, but for me, at this time, it just didn't seem to be the right thing to do. A few more months down the line . . . I'd go for it definitely!

Once again, just as they did as kids, Pete and Simon were wheedling me into doing something I didn't want to do. Will I ever learn?

Fortunately, the girls' flat was only a stone's throw from the Fat Cat bar, Llewellyn Avenue, just off the main road. So we didn't have to freeze our nuts off walking or waiting for a taxi to get there.

Apparently it was a two-bedroomed basement flat all three girls shared. How very nice for them all. Who had the single bedroom?

Inside, Pete, Simon and I sat crammed together on their three-seater couch, while the girls disappeared into the kitchen to fix some more drinks.

As I lounged there, my ears still rang from the pounding music in the Fat Cat, and Pete's elbow kept digging into my ribs. But I have to say the couch was very comfortable indeed. Its soft cushiony back and arms hugged us like an affectionate mother. I could easily have fallen fast asleep right there and then.

The peach-stained walls of the interior were typical of a girls' environment, and there was a strong scent of lavender in the air. In the corner of the room, on top of an elegant horse wine table, was a lava lamp, with its green blobs moving up and down the glass cylinder. I've always wanted one of them! However, one thing I found strange was an aluminium rocking chair opposite the three-seater couch. At first I thought it was a deck chair.

Pete nudged me, muttering out the side of his mouth, 'And you thought they were only after us for the drinks.'

'Yeah . . . you can have the ugliest one for that!' Simon reproached me.

'Shit, I've got to get up early in the morning,' I tried, cashing in my get-out-of-jail-free excuse.

'Come on, John! We're only having a few drinks with them . . . Just relax.'

'Yeah! Christ, anybody would think you're scared stiff

of them. What's the worst thing that could possibly happen ... getting a shag? Well boo-fucking-hoo for you,' Simon scoffed.

Finally, the girls reappeared with cans of lager already opened for us.

Strangely, it reminded me of a scene from the film *Witches of Eastwick* and how innocent the three witches looked to Jack Nicholson after making a wax voodoo doll of him. An imaginary newspaper headline flashed in my mind: '3 MEN FOUND POISONED IN BASEMENT FLAT. POLICE BELIEVE NOTORIOUS ANTI-MALE ORGANISATION THE RAVE VAMPS RESPONSIBLE.

'Cheers!' I said to the blonde girl Karen (the one who'd been flirting with me in the Fat Cat bar earlier) as she handed me a can of Carlsberg export.

'Keep a handy supply of these in the back, do you?' Simon asked cheekily.

'Oh, we keep a good supply of most things,' she purred, and they all giggled devilishly.

All three of us passed a look of caution between us.

Although we offered them the couch to sit on, Karen and Susan took some cushions and sprawled on the carpet in front of us. Jenny, the horsey brunette, took the aluminium rocking chair and sat facing us like a queen.

Shit, what happens now? I thought.

Susan, the blonde Simon had been chatting to all night, held up a small envelope and tipped the content into her hand. There were about a dozen small white tablets the size of Anadins. I looked down at them with concern, then across at Pete, who I think felt the same.

'What are those?' I asked warily.

'Es!' Jenny casually rocked back and forth, and took a drag of her joint.

'Ecstasy?' I asked.

'Es . . . Garrys . . . Want one?' Susan stuck her hand out.

'No thanks!' I held up my hand. I had never taken an ecstasy tablet before, and never imagined I ever would. Especially after the bad press they'd received in the newspapers recently.

'No thanks . . . honestly,' I waved my hand firmly.

'It's all right, you know, they're harmless!' Susan avowed.

'No. I'm fine!' My mind was made up, even if it meant I was the gutless bore, so be it.

Susan offered Pete one, and to my relief, he too declined.

'Tut-tut! Where are your balls, lads?' Jenny remarked in her rocking chair.

Now it was Simon's turn, and Pete and I both watched with alarm as he casually plucked one from Susan's hand and slapped it in his mouth. I leant out so he could see my look of contempt.

'You having one?'

'Yeah . . . why not? We always have them before we go out back in Manchester. I've had loads, and they've never done any harm to me.'

Shit . . . My friend the druggie, I thought.

'A mate of mine used to down about three or four a night, but the most I've ever had is two.'

'I've had about three in one night!' Jenny confessed somewhat proudly.

Listening to all this shocked me a bit, to say the least.

'You never told us you were into the hard stuff,' Pete glanced at him disapprovingly.

'Ecstasy isn't a hard drug,' Simon retorted. 'Anyway, we have the odd bit of ganja now and gain. It's not much worse than that.'

The girls themselves took one or two each, and casually

gulped them down as if they were taking paracetamols for a headache.

Some background hip-hop music was put on, and the atmosphere seemed to mellow a bit more.

As we all took turns going for a piss, one of the girls would sit in our place until the other got back. And when Pete went, Karen sidled up close to me. Under normal circumstances, I'd probably feel a bit uncomfortable about that. But having downed so much lager, I wouldn't have cared if the bride of Frankenstein came and sat next to me. I even began to like the music they had on, which had to say a lot about the state I was in.

Later, as I stood swaying in the toilet and gazing wondrously over the scented mint-blue interior, I suddenly thought to myself, What the hell am I doing here? I'm standing with my dick in my hands admiring the decor of a toilet belonging to some girls I've never even seen before, and probably never will again. What the hell's going on?

When I returned, I found Jenny and Susan performing a saucy bit of body gyrating in the centre of the room. Much to Simon's delight, of course!

Pete, however, was too busy flirting with Jenny to notice any of this.

Too drunk to care myself, I plonked back into the settee to watch the show.

The girls continued to bump and grind their soft wobbly bodies together until the music track ended, then they drunkenly collapsed on top of each other in a fit of giggles.

Bet that's given Simon a hard-on, I thought, taking another swig of lager. Karen rested her arms on my knees, and looked up at me with pupils like large shiny black marbles. 'Did you enjoy that?' she asked.

Despite being drunk myself, I could clearly tell she was riding on the ecstasy kick.

'Yeah it was great that!' I said, and her head dropped in a demure fashion.

Susan, the other blonde, sat wedged in between Simon's legs with her back against the sofa.

Pete and Jenny seemed to be chatting about anything, so I left them to it. The way things seemed to be going, I began to wonder if any of these would end up shagging tonight.

While I was still daydreaming, Karen levered herself up and sat across me with her arm draped over the top of the settee. Although she wasn't a big girl, the dead weight of her body overwhelmed me, as did the scent of the Ralph Lauren perfume she was wearing. I could hardly move.

'You don't mind me doing this, do you?' she asked.

'No . . . not at all!' I glanced somewhat warily across at Pete, who had to shift over a bit to give her more room. The look on his face said it all.

What was I supposed to do? How could any man in a situation like that fail to be tempted? Her breasts were virtually breathing down my neck, the soft cheeks of her arse were massaging my groin, my face was practically buried in her scented crotch, and the wisping sound of her tights rubbing together was driving me insane.

In my mind, I recalled the famous words of the great vampire killer Dr Abraham Van Helsing as he and Jonathan Harker encountered one of Dracula's lethal brides.

'The eyes! for God's sake don't look into her eyes!'

But I did, and I felt like a man in the desert reaching an oasis of sparkling ice-cool water. How in God's heaven could I not jump in to refresh my body? What chance did

I have of trying to suppress one of our body's most natural instincts? (Especially when you've had too much to drink.)

That's when it happened . . . I passed out! Yes, I completely bottomed out, as they say, out like a light. Not fit for man or beast!

Perhaps it was for the best. And perhaps it was the heaven-sent opportunity I'd been waiting for.

But why the hell should I be thinking like that? I'm supposed to be single, aren't I? Don't forget it was Sammy who left me for someone else. Why am I still behaving like Mr Monogamy? Why can't I enjoy all the privileges of being a bachelor again?

Why the hell should I feel guilty about going with another woman, regardless of the fact it was only because she was under the influence. Who cares? We're both consenting adults, there's no law to say we're not entitled to have a bit of adult fun without having to commit to each other. Sammy's done it, so why can't I? It's not as if I get the chance every day.

Answer: In some paradoxically tangled way I still felt attached to Sammy. I simply couldn't let go! Not until our unfinished business had been settled.

But one thing I was now certain of, when Sammy did return from her holiday next week, this whole debacle would be settled once and for all. That, I could bet my life on.

The next thing I can remember is hearing the steady hum of a taxi's engine, and the passenger door being opened. Supporting hands began helping me out.

'Will you be all right? Do you want us to come in with you?' I heard Simon say.

I took a deep breath of fresh air. 'No, I'll be fine, honestly!'

I took a step towards my front door, and my foot seemed to sink straight through the tarmac.

'Whoa!' Pete saved me from falling. 'Come on, Si, give us a hand to get him in.'

Both of them frog-marched me to the front door, and after a bit of fumbling with the key, we finally got in. They put me in my easy chair, in the living room.

'Look, John,' Pete said, a bit concerned, 'do you want us to stay, or will you be all right?'

'No, I'll be fine, honestly!' I repeated bravely.

You sure?' Simon asked. 'We don't want you falling asleep and choking on your own vomit or something.'

I smiled at their concern. 'No! You both go . . . really! I'm beginning to sober up a bit now. I'll give one of you a ring tomorrow.'

Reluctantly, they backed towards the front door. Pete's last words to me before they left were, 'Drink a few glasses of water before you go to bed, OK?'

'Yeah! Yeah!' I rubbed my eyes with the heels of my hands, and when I looked again Pete and Simon had gone.

As their taxi reversed away, I lost the light, and my living room plunged back into darkness. The darkness, a place I had come to know so well. I shook my head, feeling sorry for myself in my drunken state.

Back from yet another lager vacation, it was time to check in and collect all my heavy baggage of problems waiting there for me. The holiday's over, welcome back to reality . . . Again!

I probably would have sat there brooding all night if the thought of getting up for work in the morning hadn't wafted in front of my senses like a dose of smelling salts. 'Shit!' I mumbled, hauling my cumbersome body up from the chair and staggering off to the kitchen to down a few glasses of water before going off to bed. Did I nearly cop off with that girl tonight or did I dream it?

14

Eventually, my 5.45 alarm call found its way through the dense fog of a hangover. 'Oh . . . my . . . God!' I groaned, after only four hours' sleep, and feeling like my head was full of brambles and thickets.

Carefully, I climbed out of bed, mouth like an ashtray, and crawled to the bathroom, where I puked buckets into the pan. Yet while I was hunched over, stomach pumping out all the badness in my system, I suddenly clicked onto something (apart from the usual thought of how the hell can people do this sort of thing every weekend, and claim to enjoy it?).

I bet a pound to a penny Pete and Simon had set me up with that girl last night, just so I wouldn't ruin their chances of copping off. They probably told her to flirt with me for as long as it took, because if I'd left the Fat Cat, they would have been obliged to follow. And by God, it worked, I fell for it! I even went back to the girls' flat, something I never would have done if I was sober. That's why they kept pouring the cans down me when we got to the flat, making me plastered enough not to notice. It was all set-up.

Anyhow, I wonder if they did get off with those girls last night. Or did I botch things up for them when I passed out? . . . Christ! Simon takes ecstasy.

After I'd dredged up the last of the watery bile from my stomach, I towelled the cold sweat off my face and had a good wash. Breakfast? No thanks! Two steaming mugs of coffee will do until I get my system back in order. But can I make it through the day? Last day of the week . . . I've got to.

These days I seem to be making a habit of working with a hangover, as my workmate Mike hastily pointed out. Shit I hope he doesn't think I'm turning into a bit of an alcoholic. Naw! It's only the second time in the past few weeks . . . isn't it?

Fortunately for me, the day didn't turn out as badly as I thought it would. We only had about seven runs to make, and finished up relatively early, about half one to two o'clock. Thank God for light shifts. Hate to think if we'd had a second run to do. A second run means after we offload all our stock, we return to the depot to fill up and go out again.

However, to end the day on an especially good note, the depot manager told me I could take my fortnight break the end of next week. So I only had to work one more week . . . Fantastic!

Hopefully, during that time I'll be able to sort out my personal life, and by the time I go back to work, I should at least know where I stand . . . Fingers crossed.

Friday evening I was looking forward to a quiet night in to recuperate from last night. Feet up with a good film on the box, try to relax and forget about everything. No lager!

I thought about ringing Pete just let him know I hadn't choked on my vomit, then decided to check my mobile, which I'd forgotten to switch on today. Maybe he'd already sent me a text message.

Indeed he had, and it read, 'Give us a ring if you're still alive – u tosser!'

Dickhead, I thought, amused, and debated whether or not to ring him straight back, or first make a cuppa? Make a cuppa!

But the moment I stepped into the kitchen, I was twanged back to the living room by the ringing phone. That's probably him now, I guessed, as I picked up the receiver.

'Hello?' I answered, waiting for some sardonic reply.

'John, it's Simon!'

'All right Si? Did you enjoy last night?'

'John, it's Pete . . . You've got to come!'

'Why, what's up?' My stomach rolled with concern. Isn't it amazing when someone shocks you up like that, all your darkest fears imaginable jet past your window of thought?

'Pete's mum rang me to say that Pete's missus has come down to Llandudno to sort things out between them. She told him to meet her in the King's Head pub, the only place she knew because it was the only pub Pete used to talk about. And she's come down with the chap she supposedly had the fling with, just so he can vouch that there's nothing going on between them.'

'You're joking?' I said.

'Pete's gone straight there now, and his mum said he didn't look in a very good mood. That's why she rang me, because she's worried what he might do.'

'No shit! . . . I'll go straight down there now,' I replied.

'I'll meet you there. My taxi will be here any minute now, but you'll be able to get there a lot quicker than me.'

'OK, then, I'll see you later.' I sighed and put the phone down.

The next few minutes became a complete blur, and before I knew it, I was already booming down Conwy Road towards Llandudno.

On my way, the windscreen of my Fiesta became a kind of TV screen depicting all sorts of alarming scenarios of what might happen. The most prominent one was Pete jumping up and down on this guy's head, or vice versa. I just hoped I'd get there in time to prevent either.

Altogether, it must have taken about five minutes to reach the King's Head. I only prayed I wasn't picked up by one of those hidden speed cameras on the way.

Pulling into the car park, I half expected to find Pete and that chap rolling about on the tarmac outside, with a ring of spectators around them and Pete's missus screaming over them. But all seemed eerily silent.

I parked outside, and made my way in, car keys jangling in my hand. Two elderly customers, a man and his wife, sitting with half a Guinness each, paid me scant attention. The place appeared more or less empty. Where were Pete and co?

I walked through, looking high and low for them, and straight away picked up a kind of foreboding atmosphere. It was like the electrifying build-up before a storm breaks.

I decided to check the balcony area, while Madonna's hit 'Like a Virgin' played on in the background.

There was a loud thump, and tinkling of glassware, the sound of someone hammering their fist down on a table. I'd found them.

Round the corner at the back, Pete was leaning menacingly over the table, facing his wife and her lover. Things were evidently heating up.

I began to walk over, and Pete's glossy head turned towards me. I stopped in my tracks as if I'd been caught trying to creep up on them.

'Pete?' I called ahead to him.

'John! What are you doing here?' His mood suddenly changed.

'Just thought I'd check to make sure everything was all right.' Which was in fact the truth.

'Can you believe the cheek of these two fuckers here?' He began to boil again.

'What's that?' I played innocent, as both his wife and her lover stared my way. This was the first moment I'd ever set eyes on Pete's missus, a slim, short coconut-haired woman in her early thirties. From where I was standing I found an immediate resemblance between her and Jenny, the girl he was with last night. She had that same po-faced horsey look about her.

The wiry-framed chap she was with, apparently in his early forties, looked a tad like Dirty Den from *Eastenders*, and was obviously every bit the predatory rogue.

What a fucking nerve he has showing up here like this, I snorted to myself. It's like shitting through someone's letterbox and then knocking on the door to ask for some toilet paper to wipe your arse with. Either the guy's a complete dullard who doesn't know his arse from a hole in the ground, or he's got a death wish. Can't wait to get a closer look at him!

'Pete, do you want me to wait by the bar or somewhere?' I asked, feeling a bit awkward standing there.

'Yeah, if you don't mind, mate!' he replied.

So off I went, and as I approached the bar Simon breezed through the door.

'What's happened?' he asked, gazing about anxiously.

'Nothing at the moment,' I reassured him. 'They're up there now sorting it out themselves, I've just seen them.'

'Let's sit down here out of the way. At least we'll be able to hear if things get out of hand.'

We ended up sitting near the front window next to the elderly chap and his wife whom I saw when I first arrived.

All I had was an orange juice, and Simon half a lager, and while we waited I decided to talk about last night. 'So what happened after I passed out then? Did you and Pete get off with any of them?'

'Naw! We could have, but thought it better to get you home instead.'

'Didn't ruin it for you both, did I?' I looked down guiltily into my orange juice.

'Probably!' Simon replied wryly. 'But they gave us their mobile numbers, so it looks like we haven't completely blown it.'

I took a quick sip of my drink, ready to ask the question that had been dogging me all day. 'Remember that girl last night, the one that ended up sitting on my lap, did you and Pete set me up with her?'

Simon raised his glass for a drink, and stopped short. 'What do you mean?'

'Well, it was a bit of a coincidence, wasn't it? Especially after me saying in the Fat Cat bogs that I didn't want to start mixing with girls just yet, and then her suddenly coming on to me?'

Simon sipped his drink and swallowed hastily. 'Listen, I swear we didn't have anything to do with it, she probably liked you.'

'Yeah, right!' I scoffed.

'Well, they weren't after us just to buy them drinks like you thought, were they?'

'Perhaps it was the other two girls then! They probably got her to come on to me so they could get you both there.'

Simon shook his head. 'John, just accept it, the girl liked you, and wanted to fuck you stupid, and you blew it, you moron! When are you going to finally grow out of this silly paranoia?'

'It's not that! I just don't want to be taken for a ride, that's all.'

Simon shook his head resignedly.

'Anyway,' I digressed a little, 'what did your girlfriend say when you got home?'

'She wasn't even there! Her and her mate were out somewhere . . .' He shook his head, irritated. 'I tell you, that mate of hers hangs around our place like a fucking fly around a cow's arsehole. It's no wonder we don't get a chance alone to try and sort things out.'

'Really?' I replied, tossing a glance towards the balcony area, wondering how things were going back there.

'But as long as we're not bouncing each other off the walls, I can't really complain, can I?'

'Yeah, but it's not much of a relationship though, is it? There's not much point in being together if you don't spend much time with each other is there?'

Simon shrugged and took another sip of lager. I glanced at him for a second wondering how he could remain in such a one-sided relationship. Fair enough, he might be scared of losing her, just as much as I was of Sammy, and Pete and his wife. But if I had to put up with all that shit, I would have knocked it on the head ages ago.

I mean, even to me, it was painfully obvious Simon's girl didn't want to play for keeps, so what was the point in him wasting time on her?

She was going to dump him in the end anyway, so why delay the inevitable? Go out and find someone better, Si, don't be a mug all your life, I nearly said.

'Anyway!' Simon took a deep breath. 'It's all going to come to a head sooner than she thinks.'

This confused me, and I was just about to ask why, when we heard a clatter of glasses, followed by muffled voices. Even the elderly man and his wife, who apparently hadn't even touched their drinks yet, looked towards the balcony area.

Simon and I rushed from our seats to see what was going on. We leapt up the steps to the balcony, and found Pete and the chap squaring up to one another. Even the bartender, a somewhat young, short, stocky man, had gone over to see what was going on.

The moment Dirty Den saw us, he quickly backed off, leaving Pete glaring at him, eyes blazing with fury. It was strange to see Pete, who is usually so laid-back under these kind of circumstances, so riled up.

'OK lads!' The bartender tried to pacify the situation in a professional manner. 'We don't want to have any of this in here, if you don't mind.'

Now that I was up much closer, I had another quick look at Pete's wife, who stared right back at me. I didn't know whether to smile or turn away.

No offence to Pete, but she certainly looked a bit of a hard-nosed woman, quite capable of giving Pete a rough time at home if she didn't get her own way. She also wore a bit too much make-up – my guess to mask her mildly pitted skin. More than likely some scarring due to a bout of facial acne in her teens.

However, she did have striking eyes, which had to be seen up close to be appreciated. They were a kind of topaz-green hue, almost luminous like a vampire's, and almost as hypnotic, as I began to find it difficult to look away. Thankfully, she turned first.

I glanced back at Dirty Den, who was eyeing Pete with a cocky grin on his face. Did he mistake that gleam in

Pete's eyes as a sign of fear and not anger? For his sake, I hoped not.

The bartender stepped in closer. 'Look, lads, in the interest of our other customers, don't you think it'd be better to take your little dispute outside?'

'Yeah, come on, Pete,' Simon urged. 'Let's cool off outside, eh?'

Pete threw up his hands. 'Fine! . . . I'm calm enough!' he said, and marched out, followed by the rest of us.

Outside in the car park, I was just about to suggest that we all sit at one of the steel-framed parasol tables on the porch to sort it out, when Pete kicked off again.

'Listen, you!' He stabbed a finger towards Dirty Den. 'I need to chat to my so-called wife alone . . . So bugger off, OK?'

Dirty Den sniggered brashly out of the side of his mouth. Arrogant bastard, I said to myself.

'I think it'd be a wise move, mate,' Simon added.

'Only if Janice wants me to,' he said defiantly.

I had to smile . . . Christ, I think this guy really thinks he is Dirty Den. He was so cocksure that Pete wasn't going to give him a pasting, he thought he could show off a bit in front of Janice and the rest of us. Another mistake!

'Move it!' Pete growled, and I knew that that was the final warning.

'I think you'd better go, mate!' I raised the alarm, and I'm sure the bastard looked back at me with 'fuck you' eyes. Christ, he was pushing his luck now. Just what the hell do women see in these pricks?

That's when the first blow cracked Dirty Den on the side of his cheekbone. Talk about being gob-smacked, at least it wiped that tidy smirk right off his face!

'What the fuck's all that about?' He began flouncing about like someone who had just had a bucket of ice-cold water thrown over his head.

Janice immediately jumped in front of Pete to hold him back, while Simon and I formed a kind of barrier to make it difficult for either of them to get to each other.

'Fucking bastard! He's not gonna get away with that!' Dirty Den, cried, dabbing his cheek for blood.

'That was stupid, wasn't it?' Janice spat at her husband.

Looking into Pete's eyes, I could see there was still plenty of fire in them. Better watch out, it's not over yet. Any moment now, he's going to have another go. The only way to prevent this situation from escalating into a full-blown brawl was to get that idiot away from Pete as quickly as possible. But how were we going to do that?

'Look, mate, I think you'd better fuck off now,' I barked at him, but still he wouldn't go. I even tried ushering him off by the arm, but he just snatched it back.

What a situation it was becoming, me trying to get Dirty Den away, Simon trying to talk Pete down, and Pete's wife not knowing what the hell to do. Finally, she woke up and came over to sort out Dirty Den, so I left her to it and went back to Pete and Simon.

Bang... Without any warning, I saw a blinding white flash.

While my back was turned Dirty Den had taken a cheap shot at Pete, but had hit me instead. In a blur I saw Pete dive onto him, and that's when the real fight broke out. This time not even Simon and I could do anything to stop it. Although that didn't stop Pete's wife, who foolishly tried to get in the way and was shoved back, clanging into the steel-framed tables and chairs. Simon grabbed hold of her and pulled her out of the way.

From then on, we decided to let them get it off their

chest and be ready to stop it when one of them had had enough.

Fortunately, we didn't have to wait that long, as it turned out to be a bit of a mismatch. Pete was simply too big and too strong for the little twerp. And after he'd booted him around the car park a few times, his hapless victim was left cowering in submission. That's when Simon and I stepped in and pulled Pete away. Even though the fucker deserved everything he got, we didn't want to see him get seriously injured. In our position, Pete would have done the same.

Janice immediately dashed to her lover's aid.

'That's right . . . go and tend to your beloved. It's pretty obvious who you care about,' Pete growled, and spat on the floor in contempt.

Simon and I were left speechless and standing there looking stupid.

Just as I was about to go over to Pete, I saw Janice marching towards him with a face like thunder. Oh shit, wouldn't like to be him now, I thought.

But Pete stood his ground, and halted her with a threatening finger.

'Don't fucking start, I'm not in the mood,' he snarled, and she flinched as if she thought he was going to whack her as well.

Pete began to really lay into her, all the pent-up bitterness and anger gushing out of his system, until she was reduced to tears.

'Can't you see why I came?' she sobbed. 'Can't you see I've done everything in my power to get you back? I've tried everything!'

'No, you've fucked me up well and truly . . . that's what you've done,' Pete snapped back.

'Pete, how many times can I say I'm sorry? How long

can you go on punishing me? I had to drag Mike (so that's what his name was), no . . . beg him to come here and tell you to your face that there's nothing going on between me and him. It was a one-off! I was so frustrated not being able to be the wife you wanted, I had to find out what was wrong with me.'

'So instead of trying the conventional therapy methods, you chose to sleep with someone. What a fucking convenient excuse for a cheap shag. You had sex with him!' Pete raged like I'd never seen him before. 'He was inside you, you got pleasure from him not me. That should have been me, I married you, I'm supposed to be the only one sharing that kind of intimacy. If you can't get satisfaction from me . . . fuck off, and let me find someone who'll appreciate me.'

'If that's what I really wanted, do you think I'd have bothered to come here tonight?'

Simon and I looked at each other uncomfortably. These were things that should be said in private, not here in front of the whole world. Only they were too far gone now to care about outsiders, so it was up to us to do the decent thing.

Leaving Dirty Den slumped in one of the parasol chairs, licking his wounds, we slunk back in the pub to wait it out.

The last time I saw Pete lose it like that was when we were kids.

15

Summer '82

How long was this torture going to last? I could hardly breathe with him sitting on my chest, and the smell of grass stains on his knees was making me feel sick.

I was being pinned down, bullied by one of Jonno Edwards' right-hand lads (Jeffrey Morris – aka Sludge, because his clothes were always dirty and dishevelled, and he was a bit of a fat bastard). Just because I didn't pass him the ball when he asked.

All I was doing was messing about by myself on the soccer pitch by the kiddie's swings while I waited for Pete and Simon. Then lard arse turned up looking for trouble . . .

But why is Sludge out by himself? Where are Jonno and the rest of the cursed gang? Have they disowned him because he's such a useless fat bastard or something, and in frustration he's now taking it out on me? Hope Pete and Si get here soon, then we'll see how brave he is without his precious mates to back him up.

Sludge hawked his throat, and let the spit half dangle out of his mouth.

'You'd better not gob in my face!' I scowled back as I wriggled to get free, but he was just too heavy.

He sucked the foamy spittle back in. 'Or wot?' He grinned, thoroughly enjoying his petty torments. 'You and your two queer mates think you're so fucking clever, don't you?'

'No! I squinched my face angrily.

'Yes you fucking do! But we've got special plans for you three, especially that lanky twat Pete.'

'He'd kick the shit out of you any day!' I hissed, and that got to him. Enraged, he tore handfuls of dry grass and tried to cram them into my mouth, but I tossed my head back and forth so much, he gave up. Instead, he tore off my glasses so I wouldn't be able to see.

'Come on, four eyes, let's see you squint,' he cackled.

Even without my specs, I could see a white bogey up his nose poised to base-jump out at any second. The thought of it falling in my mouth . . . yuk!

But instead of letting fly and telling the fat bastard to fuck off me, I just let him get on with it, and be done. I'd learnt from experience that losing your temper only antagonises them even more. The trick in a situation like this, as long as they don't go too far, is to lie there impassively like a wax dummy. Don't pose any threat to them whatsoever. In the end they usually lose interest and bugger off to look for trouble elsewhere.

'Who fucking owns you?' he snarled down into my face, his head giving me temporary shade from the blinding sun.

I didn't answer.

'Who fucking owns you?' He seized the neck of my tee shirt as if he was going to bite my head off.

Now when they start getting that heavy, they're normally saying, I'm feeling a bit shitty about myself today, and simple intimidation isn't going to be enough to sugar my cornflakes. Today I'm afraid I'm going to have to break one or two heads in order to feel big again. And for starters, I'm going to take it out on this little squinting four-eyed twat here.

No, I don't think so! I may indeed be a little squinting, four-eyed twat who'd prefer to run away rather than face a fight with someone a bit bigger than me. But even twats have a breaking point.

I don't mind having the shit rubbed in my face every now and again if it means keeping nerds like that off my back. But I'm certainly not going to fucking eat it for them as well. If I was to give in now, from this day on, he, and every other fucker who wants to have a go, might as well own me. I'll be about as popular as a wet fart in a game of twister ... Zero respect. Even dogs will be coming up to me and pissing down my leg.

'Who fucking owns you?' Sludge shook me harder.

I coolly put my specs back on and stared back into his piggy brown eyes, saying under my breath, Not fucking you.

'Ha ha, dolphin head!' I heard the itchy voice of Karen Craven, the Great Orme superbitch, having a good gloat as she swanned past with her friends. Where the hell did she come from?

Shit! Could have been worse, Sharon might have been walking past. Wouldn't want *her* to know how much of a wimp I really was.

Sludge slapped my face, dislodging my specs again. 'I'm not fucking moving until you say . . . I own you.'

'I own you!' I copied.

'Tosser!' He pressed his full weight down on me, trying to crush me into submission.

'Last chance or you're dead.'

'Hoi . . . off him!' I heard Pete shout from a distance.

Ha . . . yes, my heart rose with delight. Let's see how fucking tough you are now, I said under my breath.

'Off him, I said!' Pete's voice grew louder.

'You what?' Sludge tried to sound as brash as he could.

'Fucking get off now!' I could hear Pete's Adidas trainers swish through the grass towards us.

'Or what?' Sludge retorted.

'Or we'll find out just how hard you really are, you fat git!' Pete growled.

Sludge lifted himself off me, and it was such a relief to be able to breathe easily again. I sat up to my elbows, eager to know what was going to happen next.

Just for the tale of the tape, Pete at 14 years old was already head and shoulders taller than any other lad our age on the Orme. That alone usually discouraged the average kid from messing with him. If in any trouble, it was always handy to have Pete standing in your corner.

Sludge, on the other hand, was a bit of a short arse who carried quite a bit of puppy fat, making him look stocky. He looked tough but in reality he was just an obese blob. If ever you were chased by any of Jonno's gang, you hoped it'd be Sludge, because everybody knew he was so useless at running. All you had to do was break into a quick sprint, and he usually gave up. No stamina!

'Oh yeah?' Sludge stepped back, his bottle already going. 'Come on then!' he bluffed.

Pete made a feint, and Sludge flinched. Any moment now, I heard my heart begin to sing, we are going to see Sludge scarper for his life, and oh what a splendid sight that will be.

At that moment, the worst possible thing that could happen . . . did. Jonno and the rest of his gang, including shit-face the dog, appeared on the brow of the hill leading from the estate.

'Oh shit!' I muttered.

Of course, seeing this, Sludge now had a steel backbone, and immediately took advantage of the fact that his mates were here to save him. He rubgy-charged Pete, but was caught in a body hold and flung on his arse.

Jonno and his mob stopped dead in their tracks. What the fuck's going on here? they must have thought.

Sludge wrapped himself around Pete's legs, but was kneed repeatedly in the side of his head. That's gonna hurt, I winced. Yet stubbornly, he clung on, probably thinking if only he could hold on long enough for his mates to grab Pete, it's be worth the pain.

That was when Jonno and his entourage charged like a pack of wild dogs, and I jumped up ready to run.

Realising he now had only seconds, Pete kneed and kicked his way free as if he was kicking his way out of a bramble bush. Sludge couldn't take it any longer, and let go. Pete swiftly fished up his football, and we both scarpered for our lives.

The only way we could go was up the hummock towards the old redbrick lookout turret (the castle, as we used to call it – apparently, we were told, it was used in the war to spot enemy planes flying over) and down through the top of the bluebell woods.

Once again, I had that terrible feeling of nausea in my stomach, and my legs felt as if I had balls and chains attached to them.

Mounting the hill, Pete was pulling ahead of me, and I called for him to wait, but I don't think he heard me. Behind me, I was sure I could hear shit-face the dog panting at my heels. Keep going! Keep going!

Over the brow, we burst through the thickets, the spindly branches of the whitebeam trees whipping our arms and legs for causing such a furore, and the sour scent from the ferns thick in our nostrils.

I don't know whether it was the reaction to my pure fear, but I nearly exploded into hysterics at the sight of Pete lumbering ahead of me. His lanky legs just weren't designed to handle this kind of exertion. He looked like a baby giraffe trying to run across an ice rink . . . One leg's giving way . . . is he going to fall? . . . No, he's all right! . . . Oops, he's going again. I felt like shouting to him, 'Pete, get those fucking legs sorted out for Christ's sake.'

Finally we left the thick foliage of the back woods and landed in Haulfrie. Only now did I chance a quick shufti behind for the others, but couldn't see them. Keep going!

We headed along the footpath back towards the golfie and the woods, where we could hide. Fatigue was now setting in, and my throat and lungs were on fire. I wasn't going to last much longer.

Pete, teary-eyed from running, signalled to climb over the stone wall and into old Haulfrie. But before I had chance to question it, he was up and halfway over.

On the other side, we both crashed into the brambles and collapsed, our chests heaving up and down like the driving pistons on a locomotive. My legs were pumped so much, I thought they were going to explode.

While I was busy praying they hadn't seen us jump over the wall, Pete tapped my leg. He'd heard something. I turned to him, and he held his finger to his mouth to keep me silent. Again, I held my breath, and listened . . . was that the scuffing sound of someone's feet I could hear?

The closer the sounds came, the more our eyes bulged

with terror. Any second now Jonno was going to leap over the wall and catch us. If he did, we would be completely at his mercy.

A face shot over the top of the wall, almost giving us heart attacks. 'Ha! . . . Caught ya!' Simon cackled.

'You prick!' Pete swooned with relief, and our bodies went limp.

'What the hell are you two doing down there then?'

Pete looked up at him reprovingly. 'Where's Jonno and the others?'

'I don't know . . . They're not here . . . Why?'

Wearily, we climbed back over the wall and filled Simon in about what had happened.

Afterwards, as we headed towards the woods, Simon, still thinking about it, snatched up a small twig and snapped off the end. 'They probably gave up the chase by the turret.' Then snorted. 'Shit! I'd hate to be you two when they do catch you, though.'

'How did you know we were there, anyhow?' I puzzled.

'Well, Pete said if you weren't on the soccer pitch, you'd be down here by the squirrel tree. So I decided to check here first, and just caught you both jumping over the wall. I was gonna call you, but thought, fuck it! I'd give you a bit of a scare instead.'

'Fate or what?' Pete added.

'Where've you been, anyhow?' I asked.

'Me mum's come down for a visit, so I stayed with her for a bit.'

'I thought she was supposed to be coming down next week?'

'No, it's this week!' Simon dropped his head. 'She's staying until tomorrow.'

I could see Simon was getting a bit broody about his mum again so I didn't ask him any more questions.

That was until Pete tactfully suggested we climb the squirrel tree, which I agreed to do as long as they didn't try to coax me into going to the top again.

Sitting on my perch about two-thirds of the way up, I looked down gingerly through the ladders of branches, and imagined if Jonno and his gang suddenly appeared at the bottom. If they did, I knew they'd either climb up and throw us down, or simply stone us off with fir cones. Shit! – I clung even tighter to my branch – they might even be down there now, hiding in the thickets ... watching and waiting.

It was now just after midday. The sun was right overhead and cooking up the Orme like a Sunday roast. But up in the squirrel tree, it was refreshingly cool and shady. I myself preferred the glorious summer Technicolor mornings, like those chirpy cornflake ads they have on the telly. In the afternoons, when the sun gets hotter, all that rich colour gets bleached out, and it's just too bright for me.

I glanced up ten feet or so, to listen to what Simon and Pete were talking about. Apparently, Simon was telling Pete all about the musical show his mother was doing down in London at the present.

'Hey, Si, do you miss your mum when she goes back to London?' I thought I'd ask as he seemed in the mood to talk about her again.

'Yeah ... sometimes I wish she hadn't come, though.'

'Why's that?' Pete asked, his legs dangling over both sides of the branch and his heels kicking the scaly trunk, and sending down chippings of bark on my head.

'Well, I just start getting used to her not being here, then she turns up, and it's like reopening an old wound again.'

'Would you like to have her home for good?'

'Oh yeah! I wouldn't have to dread saying any more goodbyes to her, would I?'

'Suppose not!' Pete agreed.

I tried to cheer him up a bit. 'Hey Si, just think, she won't be touring forever! She'll probably settle down for good, and you'll go to live with her.'

'Yeah, but what if that means going far away from here, away from all my friends?' That seemed to silence us all for a few moments.

The dreaded thought that one day we would all go our separate ways had always haunted me. I had known Pete and Simon virtually all my life, they were like family to me. And to imagine them going off in that big wide world and leaving me here all alone, had often kept me awake at nights.

The only consolation I had at the moment was that we still had plenty of messing-about years together ahead of us. So I didn't need worry about it yet.

'What about your mum, John?' Pete shouted down to me. 'Do you think she'll ever find someone and settle down?'

I leant my head against the bark. 'She's had one or two guys in the past, but nothing serious . . .'

'Does it worry you though that if she does, you might become second best?' Simon asked.

I looked up at him. 'Yeah, I suppose it does. Whenever she's had a man home, I always listen outside the living room door in case they're planning some sort of life without me.'

'Shouldn't listen behind closed doors!' Pete slammed. 'Me gran clipped me across the earhole for doing that once. She said, Don't you know curiosity killed the cat?'

On the top of the golf course we heard the faint hum

of the council Land Rover mowing the greens and fairways with its trailer of grass cutters.

Most of that afternoon we spent plotting our route for Thursday night, that's if we could get away with sneaking out again (may have to work on that one a bit).

Instead of going through the glade to Lovers' Green like last time, we decided to tunnel through the back of our den. That way we could creep up from the back of the green, and get a much better view. All that seemed reasonable, providing we could clear away as much of the foliage as possible. This included any batches of dried twigs, protruding stumps, entangled vines, anything that might cause noise and give us away.

So without further ado, we got cracking. Christ, what a hassle we had. It was ten times worse than having to do a bit of tidying up in the house for my mother. I vowed I'd never complain to her again!

Finally, after snapping, kicking, and tugging out the roots of the most stubborn dead plants and vegetation underfoot, we'd done it. We even did a few test walks up to the green just to make sure.

Pete stood, hands on hips, chuffed with himself. 'Just don't fart, Si. That's the only thing that'll give us away now!'

'You can talk, fart-arse,' Simon snorted, and I had to smirk.

I glanced down at my raw grubby hands, and had a sniff. They smelt like the inside of a rotted greenhouse.

'What else are we gonna do then?' I wiped my runny nose, hoping they were just as fed up as I was.

'What about making an emergency exit?' Simon suggested.

'Fucking hell!' Pete chucked a twig at him. 'We're not planning to escape from Colditz, you know! Why do you have to complicate things? We'll just go back the same way through the den. There's no other way we can go, in any case.'

'We could tunnel through the bushes towards Beaver Lodge.'

'Bollocks to that!' I jumped in. 'I'm not spending another two hours making another path we may not even use.' And Pete agreed.

With part 1 of our route sorted, next we had to plot our retreat. This time, we wouldn't double back up the golfie to the estate. Instead, we would sneak past the front of the green and head towards Beaver Lodge and Rofft Place Terrace, into the residential area. It was quicker and much less of a hike, especially if we had to leg it in a hurry again. I just wished we'd have done that last time.

'Hang on a minute.' I lifted the finger of enquiry. 'When we do make our getaway? What if some of them are waiting for us at the entrance to Lovers Green and block our way past to Rofft Place?'

Pete picked up a club-sized branch for a weapon. 'We make sure we're tooled up to whack our way past if we need to. They'll scatter like chickens.'

'You hope!' I sneered. 'So where do we put them then?'

'On the day, we bury them in the den ready.'

'Why don't we just keep them on us the whole time, just in case?'

'Because it saves us carrying them around all night,' Simon chimed in. 'And just say we got seen carrying all that stuff on our way into Haulfrie, we'd get reported.'

Fair enough, I thought, and simply stood there enjoying the summer tranquillity. Above us, a cool gentle breeze sighed through the tops of the whitebeam trees. I looked up to catch the jiggling leaves glittering like emerald gemstones against the glare of the mid-afternoon sun.

The next time I look at those, I'll probably be praying for my life, I thought, and shook my head to myself.

Content we'd done everything we'd set out to do that afternoon, we headed back up to the estate. Above us, dark clouds had begun to bubble up in the sky, blocking out the late-afternoon sun. Finally we were enjoying some shade. What a relief!

On our way, we stopped off by the trailer of grass cutters left there by the Land Rover man. While I fingered out some clotted grass from one of the coiled steel blades, Pete and Simon argued about why Mr Golf wanted to have his course trimmed in the middle of the season.

In the far east, over the coast of Rhyl and Prestatyn, the skies began to bruise ominously.

'Looks like that forecast you heard was right, Si.' I nodded in the direction of what was looking like a bad storm heading our way.

'Perhaps that's why Mr Golf chose to close today – he knew about the storm,' I suggested.

For the next half-hour or so, we stood watching it drift over, as if someone was slowly pulling a plum-coloured curtain across the heavens.

I don't know about anyone else, but the three of us have always loved a good thunderstorm. Whenever you see that minty-blue sky turn a dark, poisonous, hue, and you feel that electric buzz in the air, watch out! Here comes another awesome display of Mother Nature's raw earthly power.

Then we'd ask ourselves, Is it going to be a mild one, or a right banger that'll split the heavens in two? If we stay out here, will we get struck? And if we did, would we survive, or get totally incinerated like flies on an electric Insect-o-Cutor ring?

Myself, I much prefer the thunderstorms in the daytime, as opposed to the night. To be woken up by that earthshaking boom always reminds me of those late-night horror films when all the dead rise out of their graves. So now, whenever I wake up in bed during a storm, I always imagine an army of zombies all gravitating outside my bedroom window, waiting to get me.

Call me a silly sod . . . I just can't help it!

After we cheered the first few flashes of lightning and distant rumbles of thunder, I suggested we all went back to my house to watch the storm with a cup of tea. My mum wasn't due back from work for another few hours, so we had plenty of time.

So that's how we spent the rest of that mid-August Tuesday afternoon. By the way, the storm turned out to be one of the best we'd ever had. It lasted for about two hours, sheet and fork lightning every 30 seconds, followed by crashing thunder, like giant cannon balls being rolled across the Orme. Smashing! You can't beat a good old-fashioned midsummer thunderstorm. Wouldn't you agree?

But talk about the afternoon ending with a bang. After the storm passed on, the topic of Jonno and his gang cropped up again, and how we were going to stay out of their way for the next 20 years or so.

Then Simon told us that on his way down to meet us, it was lucky it was Sharon and her boyfriend he bumped into, and not Jonno.

Sharon Roberts has a boyfriend? I nearly choked on my boiling-hot tea. My sweet innocent bohemian girl

Sharon, who only yesterday, was playing with her dolls in the dirt; and now she's putting it about with the nearest cheese dick she can find? Do I sound bitter or is it just me?

'Sharon has a boyfriend?' I squeaked, trying not to sound too shocked.

Simon shrugged. 'Well, they were walking hand in hand.'

I couldn't believe it! Some twat's beaten me to it! Now I'm going to have to put up with seeing them canoodling around the estate, like a pair of soppy lovebirds. How can she do this to me? She must have known deep down that I liked her and was just waiting for the right moment. What a bastard!

Well, if she couldn't manage to wait just a little bit longer for me . . . Fuck her! She's not worth it! Let him have her, whoever he is.

I felt so pissed off, I nearly shouted 'Fuck!' all over the place, but if I had, Pete and Simon would have sussed me out. My only outlet for this raging jealousy was to blurt out the most insulting and cruel thing I could possibly think of.

'Well, to go out with that freak, whoever he is, he's got to be the dopiest fucker in the world.' Yet, the second after saying it, I wished I could've taken it back. But it was too late. The damage was done.

Even Simon chastised me for it – Simon, who is usually the king of put-downs.

'You tight bastard! What the fuck's she done to you?'

She hadn't done a thing, and I panicked for an excuse. I was just saved by the bell when Pete diverted our attention to an advertisement for one of those ghetto blasters on the telly. 'I've got to get me one of those for Christmas,' he drooled, and I was let off.

Thinking about it later, it would have served me right if Simon had reminded me that I was certainly no Prince Charming myself. But he didn't. Why? Because he is one of my best mates.

16

I still cringe painfully about what I said about Sharon all those years ago. I just thank God it wasn't to her face, especially as she's been DEAD now for going on 15 years. God rest her soul!

I couldn't believe it when I first heard she had died. At the time, it came as a tremendous shock to everyone who knew her – such a tragic loss.

Apparently she became a drug addict – acid, marijuana, cocaine, crack, you name it. She took the lot. She died from an overdose at the age of 20, and was buried in Llanrhos cemetery, a mile or so out of town.

To this day, it remains a mystery how on earth she ever managed to get into drugs. Anyway . . . wherever you are now, Sharon, God bless you, and I'm sorry I said those things about you. They weren't true!

Christ . . . Pete and his wife are still outside in the cark park trying to sort out their differences. They've been out there over 20 minutes now, they must be freezing!

Simon and I have had to have another drink, although only orange juice for me, I'm driving, remember? Strange, Simon hasn't said much since our second drink. Maybe he's still mulling over what has happened tonight.

Yet deep down, I'm not sure, it's so hard to tell with him, it could be something else. Don't think I'll bother asking, not now, and even if I did, he probably wouldn't tell me anyway. Knowing him for as long as I have, he's always bottled things up inside. Sometimes getting him to talk openly about things is like trying to tear bits of skin off his body. Of course it could be my imagination . . .

'Want another drink?' I asked, but he just shook his head.

At that moment, Pete breezed through the door. By the flustered look on his face, I couldn't be sure if it was the biting November cold, or he'd done something terrible to his wife.

'All right?' I asked, and Simon instantly flickered back to life.

Pete flopped down in one of the old wooden chairs beside me.

'They've gone back home now . . . sent them packing,' he said with an accomplished sniff.

'So what's the upshot of it then?' Simon asked.

Pete shrugged his heavy shoulders and sighed, his breath stale from all the arguing with his wife. But we didn't mind.

'I've told her I want a divorce. That's it . . . over! I'm getting in touch with a solicitor on Monday, to start proceedings.' His mouth seemed to be twitching slightly.

I have to admit this saddened me, as it not only meant a truckload more anguish for everyone intimately involved, including Pete's son, whom I'd never even met. It also meant that there wasn't much hope for me either. Being in near enough the same boat as Pete, I couldn't blame him for making that kind of decision. Yet deep down there was a tiny part of me rooting to see a reconciliation, something to prove that even in the most unforgivable situations, there was still room for mercy. Perhaps if Pete himself was able to forgive and forget, then maybe I could. So what now?

An uncomfortable heavy silence followed, as if we were all mourning the sudden death of a close friend. In this case it was the demise of Pete's marriage.

This damn melancholy was becoming much too familiar, and once again it brought forth the thought of Sammy. In a few days, she would be back from her holiday, and what then?

I wondered if she had actually gone with her friends after all, or was that a merely a smokescreen so she could go with her lover? Then again, if she had told the truth, would she have ended up having a holiday romance anyway? *Would* she have a holiday romance? Well, why not? In her mind she was more or less single now, and may as well go out and enjoy herself.

Yeah . . . And I might as well have copped off with that girl the other night, if that's the case! No, don't get started again, change the subject . . . I know . . . What about inviting Pete and Simon back for a chat?

'Want to come over to my house and have a few cans?' I said with a bright look.

Pete grimaced. 'Naw thanks, mate. I don't think I'd be very good company at the moment. I just want to go home and have a good think.' Which, under the circumstances, was understandable.

'Si?' I asked, but he wasn't with it either.

'Think I'll give it a miss tonight as well.'

(What the hell was eating *him*?)

Oh well, at least I still had my cosy Friday night to look forward to. What was left of it.

To save Simon getting a taxi, Pete offered to give him a lift home. Before they left, I told them they could drop over tomorrow night if they wanted to. Pete said he'd give me a ring to let me know, which I suppose was an easy way of saying, Probably not! Although when tomorrow comes, they might feel different and be thankful of a shoulder to cry on. We'll see.

As I made my way back home, I wondered what was going to happen when Sammy returned from her holiday next week.

Surely she's had time enough now to know what she wants to do. As for me, I've already been to hell and back over this, and have more or less given up hope of a reconciliation. I wonder what she thinks . . .

That night, I woke with another start, drenched in perspiration and gasping like some poor animal beaten within an inch of its life. All I could see was those masked faces again, and the bulged eyes glaring from behind the cut-out slits. Frenzied eyes belonging to minds barely in control of their sanities. Eyes that feed on people's pain, people's fear. Eyes that say, Oh if he gives me that velvety scream again I'm going to do it! I can't help it!

What is it with these nightmares? I've got to do something about them, otherwise I'll end up with a heart attack or something.

Ever since I broke up with Sammy . . . no, ever since I met back up with my two long-lost mates, these dreams have been getting worse. It's like fragments of a broken jigsaw, fitting back together, piece by piece. But when the puzzle finally unfolds, I know exactly what I'm going to be able to see. That terrible night back in '82.

How could we have been so naive to imagine that if we just forgot about it long enough, it would simply fade away from existence, and that would be that?

Is that why Pete and Simon moved away? Is that why we have stayed apart for so many years, scared the mere sight of one another would trigger recollections of that horrific day?

Not since we were those foolish, hapless teenagers have we ever mentioned it to each other. Maybe now it's time to make a stand and face it once and for all. But will they? Will Pete and Simon finally go back to the night of 26th August 1982? . . . They have to! Our sanities, maybe even our lives, depend on it.

Later that morning, I paced my kitchen, cordless phone in hand, trying to think how I was going to coax Pete and Simon back here for a bit of regression therapy. I'll just tell them that we've got no chance of sorting out our futures until we first mend the past, I decided.

Ring! Ring! went the phone in my hand and I nearly dropped it with fright. My first thoughts were of Sammy calling. Couldn't be, could it?

'John?' Pete's tepid voice poured down my ear.

'Pete,' I cried in delight. 'I was just about to ring you. How's things?' I didn't want to jump straight in and nab him the moment he spoke.

He made a dull rasp. 'Don't ask, mate! She hasn't phoned, and I haven't phoned her. Listen, the reason I'm ringing . . .' He paused uncomfortably, as if he was going to ask a big favour of me. '. . . I think it's time all three of us, you, me and Si, had a sit-down and chatted about the past . . . You know, that time.'

My heart thumped into my ribs for joy. 'Well, fuck me, Pete! I've just spent the last hour or so pacing about the house wondering how I was going to ask you the very same thing.'

'Fate or what?' he snorted.

'I'll fucking say it was!' I blew with relief.

'Thing is,' Pete sighed, 'I don't think Si's all that keen on the idea.'

'Well, it's got to be all three of us, Pete. Can't leave Si out of it.'

'I know! I know! I'll have a chat with him – he'll come!'

'When do you want to do it then?' I asked.

'How about Monday night? I've got a few things to sort out this weekend, and I don't think I could do it straight after last night anyway.'

'Yeah, I understand.' I grimaced, having hoped it'd be sooner. 'It's all set then. Can't wait to finally get it off our chests. Hopefully the nightmares will end with it,' I remarked.

'You too? Shit, we definitely need to talk . . . We'll pop over about seven-ish Monday night then?'

'OK, mate, see you then – and cosh Simon over the head to get him here if you have to.'

'Will do . . . See ya.'

I put down the phone, and already felt a ton lighter. At last it was going to happen. I felt like someone with chronic kidney failure, just told the promising news that a donor may have been found . . . Halle-fucking-lujah!

Saturday came and went like a half-hour dinner break in a ten-hour work shift. Things were really moving now. Sunday I went over to my mother's, and even had dinner there. I know she still loves the opportunity to cook me one of her sumptuous Sunday roasts. And I was only too pleased to wolf it down. You can't beat a bit of Mum waiting on you hand and foot, especially when you've been used to cooking your own tea for the past 15 years or so.

Yet when she asked why Sammy wasn't with me, I had to weave a little yarn about her doing a bit of overtime in work. That seemed to work for now, but talk about spinning these little lies ... If things didn't get sorted soon, I would run out of thread.

Monday morning, despite getting up early, I simply couldn't face work, and phoned in telling them I had a stomach upset (skivers). Hopefully that'd buy me enough time until Friday, when my holidays began.

That morning I decided to have a good breakfast, sausages and beans, then sat to watch the early morning chat shows on the TV.

The caption at the foot of the screen told me that it was a live debate about spouses who have a confession to tell their partners. Sounds more like *Jerry Springer*, I remarked. And why were they doing a live debate?

Sitting on the stage were these two gothic-like girls of about 20 with long straggly black hair; and punkish-red hues running down one side of their heads. On their faces, both wore eyebrow piercings and nose studs. Christ ... what a pair, they looked like two Ozzy Osbournes.

The groomed lady host turned to one of the young women. 'So, Joanne, you're fed up with your boyfriend of ten months and have come here to tell him what?'

Joanne and her friend shared an audacious little smirk. 'I'm here to tell him I'm in love with another woman, and want to leave him.'

A murmur of disapproval rose from the audience, and I sniggered to myself.

'Well, before we meet your current boyfriend, would you just like to explain what sort of a relationship you had with him over the past ten months?'

'Sure! He has never been there for me, he never showed me much affection, he never used to tell me how nice I looked. He never took me out anywhere. He just totally neglected me, treated me like a pet who is supposed to be there whenever he wanted. So out I went looking for someone who could appreciate me.'

'Did he beat you or anything?'

I tutted with annoyance. Christ, she's trying to get him condemned before he even gets out.

Joanne paused hesitantly. 'Yes! Just the once, and it was with a closed fist.'

A few recriminating tuts from the audience.

'Well, no matter what the situation is, there's no excuse for a man to raise his hand to a woman.' The host shrugged dispassionately. 'So on that note, I suppose it's time to meet him. For the past ten minutes or so he's been sitting in our green room, and hasn't heard what's been going on out here. So now we'll call him in . . .'

Now that you've painted him out to be a complete bastard, I muttered at the screen.

'Please welcome . . . Simon.' Despite one or two hisses, most of the audience clapped charitably.

I snorted to myself, wait till I tell our Simon. At least he's not stuck in a situation like this . . . But to my total shock and horror, Simon, OUR SIMON walked out onto the stage, and eased himself into the empty seat provided for him.

What the f—! I tried to say, with half a sausage dangling out of the corner of my mouth. I didn't know whether to laugh or shout. I had to shake my head repeatedly to confirm what I was seeing was real. It was like someone slapping me across the face with a wet salmon.

Simon, wearing a lime-green shirt, averted his eyes from the glare of the television cameras as if he could sense I was watching.

'Welcome, Simon!' the host began. 'How long have you and Joanne been together then?'

'About ten months now!' Simon hawked his throat uncomfortably.

'Good relationship?'

Simon shrugged his narrow shoulders in a fair gesture. 'Not bad, I suppose. Good times, bad times.'

'Fucking hell, Si! You kept this quiet!' I fumbled about on my hands and knees to find a blank vid to bang in the machine.

The presenter fiddled with her cue-cards. 'Would you say that you're still fairly close?'

'I enjoy her company when we can see each other.' Simon gave Joanne a mild look of reproach.

'Do you love her?'

'Does she love me?' Simon looked suspiciously across at his girlfriend.

'OK . . . Over to you, Joanne.' The presenter nodded.

Simon, appearing a bit flush-faced, turned to his girlfriend, and I thought . . . Shit no! Not here! Not like this, in front of millions of people.

Joanne looked at him somewhat sheepishly. 'Simon, you know that we haven't been spending that much time with each other lately, and whenever we do, we usually end up arguing. Well . . . I'm here to tell you that I've fallen in love with Donna, and want to be with her permanently.'

The nation and I held our breaths.

'OK, fine!' He shrugged nonchalantly, and the crowd didn't know whether they should clap or what. Joanne eyed him suspiciously, waiting for the punchline to the joke he was surely playing.

'You, you don't mind?' She smiled sardonically.

'Wait a minute,' the presenter interjected in amazement. 'You're telling us you don't mind that your girlfriend is dumping you for another woman?'

'No, not really!' Simon shrugged, and I had to laugh, probably with relief.

The presenter, the audience and Simon's girlfriend were clearly stumped. This wasn't supposed to happen! Simon was supposed to crumble into a pathetic blubbering wreck, just like all the other hapless male victims before him. Come on! The sadistically anti-male audience want to see this guy at least get verbally castrated.

'May I ask why you are handling it so well?' asked the talk-show presenter.

'Well, the truth of the matter is . . .' He shifted confidently in his seat. '. . . It's something I've been expecting for a while. Over the last ten months I've been with her, all she's ever wanted to do was get stoned with her university friends. I was the one who had to go and get her when she rang me up too pissed to get a taxi by herself. All the times I've offered to take her out, she's always had an excuse to go with her uni friends instead. So in the end I gave up asking. Then I found out she had started cheating on me, and has done so on many occasions with at least half a dozen lads. Being the foolishly forgiving person I was, I kept taking her back. But about a month ago, I had suspicions about her cheating on me with her so-called girlfriend. So one night, I crept home and saw them with their hands down each other knickers . . . Didn't know that did you?' Simon sneered across at Joanne, who didn't know what the hell to say.

A few embarrassed sniggers rose from the audience, and the presenter figeted anxiously with her cue-cards. This was, after all, live television with no edits or bleeps.

'Urm? Can we keep in mind that this is live television,' she bleated.

Simon shrugged smugly. 'So out I went, and found someone else for myself.'

Yeez! I thumped the air in delight, but who was this so-called new person in Simon's life? For the time being, that didn't matter.

'Fine!' Joanne clutched the hand of her female lover.

Still determined to make Simon out to be the villain, the presenter cashed in her ace card. 'But you did hit her though, did you not?'

'That's right, yes I did!' Simon confessed. 'One night after catching her with another guy, she in frustration – '

'That's not true! That's not true!' Joanne stormed, but Simon ignored her.

'. . . She came at me with a hammer and broke my wrist before I could overpower her.'

Fuck, Si! You never told us any of this, I muttered.

'Oh, that wasn't the one and only time,' Simon continued. 'She's thrown objects, spat, sworn at me in public when she's been copped, and I have plenty of witnesses who I can call on to testify to that.'

'Well, a lot of this information which I'm receiving now wasn't actually given to my researchers, so there's very little I can do about it,' the presenter admitted.

'No, I wanted it to be a surprise! I didn't want to give anyone the chance to try to sabotage my chance to tell the true untold story,' Simon explained.

Fucking brilliant, my son! I said proudly.

'And I just want to add that I hope she seeks medical help with the drug problem she has at the moment.'

'I see!' The host glanced nervously at her camera crew, just as Joanne's temper snapped. Without any warning, she leapt onto Simon like a fighting hell-cat, but was quickly subdued by the off-camera security.

After things cooled down, the presenter announced that she was going to take questions from the audience. With the microphone, she turned to a bespectacled middle-aged woman with her hand up. The woman stood up, smoothing down her black skirt.

'Well, before Simon came on, I was ready to wish Joanne and her new partner all the best, but now . . . I just hope Simon gets rid of that so-called woman up there and enjoys a much better relationship with the woman he's found.'

With that a rousing applause swept through the audience, much to the smacked-arse looks of the presenter and the two girls on the stage.

Flustering around for some feminist support, and keeping away from the dangerous opinions of the men, the presenter found another woman. This time, a podgy, gum-chewing ladette in her late twenties stood up and took the mike.

'Simon, you've just said that you don't mind Joanne going off with this other woman because you now have a woman of your own. So, in fact, you're just as bad, if not worse than Joanne. At least she had the fortitude to come clean and admit she has someone else. If it hadn't been for this show, I bet you'd have carried on going behind Joanne's back.' No claps from the audience.

Get out of that, was the look in the dark eyes of the presenter.

'Are you joking me or what?' Simon fired back. 'You're

saying that after putting up with all that crap from her for ten months, I was wrong to find someone who'd appreciate me, and now I'm the villain? Where are you from – Men-Haters-R-Us?'

A few raised chuckles from the audience.

Go on, lad! I chanted.

The woman snatched back the mike. 'No! I'm just suggesting that maybe you didn't treat her right in the first place, which would explain why she felt inclined to look elsewhere.'

'Good point!' the presenter added in support.

'Hang on a minute! You're not turning this thing around to make me look like the scoundrel. I've seen this happen too many times on this one-sided male-bashing show (brief camera shot of presenter trying to look bashful). Most of the time the topics featured are mainly about the faults of us men. OK, we have our imperfections . . . sure! I admit that, but we're not the only ones. You women are no saints yourselves (boos from some of the females).'

'That's not true! It's not all bad men, we do cover bad girls as well!' The presenter haughtily clacked her way down the stair aisle towards the stage.

'Oh yeah! . . . Every once in a blue moon, and what usually happens when you do?'

The host glanced covertly at her producer again, wondering whether or not to pull the plug on this guy.

'. . . I'll tell you what! I guarantee in the bad girl show, you'll only pick couples where the chap turns out to be another bloody Charles Manson or someone. So in the end it doesn't matter what the woman was accused of doing, because it's nowhere as bad as the way her monster husband is treating her . . . Right? So once again, this proves it's women who are always the long-suffering victims of us men-beasts. Am I right? (Deserved claps from some of the bold males in the audience.) I mean, we can't win, can we? Even if Joanne stabbed me in the back with a knife every time she got back from shagging some other bloke, you'd say it's my own fault.'

By now, I was dancing an ecstatic jig around my living room.

But Simon hadn't quite finished yet. 'I bet in the audience here, there are at least a handful of women, as well as men, who have cheated on their partners. Yet how many of them would actully put their hand up right now and admit it was their fault? Go on, raise your hands,' Simon challenged, but nobody did.

'Yes, but we're not here to discuss that topic today, that's another show. And it happens to my show!' The presenter stood her ground and tried to rally support from her audience (just a few claps).

'Yes! And no doubt it'd be another show doctored to deliberately humiliate and debase us males.'

Go on! I fisted the air.

'OK, thank you for your opinions, Simon, but I'm afraid we've run out of time.' The simmering presenter struggled to keep her composure. 'Time for a break, when we come back, we'll be talking to a woman who's been married for nearly a year and still hasn't had her marriage consummated ... Back in a moment.' Then she sulkily marched down the aisle off-camera.

At-fucking-last! Someone has said what needed to be said about these hypocritical, male-bashing talk shows. Halle-fucking-lujah! Simon, you're my hero!

17

The rest of the day, I tried to contact Pete to tell him about Simon on the telly and how admirably he had stood up for himself. But I couldn't get hold of him. Typical!

Shit, just thought . . . I hope Simon makes it back in time for our important meeting tonight.

At about 6.30 Pete finally returned my call, and it turned out that he didn't even know Simon had appeared on the show. However, I reassured him I had managed to tape at least three-quarters of it, and he'd be able to watch it later. He said everything was still on for tonight, and he'd turn up, hopefully with Simon, at around 7.30 as planned. Great!

And you'll never guess who phoned me five minutes after I'd spoken to Pete? No, not Simon . . . But Sammy! Yes, Sammy! A total surprise, to say the least.

Basically, she'd just arrived back from holiday, but while she was there she'd had a long think about what she wanted to do about our relationship. Now at long last she was ready to have that talk with me. Yet the moment I heard all that, I felt like someone just called to the hospital to get the worrying results of a CAT scan. My palms went clammy and my legs felt like dead weights. What would be the outcome?

Sammy didn't want to say too much over the phone, but did tell me that she would come over later in the week to have that little discussion. Was that a good or bad sign?

I asked when she would like to come over, and she suggested Friday evening, 7.00 p.m. So it was confirmed. Just as I'd hoped, it looked as if this was definitely the week everything was going to come to a head.

At 6.50 that evening, I sat in my living room with a mug of tea, a time I purposely set aside for reflection. I just wanted to mentally prepare myself for what we were about to go through. I really didn't know what to expect, or how we would react to reliving possibly the worst period in our lives.

Indeed, it might be the only way to completely cure all those terrifying nightmares, and hopefully pave a way out of our own maze of domestic problems. Or it might turn out to be the one card on the pyramid that sends the whole lot crashing down (if you know what I mean).

I had to admit I felt nervous, probably more nervous than facing the prospect of losing Sammy at the end of the week.

At 7.25 p.m. I heard a car pull into our close, and went to the front door, ready to let them in. I waited for the passenger doors to bang shut, then opened the door. Pete and Simon marched solemnly through and into my living room as if they were going to war. First of all, I shook Simon's hand for his excellent performance on telly that morning. (The fucking dark horse – I bet that's what was secretly eating him up in the King's Head on Friday.)

Apparently, he only had a few days' notice to appear on the show. And what about the incredible revelation that his girlfriend turned out to be a lesbian ... Didn't he take it well, despite the incredible irony?

After fantasising about wanting to see two women together for so long, who would have guessed fate would have his girlfriend dump him for another woman. That's got to be poetic justice!

But what about the new girl he mentioned on the show? It turned out to be Susan . . . Remember her? The night all three of us went back to those girls' flat in town. The girl with the ecstasy tablets who sat between Simon's legs. (Not too sure about the tablets though.)

However, I hope it works out for him, I thought. By Christ he's earned that privilege after what he's been through with Joanne. That's another thing . . . He never told us she was that bad!

Needless to say, before we took our long-awaited trip back into the twilight zone, we just had to watch a rerun of the show just for Pete.

Afterwards, I turned to Simon because I knew he was the least keen about coming here tonight for this. 'Sure you're all right about doing this?' I asked him.

'Not really!' He sighed restlessly. 'Apart from having to rush back from the studios in London where my girlfriend dumped me in front of a million people, then relive probably the worst childhood nightmare . . . Let's just say it's not going to be one of those days I'm going to take a picture of and put in the photo album. Aside from that, I'm supposed to be meeting Susan at around ten o'clock tonight.'

'Fuck Susan!' Pete snapped in annoyance. 'Remember us, and where we've been. You've only just met her, for Christ's sake . . . This is ten times more important. If we don't finally get this off our chests, we may not have much of a future.'

I had to nod in agreement.

'OK! OK!' Simon sighed apologetically.

After fetching a six-pack from the kitchen fridge, I bolted the front door and made sure the living room curtains were shut so no one could peep through. Then I closed the living room door and turned down the television. Finally, after some 20 years of running from the demon that had been chasing us, it was time to stop and fight.

We were ready!

18

26 August '82

Pete's old ridge tent was a trifle snug for three people, and it smelt horribly dank inside. Silly bugger, I thought, I bet after the last time he used it, he forgot to hang it out to air-dry like you're supposed to.

It was so ancient, it must have belonged to his grandfather. There was no groundsheet, which meant by morning we'd all be sleeping on wet grass. The only flysheet it had wasn't waterproof, so if it rained, we were fucked. And the zip on the entrance was broken, so one of us would have to sleep all night with one eye open in case someone was creeping around outside.

I was crammed to one side, with my head pushing out the nylon wall. I hated it when that happened, because I always imagined someone outside being able to smash me with a heavy club or something. Pete was in the middle (owner's privilege) and Simon flanked me on the other side. Realising we'd have to stay like that all night was like being squashed in the back of tiny car on the outset of a very long journey.

Although it was just past the peak of summer, we had all brought along our sleeping bags in case it got chilly during the night.

Provisions? Yes, I had brought a flask of coffee, Simon had brought the sandwiches (I wished I'd made them, I thought, I bet they're soggy as shit by now) and Pete had provided the bags of crisps. Ever tried a packet of cheese 'n' onion in the middle of the night? It's like eating an apple after you've just brushed your teeth. Or having a dollop of ice-cream on top of your roast potatoes. Basically, you just don't do it.

Going camping was at least a better idea than trying to sneak out like we did the last time. Camping! Why hadn't we thought of that before?

The only misgiving we had about sleeping so close to each other was that we all had to lie on our sides in case we fell face to face with one another in the night. Also, we made sure we kept strictly to our own space, as it was forbidden for loose arms to drape over anyone during sleep. That would be extremely queer! And on no account was anybody allowed to fart.

Just for the record, those were lads' camping rules that had to be strictly adhered to at all times.

'Fucking hell, Pete, it stinks in here!' I cried.

'It's probably got a bit mildew over the years.' Pete tugged his sleeping bag out from under my feet.

'I'd better not be sleeping on some dog shit or something,' Simon groaned.

'Hey, I think Hayley's having some friends to sleep over tonight . . . Shall we have a peep before we go down into Haulfrie?' I suggested.

'Perve!' Pete said, banging the base of his rubber-cased torch (the one they supposedly use in the army). 'Shit, I bet the batteries are dead.'

'Yeah!' Simon buzzed at my suggestion. 'You never know, they might all end up shagging each other!'

Pete and I shook our heads at one another, as the

torch came to life. A weak orangy glow made our faces look like ghostly masks.

We stayed inside the tent until about midnight, roughly the same time we all met up for our rendezvous the previous Thursday. As we stood up outside and waited for our eyes to adjust to the pitch blackness, I thought the air seemed much colder than last week. Perhaps this was the onset of autumn.

While Pete dived back in to hide his torch under the sleeping bags, I shivered in anticipation of what we were about to go through tonight. Then prayed to myself for Lovers' Green to be dark and empty so we could all come back safely and sleep out the rest of this cursed evening.

We had set up camp on Quarry mountain (the one that resembled the *Titanic*) overlooking the estate below. The panoramic views from there were quite breathtaking. All the east and west coasts were fringed with thousands of dotted lights like strings of diamond necklaces. Even the estate itself, ablaze with the copper streetlights, looked like a floodlit football pitch.

As we marched down towards the quarry, I asked if the weapons we might need for insurance were in position, and Pete gave me a grouchy 'Yes'.

Carefully, we climbed down the rocks on the lower part of the cliff and onto Tyn-Y-Coed Road just above the new estate where we lived.

'Shit, we should have come down the mountain behind Simon's house,' Pete said with unease. 'Me old folks told me not to wander around in the early hours in case I get into trouble. It'd just be my luck if one of them saw me walking past.'

'Naw! Would've taken us ages to get down the side of the mountain in this dark!' Simon grimaced, then rubbed his hands excitedly. 'So are we gonna have a little peep at Hayley and her friends or what?'

Pete and I shared an agreeable shrug . . . Why not?

Hayley lived in one of the old council houses, just off the estate, with its back facing the golf course. This was perfect for us, as we could hide in the darkness and not have to worry about someone seeing us from behind.

As we stood outside her back garden, we gazed up at the cosy pink light pouring down from her bedroom and pooling on the lawn.

'Fucking hell, they've got the curtains open in the bedroom and the top window's open!' Simon said excitedly, and scrambled up the loose wall, disturbing a few boulders.

'Well, be quiet then!' Pete hissed, climbing after him.

'See anything?' I asked.

'Just heads!' he said, somewhat deflated.

Pete and I steadied ourselves beside him and gripped the mesh fence above the wall, put there to shield the houses from low-flying golf balls.

Two then three heads began bobbing up and down in the bedroom.

'What the hell are they doing in there?' I said.

'Just messing about . . . Dancing, probably.'

Someone came to the window, and we jumped back to the ground with a heavy clump. Taking a moment to brace ourselves, we chanced another peep. Simon began to laugh in little hiccups.

In the bedroom window, Karen, my nemesis, appeared wearing one of those long nightie tee shirts.

'Shit! Why does she have to be here?' I groaned, as she leant one knee on the window sill and blew cigarette smoke out of the top window flap.

'Who the hell does she think she is?' Pete snorted.

'She's got no tits, has she?' Simon rasped. 'And she looks a bit of a mess without her make-up and hairdo.'

Someone else came to the window, one of her best friends, Mandy, also wearing a tee shirt, although her tits swelled out a bit more. You could even see her nipples standing out like studs on a football boot. Obviously, they weren't wearing any bras.

'Go on, show us your tits,' Simon purred.

Both of them turned their heads to talk to someone in the room, probably Hayley herself, though we hadn't see her yet.

To our complete delight, Karen suddenly lifted her top and two tiny dimples popped out.

'Whey-hey!' Pete and Simon sang quietly.

It appeared she wanted to show Mandy something on one of her puny breasts. We couldn't believe it! There she was, actually standing there, bare tits and knickers in front of us (incidentally, her knickers were white with red specks), completely unaware that we were perving at her. If only she knew, she'd probably chase us with a meat cleaver.

Then she turned this way and that, parading them about, with hardly enough meat on her diddy little tits to make them jiggle.

'Fucking beanbag tits!' I sniggered in revenge at all those cruel jibes about my dolphin head.

She stopped and pointed at something on the flank of her breast, like a mole or something. That's when Mandy just as casually lifted up her top, and her two rock-hard boobs flicked out like a gunslinger drawing his two Colt 45s.

'Wow!' Simon drawled.

Pete turned to Simon. 'Bet if you were here by yourself,

you'd be tossing off by now, wouldn't you?' But Simon took no notice.

I saw something bounce off Karen's head, probably a cuddly toy. She picked it up and playfully tossed it back.

'Come on, let's go!' Pete became a touch anxious.

'Hang on a minute! Hang on!' Simon protested, as Karen and Mandy began giggling about something.

'Hey, do you think they know we're here?' Simon ducked down a tad.

But whether they did or not, it didn't prevent Karen whipping down her knickers and sucking glass with her scrawny little butt-cheeks.

'What the fuck's she doing?' I looked on bemused.

It looked like Mick Jagger kissing the window, and judging by Pete and Simon's silence, they were just as confused.

That was until we saw the glass mist up, and it became obvious she'd just farted on it. The two girls collapsed in fits of laughter, their hyena voices pouring out of the top window flap.

'Dirty bitch!' Pete remarked.

'Go on, Mandy, why don't you show us your arse?' Simon prayed, but she didn't.

'Just think,' I snorted, 'all that swanning about with her nose up in the air, thinking she's better than everybody else, and underneath, she's just a dirty slag!' It gave me a deep feeling of satisfaction.

'Bet she's left a bit of shit on the window! Why don't you go and sniff it, Si?' Pete teased.

'Why don't you?' Simon countered.

'Where's Hayley? Haven't seen her yet,' I added.

'She's probably the only one sensible enough not to

strip in front of a window with the curtains wide open,' Pete replied.

'Shh! Keep your voices down,' Simon urged. 'They'll hear us.'

'Hey!' Pete shoved him. 'You weren't worried about that when you nearly trampled the wall down to get your rocks off, were you?'

Suddenly, we heard a sharp click coming from the neighbour's back door. In panic, we all scampered off and hid behind the golf shed near the number nine green.

Simon and Pete collapsed against the concrete wall, pissing themselves laughing, while I stood praying nobody had seen us.

Heart going like the clappers, I had a peek, then Pete joined me. All was just as dark and serene as before. Couldn't even see anyone in Hayley's window any more.

'Come on!' Pete tapped my shoulder. 'Let's go before we do get caught!'

So once again, just like last week, we took our chances down in Haulfrie Gardens, the black wilderness. The lion's den!

At the bottom of the golfie, we stopped to listen if we could hear any voices coming from Lovers' Green. We heard nothing! It was so peacefully quiet, you could almost hear your own heart beating.

Christ, we shouldn't be here now, I sighed to myself. Nobody should be here now. Even the pine trees above us standing guard like cloaked giants seemed to be hissing down at us in contempt. Or was that just the breeze rustling the leaves?

Nervously, I began to sing that old 'Teddy Bears' Picnic' song in my head. We could be in for a much nastier surprise in the woods today . . .

Shut up! I told my conscience, and tried one last time to deter the others from going to the green. 'Hey, let's have one more look in Hayley's bedroom, and then go back to the tent for a good old nosh-up.'

'Come on, John, don't be a wimp all your life.' Simon marched on. 'We might as well have a look ... We've come this far.' Pete shrugged.

I sighed hopelessly, and dragged my heels after them.

As we passed the mighty squirrel tree, I gave it a wary glance. It looked so surreal silhouetted against the dazzling lights in town. Like a giant skeletal spine with limbs. I imagined trying to conquer it now, and shuddered at the thought.

As we reached the last bend before the green, my scalp felt as if someone had just poured freezing water over it and my whole body tingled with the terrible anticipation that someone was about to jump out from the bushes.

We peered into the glade, and again saw the glow from their campfire cast in the branches of the pine trees.

My heart turned to ice. They were there, after all! But why was it so quiet?

'Come on! Let's go through the den.' Pete backed us up and carefully led the way through the dark thickets. I'd never crept through the bushes at this time of night before. The leaves felt like cold velvet against our faces, and the branches like sharp claws tugging at our jackets.

Soon we found the entrance to our den. For one dreadful moment, I imagined someone might spring out from the yawning black mouth.

I pushed Simon to go first, and before he had chance to protest, he was already inside. Pete and I followed.

Hunkering inside, it was so dark I could hardly see my mates. For all I knew they might have turned into grotesque demons who had trapped me into coming here.

'Where are our weapons, just in case?' I asked nervously.

'You've just passed them, fool!' Pete hissed. 'They're by the path, where we put them.'

'Still can't hear anything on the green,' Simon muttered.

'Are we ready then?' Pete puffed tensely.

No I bloody wasn't! I didn't even want to be here. Couldn't they go alone and leave me here, safe in the darkness? No! Gotta go . . .

When you dance with Satan, you have to wait for the record to stop . . . No shit!

Pete began burrowing through the back of our den, wincing in annoyance as some foliage crackled. Simon was behind him, and then me. The path we had cleared to prevent being tangled in the overgrowth had worked a treat. Of course there was still a landmine of dry, dead twigs lying about, so we had to be careful. Just one sharp snap at this time of night would sound like a gunshot, and that would be it.

Climbing the embankment up to the green, we dropped stealthily on all fours. I don't know why, but I turned to glance at the tall whitebeam trees I'd noticed the other day, and remembered the cancerous dread I felt for this evening.

Pete swiped his arm back, and we stopped. 'I can hear talking!' he whispered, so we listened.

We could hear nothing. Maybe it was just voices from town carried up on the night breeze. Pete craned his neck over the verge of the green, his face splashed yellow by the glow of the campfire.

For today's the day the teddy bears have their pic . . . nic, I sang in my head. The suspense was killing me.

Simon asked what he could see, but Pete ignored him. Impatiently, Simon nudged him.

'There's nobody there, you impatient twerp!' he spat, and Simon swung a bemused glance at me.

Boldly, Pete dared to stand up for a better look.

'Are you sure there's nobody there?' I asked.

'Can't see anyone.' Pete shrugged, so Simon and I stood up.

I prayed it'd remain that way long enough for my two companions to get bored, then we could all go back to the tent.

Like worried sheep, we gazed around the green, the roasting campfire turning the whole glade into an island of flickering light. But where the hell was everybody?

The only thing we could find was a cassette player that had been left by the shrubs at the entrance. No litter or empty beer cans strewn all over the place. Whoever they were, they had to be the tidiest revellers to date. I started to relax a bit. Perhaps it wasn't going to be as bad as I'd feared.

'Hey, let's go and have a look at that ghetto blaster.' Simon leapt up, but Pete caught him.

'Hang on a minute! . . . I don't like this.'

'There's nobody there.' Simon shrugged confidently, but Pete wouldn't let go.

'I don't know . . . It looks a bit too tidy for my liking. Let's just wait for a bit.'

Simon tutted impatiently.

'Well, I don't mind waiting!' I hastily agreed.

'I hope we haven't come all this way just to bloody look,' Simon groaned.

'Don't you know curiosity killed the cat?' I put in.

'Bollocks!' Simon dropped back down.

We waited, and waited, but still nothing.

'Maybe they've had their little party and fucked off,' I suggested.

'They're not going to go away and leave their stereo behind, though, are they?' Pete replied.

'Well, I'm not fucking sitting here all night.'

'What do you want to do then, go and sit by the fire listening to music until they get back?' Pete shook his head.

'No! Obviously there's nothing going on at the moment, so why don't we go back for another perve in Hayley's window and then try again later?'

'I'm not coming all the way back again,' I protested.

'Well, you wait back at the tent then, and me and Pete will go.'

I turned to Pete to await his decision.

'We might as well come back later,' he announced, and I tutted angrily.

'Listen, John, we haven't come all this way just to go home now, it'd be a complete waste of time. Look, we'll give it one more try later, and if there's still nothing going on, I swear we'll all go back to the tent for the rest of the night, and that will be the end of it . . . OK?'

I didn't answer.

'Fair enough?' he pressed.

They knew I'd agree, but before I did, I let them see and hear how pissed off I was about it.

As we were about to leave, Simon defied Pete by racing onto the green like an impetuous little school kid. We called after him but it was too late. Swiftly, he pounced on the stereo, and scuttled back with his trophy. But Pete stood in his way.

'You're not fucking taking that!'

'Ahh . . . come on, I've got to have something to make it worth my while.'

'Yeah, and when they come back and see their stereo gone, they're gonna know they've got prowlers.'

'You can't take the stereo, Si, not if we're coming back,' I chided him.

Simon rolled his eyes, and sulkily lumbered back.

'Fucking idiot!' Pete shook his head in annoyance. 'I'm beginning to wonder if it is a good idea coming back now.'

I gave him a 'there's still hope for me then' type look.

Simon put the stereo back then seemed to freeze solid. I thought he'd seen something else to steal. Slowly, he turned and walked back as stiff as a board.

'What's up now?' Pete asked.

'There's someone up in the trees.' He grimaced nervously, and a bolt of fear shot through my stomach.

'Bollocks! Stop pissing about!' Pete told him.

I hoped to Christ he was, so I called his bluff. 'Where then?'

'I can't fucking point, can I? Over there behind the green.' He shifted his head.

To be honest, if you looked close enough, it was easy to see all kinds of odd things in the darkness beyond, especially with the play of flickering light off the campfire. Even the trees with their long skeletal arms looked in some supernatural way as if they were jiggling about in a macabre dance.

'You're just imagining it!'

'Go and stand where I was, then.'

I was just about to call him a paranoid moron when we heard an almighty CRACK, like King Kong snapping off one of the thick pine branches. My arse nearly fell out from under me, and we tore back to our den like mini-tornadoes. On the way, I must have been pricked about a hundred times from the bramble bushes, but didn't feel it. Lucky I didn't lose my glasses as well.

Inside the den, we all collapsed into one another, puffing with exhaustion and fear.

'What the fuck was that in the trees?' I shrieked, shaking like a leaf.

Simon took a deep breath. 'Could've been a bird.'

'Yeah, a fucking pterodactyl more like,' Pete huffed.

'Let's go now while we still have the chance.' I scrabbled out of the den.

'Wait! Wait!' Pete wrenched me back in.

'What?'

'There's someone on the path.'

I froze stiff, and the bitter taste of fear squirted in my mouth again.

We couldn't see anyone; it was so dark in there, it was like being underwater in very murky water, with bushes of reeds in front of you.

But you could certainly hear something! Footsteps, dozens of footsteps stealthily moving up and down the footpath, trying not to crackle the brushwood underfoot.

They knew where we were all right, they had us trapped, but they didn't want us to know it. We were like wild rabbits hiding in a deep warren, with about a dozen ferrets poised at all the holes ready to shoot down.

'Fuck, what are we gonna do?' I shrieked.

'Just stay here, don't move!' Pete's voice sounded as if he was going to cry.

'Shit, the weapons are by the path, aren't they?' I recalled.

'Well, I'm not fucking getting them!' Simon sniggered nervously.

I wished to God I was back at home safe in my bed. Why the hell did I agree to come here? ... What if they charge in to get us? ... What's the plan? ... Just run anywhere, every man for himself? Christ! ... They may be axe-wielding maniacs.

But whoever they were, and whatever they were, they suddenly stopped moving. Shit! They're going to get us!

With a trembling hand, I tapped Pete's arm, reassuring myself he was still there with me. 'Pete? Pete? When you run, don't leave me behind ... I don't want to be left behind.'

Pete whispered with a shaky voice, 'We all go together.'

On Lovers' Green the stereo came to life and warbled until the tape reels reached the right speed. It sounded as if the batteries were running low, and reminded me of one of those monophonic record players when you switch the speed from 33 to 45.

As for what crazy, weird music it was playing, I'd absolutely no idea.

Then everywhere became a complete zoo of vocal sounds and shouts, some animal, some human – even non-human. Or was my imagination running away with me?

But if that wasn't enough to scare us half to death, all the bushes around our den began to thrash so violently, you could have sworn a tornado was passing us by. The sound was almost deafening.

Whoever they were, they wanted to literally tear us out of the forest. Yet, still we couldn't see them.

I was so scared, I gripped Pete's jacket, and felt hands gripping my own. I hate to admit it here and now, but that was when I pissed myself. The wetness in my crotch quickly cooled and made me cringe with shame.

All we could do was sit there, three quivering blobs of fear.

I began to sob, and didn't care who heard me. At 14 years old you think you're pretty tough, but let me tell you, you're not! When you can taste death like that, you're crying for your mother like a helpless baby.

Paralysed with terror, we couldn't move even if we'd wanted to. I remember thinking I didn't want to die, not here, not now.

I didn't have time for any other thoughts, as that was when our den roof was completely ripped off, and we fled for our lives. But we didn't get far. Something immensely heavy came crashing down on us, knocking the very lights out of our world. Now we couldn't feel anything.

We were caught!

19

When I say I blacked out, I didn't completely lose consciousness as such. For I knew what was going on, at least it felt as if I did, it was just that my mind wouldn't accept it.

Most people react the same way when they go through a life-threatening experience. They simply block it out, because it's the only way they can handle the overload of stress.

Personally, I think it's the body's own shutdown mechanism in preparation for death itself. You've blown the main fuse, shorting everything else out. You're incapable of doing anything more, so why worry about it?

In situations like that, I believe you even welcome the reality of death. At the very minimum, death means you won't have to suffer all that trauma any more.

The very next thing I can remember was sitting back on Lovers' Green with a nylon hood or cowl over my head (which stank to high heaven, like dank old rotting wood. Someone must have locked it up in trunk for about a thousand years) and I couldn't move my hands.

As far as I was aware, Pete and Simon both sat with

their backs against mine. Our wrists were tied together behind us.

All around us were cackling, jeering, hissing voices. I don't know how many, and I didn't have a clue what they were up to.

The music on the stereo was now pumping out some dreadful thrashing rock. I looked up, and through the thin material of the hood, I could just make out the campfire, which looked like a cobweb of fluttering light. (I assumed Pete and Simon were also wearing hoods.)

My wrist started to hurt a bit. Whatever they had used to bind us certainly felt tougher than rope. I wiggled my fingers over the double knot they had tied, and it felt like washing-line cord.

But aside from that, what the hell was going on here? And why were we being held like prisoners? OK, we were nosy little bastards prying where we shouldn't have been, but that didn't give them the right to blindfold us and tie us up like animals.

Maybe all this was a joke, or they were just trying to scare us.

Well, if so, they've succeeded, I thought. I solemnly swear, if they let us go now, I'll never come back here again, and won't tell a soul.

Or suppose they have no intention of letting us go?

'Pete? . . . Si? . . .' I murmured in alarm. 'What's happening?'

'Haven't got a clue,' Pete replied.

'What are they gonna do to us?'

'Fuck knows! But they'd better let us go soon.' Pete tugged angrily at the cord.

Simon, however, was oddly silent under the circumstances, which made me curious. 'Si, what are you doing?'

'Shh . . . I'm thinking!' was all he'd say.

'Shit! Well, think fast,' I hissed, as I heard swishing footsteps approach then stop in front of me, eclipsing the glare from the fire. I stiffened like a board again, not even daring to breathe.

I sensed that at least two or three people were now standing in front of us. Shit, this is it! Now they're gonna kill us, or at least maim us! My whole body braced itself for whatever they were going to do to us. I was so terrified I wanted to cry, but couldn't get it out.

I flinched as something touched the top of my head, then my hood was whipped off. The whole surrealistic scene flooded into my tear-welled eyes.

A fancy-dress rave! A Mardi-Gras. Painted white faces, plastic, and rubber-skinned features with maniacal smiles ... Masks! That's what they were all wearing, strange masks. What the fuck?

Why were they wearing masks? There were about a dozen of them, some squatting around the campire, others standing about, all with crazy faces looking at us.

There was Ronald McDonald and Porky Pig with an extra large snout, something that looked like a badger without any ears, half a dozen smiley-sad faces, and what I can only describe as a drag queen mask.

'Fucking hell! It's the texas chainsaw family!' Pete quivered.

One of them crouched down in front of us, making us cower like frightened puppies. It looked like one of those 1970s wrestler's masks, the Kendo Nagasaki one, but with a ridiculous dark-permed wig and red blusher make-up on the cheeks. Must be some sort of a transvestite.

The thing stared straight into my face, and I could smell strong oilseed. I felt the skin on my back crawl. It was like a demonic woman baby-sitter pushing her elongated face into your pram to eat you. I tried to tell myself they were only humans behind the masks, not to be afraid. But all I could see through those tiny little slits were simply glazed jelly-balls. They weren't eyes at all.

'We don't usually get visitors!' It tried to mimic a thick South Welsh accent, to preserve its identity.

'Hey, you fucking better let us go!' Pete stormed.

The thing tutted in contempt, and caressed Pete's chin. 'Don't you know it's not safe to venture out by yourselves after midnight? Especially three little piggies like you. Didn't your mummy ever tell you about us?'

'We haven't done anything to you, you can't fucking tie us up like this! . . . Let us fucking go!' Pete wriggled about, losing his temper.

I was worried that this would antagonise them even more, so I jumped in. 'Hey, we didn't mean any harm, we were just being nosy, that's all.'

The thing turned back to me.

'If you let us go, I promise we'll never come here again, and won't tell anyone . . . *anyone*!'

'But we gave you a chance not to come back last week, and you have.'

'What?' Pete snapped, confused.

'Didn't think we saw you, did you? But we did! We've got many watchers in them thar woods (another pathetic accent change). Yes, we spotted you running away last time. But obviously you must be interested in our little group, otherwise you wouldn't have come back.'

'We don't want to join your fucking group!' Pete barked.

'You will!' The thing said chillingly as it stood up, and held out an introductory arm to the rest of the members by the campfire. 'See? We've all been waiting for you.'

In reply, they nodded and saluted us with their lager cans.

'We have everything ready for you, the party will begin when our final guests arrive,' it teased, then swaggered off with the others back to the campfire.

'Pete, get us out of here!' I bleated.

'What are they gonna do to us?' I heard Simon say.

'Pete.' I nudged him, but he didn't reply. He was either too busy thinking, or praying.

Myself, I felt as if I had lump of hot wax at the top of my breastbone and slowly dripping down into the pit of my stomach.

This was too much. Was I dreaming all this or not? Was this actually happening? I felt so tired and drained, I just wanted to go to sleep.

I turned to look at the freaks by the campfire again, and one of them with a mad-grinning face looked back at me. The dancing light from the fire made his mask appear even more sinister.

Once again, to keep my sanity, I had to tell myself that these were normal everyday folks, but with false faces. For instance, Ronald McDonald might be a guy who worked in a supermarket. Porky Pig was a female and could be a receptionist during the day.

The thing? I speculated. Fuck knows, perhaps he works as a bank clerk in Barclays, or he might be a 'doley' who lolls at home all day watching schlock horror movies and porn flicks.

Or maybe these degenerates dwell in some dark basement somewhere, and only come out at night.

But don't these people have any moral rules or what? Don't they care about what they're doing to us? Haven't they got any younger brothers or sisters, even children of their own? Don't they know how scared we are? Obviously not!

If only Pete's dad would rush in now with the police,

and save us. I'd never complain about anything again, not even my dolphin's head.

Just as I was about to think it couldn't get any worse, more freaks arrived, and the three of us gulped ... Oh shit!

In all about six more poured onto the green, and a joyous reception rang out for them. However, instead of masks, this group wore balaclavas over their heads. And on their way to the others, they spotted us by the bushes in the corner. One of them pointed a threatening finger, and gave a sick cackle.

My blood chilled even more. 'Shit! what are we gonna do?' I cried.

'Why don't you come up with something?' Simon snapped at me.

So I snapped back, 'Hey, it's your fucking fault we're here in the first place.'

After the group had settled, we watched them begin to shoot up with drugs. Some began snorting crack from the back of their hands, some popped amphetamines down their gullets like seagulls at a picnic leftover. The rest were seemingly content enough to just sit there and chill.

That's when I started to feel scared again. The feeling I had was like going to the dentist for a filling when I was young. First it was the nail-biting waiting room, followed by the shit-scared walk to the dentist's chair for the numb-up injection. Once that had been given, I knew I had at least five minutes or so before the dentist returned and said, 'Right, let's make a start.' That's exactly how I felt waiting for the freaks to come up from the drugs. I mean, they were loony enough without drugs, what the hell were they capable of doing with them?

'Shit! They're gonna go mental now!' Simon cried,

and we all tugged so hard to free ourselves, we nearly dislocated our shoulders.

It was no use, so we gave up.

As we sat there limp, I noticed a group of them beginning to pass an empty plastic container between them. In turn they all seemed to be urinating into the neck, until it became three-quarters full. A minute or so later, they all walked over to us. We stiffened up in anticipation.

One of them (badger mask) held three plastic drinking cups in his hand. Three drink cups, three of us . . . Oh shit!

The thing stood over us. 'If you really want to get away from us, here's your chance.' They began pouring the urine into each of the cups. 'If you drink these, every last drop, we'll let you go.'

'Fuck . . . off!' Pete blasted, and was clipped across the head for his outburst.

'You've got to be joking us!' Simon shook his head incredulously.

'That's the deal! We'll only be convinced that you don't wish to remain here with us if you can down one each.'

The other freaks nudged and whispered excitedly to each other.

'Why do we have to do that? Why can't you just let us go?' I squeaked.

'Because if you want something so badly, then you have to be willing to make sacrifices for them. And in this case, it has to be your dignities.'

'I'm not drinking that!' Pete said sternly.

'Well then, you'll be letting down your two friends, because you all have to do it.'

I stared at the plastic glasses in front of us, all full of yellow fluid, like still ciders.

'You've got sixty seconds to make up your minds.' The thing folded his arms arrogantly.

Shit, is this our only way out? Half a dozen gulps of this filth, and we can walk? The nightmare will end? . . . What will it taste like?

The cups were pushed under our faces, the thick liquid barely swirling inside. I squirmed back as if the piss was going to jump out at me. Could I honestly go through with this? Was getting away from here really that important? Were we willing to do absolutely anything for our freedom?

Never in a million years would I ever have dreamt about doing anything like this, but never had life meant so much to me. 'Pete? Si?' I called for their support.

'I can't! I can't!' Pete turned his face away in disgust.

'Pete, it's our only way out!' I began to sniffle.

'Time's nearly up, lads!' the thing alerted us.

'For fuck's sake,' Simon said in a trembling voice, 'let's just do it and go home.'

'I can't! I can't!'

'They'll let us go!' I begged.

'We'll do it.' Simon gave in, and I could feel Pete's head rolling around in torment.

The cups were forced under our mouths, and I just caught a whiff of the sour piss. Utterly repulsed, I felt my stomach contract in outrage, as it screamed at me, Don't you dare let that filth come in here.

Having no mercy whatsoever, they poured the warm fluid down our throats, as the tears streamed down our cheeks.

My eyes snapped shut, and my body seized as the strong salty taste hit me like a 40,000-volt charge. I gagged, and literally spewed my guts out. Behind me, Pete and Simon did the same. I retched and retched until every last vile drop had been pumped back out of my system.

'Come on! Come on, finish it!' they cried, forcing the cups to our mouths again, and a further stagnant whiff sent me heaving once more.

None of us could take any more, our bodies simply said, No way! To get another drop in our mouths, they would have had to kill us. Satisfied, the freaks danced and whooped jubilantly back to the fire.

For a while, the three of us were completely out of it, the torment we suffered inside our bodies far worse than anything that could happen outside.

Every time I breathed, every time I swallowed, I could taste that repugnant stale filth. And every time I had to fight against the urge to vomit again. I had to tell myself, swear to myself that it was all gone, no more, don't even think about it now.

'John? Si? . . . Yer all right?' Pete asked drowsily.

Both of us said we were.

'Hey, come on, you said you'd let us go now,' Pete shouted to them, but got no response.

Simon, amid repeated gobbings into the bushes, mumbled, 'They're not gonna fucking let us go!'

Before we had time to recover, they swooped on us once more. About half a dozen of them forced our mouths wide open and stuffed some kind of tablet down our throats. It was like having half a dozen dentists in your mouth racing to administer the fastest Novocaine shot.

'Swallow it! Swallow it!' they demanded.

I held mine inside my mouth for as long as I was able, but Pete and Simon spat theirs back out. Their punishment was a vicious hammering which knocked their heads back against mine like skittles in a bowling alley.

Yet, despite this spiralling all-round lunacy, I almost laughed when I heard one of them cry out, 'Argh yer bastard' when either Pete or Simon bit on them as they tried to put in another tablet.

Call me wimpish, but I just couldn't handle it any more, and I swallowed whatever it was they'd put in my mouth. At the time, I prayed it was something that would put me to sleep forever and end this unrelenting, surreal nightmare.

Little did I know, this surreal nightmare had only just begun!

After we had swallowed the pills, the freaks fanned out around the green.

'Shit! What have they just given us?' I flapped.

'What do you think they've given us? . . . Drugs!' Pete slumped back against me.

'Shit! Shit!' I panicked even more. 'What's going to happen to us?'

'Whatever it is, you probably won't give a shit about it soon, anyway,' Simon groaned.

Christ, we could be in serious danger here, I said to myelf. It isn't as if we've been given an overdose of Anadins. We're talking about serious drugs here. What if something goes wrong? Would the freaks phone for an ambulance for us? Would they fucking likely! They'd just leave us here to die, and scarper off . . . Bastards!

I felt poised on the cusp of a white-knuckle roller-coaster ride that I didn't want to be on. So I closed my eyes and prayed.

All I can remember after that was feeling as if my head was trying to spin off my shoulders. My name was no longer John, I didn't know how old I was, if I had any parents, or where I lived, for that matter. And didn't really care. Just as long as I wasn't thinking about what was happening to us, it was all right.

The campfire became a roaring bonfire, and these wiry figures, flapping like birds, took turns leaping through the flames, sparks bouncing off their limbs.

Grotesque faces, piggy, wolf, goat and badger, prodded, and glared into my head, trying to see through tissue and bone to find my soul. These poisonous-looking creatures picked me up and took me for a spin through the forest. They tossed me up as high as the tops of the pine trees, where the needle pines brushed my face, then back I fell into a blanket of bucket-sized hands.

Malefic grins, painted joker smiles, expressions that supped on pain and torture as a connoisseur samples vintage wine. But every time I screamed the voices reassured me, promised me that it was going to be all right. Then they'd give me that horrible grin again, and I'd yell, and so it went on!

These were the things nobody, let alone young kids, should ever have to see. These were the things that slink about in the night, when everybody else is supposed to be fast asleep. These were the things that made you hide petrified behind your bedcovers in the night. These were the demons your mother always warned you about when you were young.

Surely this was hell. Surely that was where I was.

Next, I remember being inches away from the wrinkly jowl of an old woman, her tissue-like skin so delicate I could tear a finger through it. She laughed so loudly and so widely that I feared she was going to eat me whole.

We were moving rhythmically. I felt warm all over. I didn't like it.

Her slug-like tongue, smelling of wet shit, plied my

face, and I yelled out. Moments later, I heard the echo of those cries again and again from my two companions, Pete and Simon.

Still those gangly phantoms leapt through the flames.

Today's the day the teddy bears have their picnic...

Once more, I could feel my hands tied behind me, and the support of my mates' backs against mine. For now, the only movement I was aware of was my chest breathing in and out.

Drowsily, I lifted my head, and gazed around with jelly-type vision. The freaks were still partying by the campfire.

'John, you all right?' Pete nudged me.

'We were getting a bit worried about you,' Simon sighed.

'I'm all right!' I shook my head. 'Did I dream all that or what?'

'No! You didn't dream it, not unless we all dreamt the same thing.'

'Fuck!' I murmured, letting my head drop forward again.

When I looked up, I found another freak standing in front of us, one of the balaclava group, a small impish figure in black apparel. It just stood there studying us, and tilting its head to one side.

'What do you fucking want?' Pete barked at it, and it wandered back to the others.

'Fucking bastards! I wish I had a hammer, I'd...' Simon was so angry could hardly get his words out.

'Hey, you two.' Pete sniffed the tears away from his nasal passages. 'Don't ever tell anybody what happened to us here tonight!'

'What, and let these fuckers get away with it?' I seethed.

'John, if we tell our parents we'd have to go through

the whole thing with the police, and I don't think I can do that. And besides, I'd never be able to look my mum and dad in the face, knowing what they know about me.'

Shit! He was right! Imagine the looks we'd get from everyone. It'd be just as humiliating as actually living out the terrible ordeal itself.

That's if we were to survive this night. . .

'So what are they gonna do with us now?' I asked, but got no reply, and perhaps it was better I didn't.

Now the thing and badger man came for a look. The thing bent forward with his wig of black permed hair and rubber features smeared with women's make-up. I didn't know of which I was most afraid, the mask he was wearing, or what was behind it. A latter-day Frankenstein monster.

'So are you gonna let us go now?' Pete asked.

But he just laughed and walked away, saying to the other discreetly, So how are we gonna to do it?

Terror strummed at my stomach again. *So how are we gonna do it?* Do what? . . . What did that mean? How are they gonna let us go? Or how are they gonna get rid of us?

'Pete? Pete?' I cried.

'I know! I know! . . . Shit.'

'They can't just kill us!' Simon shrieked.

'We don't know that, let's not get carried away.'

Beside us, the thickets crackled lightly. What the fuck was this now?

We all looked to see something black and large slowly emerge from the bushes . . . Another fucking monster? . . . No! It turned out to be one of the balaclava members holding a gleaming pocket penknife in its hands. Without another word, it set about trying to cut us free, using our bodies to hide from the freaks. I couldn't figure this whole thing out at all, neither could the others. But if it meant we might get out of this, after all, we were in.

Maybe this was the chance I had been praying for.

The strange impish creature spoke to us in a very peculiar tone, like a poor man's Great Gonzo from *The Muppet Show*.

To me it sounded like a young lad of about our age ... weird!

But what it told us chilled us more than anything we'd seen or heard tonight. 'I know what they're planning to do to you!' It said to us as it sawed through the cords. 'They're tossing up between slitting your throats, dicing you, and feeding you down one of the potholes on the Orme, or sell you off to a rent-boy agency in London.'

'What?' Simon nearly shit his pants.

'They can't risk letting you go now, that's how they nearly got caught last time.'

'Last time?' I nearly screamed.

'Hang on!' Pete warned. 'Two of them are leaving the green.'

The imp froze. It was the thing and badger man swishing through the bushes at the entrance of the green.

'I'll have to be quick!' it continued. 'After I cut you free, wait for your chance and run! ... Run for your lives!'

I felt the cord binding my wrists die, and release the ache. Finally we were free to go. The imp said no more, and slunk back into the overgrowth.

If it was up to me, I'd have sprinted for it there and then, but Pete made me wait. After all, we might only get one shot at this, and we couldn't risk getting caught again, that'd definitely be it! Best to do it properly.

As Pete gave the instructions, the adrenaline started to flow. We were going to get out of here . . . Yes!

'Listen, you two, when we make a break for it head towards Rofft Place and back onto Llwynon Road.' The consternation was thick in his voice. '. . . It'll be lit there and we should be safe. They won't follow us onto the main road in case we shout for help.'

I began taking heart-thumping deep breaths, praying to God we would succeed. I eyed up our escape route ready – it was more or less a clear run. Our main concern now was the thing and badger man. Where the hell were they?

We'd have to wait for them to rejoin the group before making our attempt. Couldn't have them jumping out on us.

That itself took another five excruciating minutes. But it was worth the wait seeing them re-emerge and stroll over to the edge of the green, to gaze out across the dazzling town below. My heart fizzed in anticipation.

'Right! Are we ready?'

'Yes!' I replied, mouth cotton-dry and arsehole sucking in cold air. Now I knew how Olympic sprinters felt on the starter blocks.

'GO!' Pete pistoled us off.

A dreamy sprint ensued. Were we actually running away, or was it just wishful thinking? Yes we were, because I felt the thorny shrubs at the entrance gore my hand as we tore through . . . Don't even look back! . . . Don't want to!

My mind went blank from blind fear . . . or the after effects of the drugs . . . I turned left towards the woods. Pete and Simon headed towards Rofft Place.

'No, John! . . . This way!' Pete screamed at me, but it

was too late, I had to keep going. Only a complete dickhead like me would have gone the wrong way.

Now I had to out-sprint these maniacs back through the entire woods, in the middle of the night, all alone. Just as I had the beloved vision of home in my sights.

Snivelling back the snot and tears, I thundered down Haulfrie's maze of footpaths. How far would I get before I was caught? Would I even reach the bottom of the golfie?

I didn't know how much longer I could keep going, my batteries were already running very low. Should I just stop and end the suffering? What was the worst they could do? Kill me and end the torment, anyhow?

The bottom of the golfie was only yards away when I heard the guttural snarl of a dog coming down the path to meet me. Shit, can't go up, can't go down, this is where it ends.

Primal instinct, my only remaining drive, took over. The squirrel tree was my one last hope. I bounded down the embankment, churning great waves of soil, thinking I'd probably get my first foothold and they'd grab me. The dark wooded giant stood before me, and I leapt for the first branch, kicked at the trunk for purchase, and hauled with what meagre strength I didn't know I had. The strain was almost too much to bear, and if the next branch hadn't been so close, I would have given up. I grabbed it, hands painfully snagging the broken twig stumps, and hitched my feet up out of reach of grabbing hands that could come any second. In a frenzy, I climbed as fast as I was able, my chest on fire. I thought it was going to explode. I managed to scramble up to about ten feet, still amazed I had made it this far, and almost fainted. I think I pissed myself again too.

I looked down but saw no wild dogs waiting to savage me, or any freaks with murder on their minds. Where were they all? I was sure they were breathing down my neck.

Nauseous with fatigue, I hooked my chin over a branch the size of an elephant's trunk. My feet trembled so much it was like standing on a pneumatic drill. The bough felt cold, but the whiff of pine leaking from the pustules on the bark was like smelling salts and brought me around a bit.

Once more, I was just about to reconsider the possibility of actually getting out of this alive, when I heard crunching leaves beneath me.

'Hello, bayeee ba!' a voice bellowed up to me.

It was staring at me, someone in a balaclava. A fresh surge of boiling hot terror made my nails dig deep trenches in the bark.

Whoever it was slowly raised their hand and whipped off their disguise. It was Jonno Edwards, the notorious Jonno Edwards, the face of doom itself . . . So it was his dog, shit-face, that had growled at me on the footpath near the golfie. I should have guessed.

There and then I could've easily melted into liquid and drained down the trunk onto the ground in front of him. But that inextinguishable instinct to live kicked into touch once more, and I began to climb. I climbed . . . Shit! What am I doing?

Jonno slipped what looked like a bread knife between his lips, and started after me. I was now utterly convinced I was going to die. I had diced with fate too many times, and now I had lost. Time to pay up. Although I might as well have just stayed put and got stabbed. What was the point of climbing any further? Why prolong the inevitable? But climb I did.

'Hey, four-eyes . . . Is it true you're the only one who hasn't conquered this fucking tree yet?'

I didn't reply.

'That's probably because you haven't been pushed hard enough. Tell you what, I won't stab you while you're climbing, but if you stop, you'll get it.' Laughter began to piss out of his mouth. 'You never know, you might finally get to the top before you die.'

Shit! I sealed my eyes. Don't listen to him!

The higher I climbed, the more my head span and the slower I became. I was now just past halfway up, some 45 feet above the ground. Shakily, I reached for the next branch, and froze. I couldn't go any further. I looked down beneath me, and saw those lethal spiked railings at the bottom. I closed my eyes again.

'Keep going, you fucker!' Jonno growled, with the knife in his mouth, but I ignored him. 'I said keep fucking going!'

As he drew closer, I could feel the tree totter more and more. I opened my eyes, and saw he was only a few feet beneath me, knife blade clanking against the branch. I tried to hitch my legs up out of his reach, but still couldn't prevent him sinking the blade into my calf muscle. I screamed before I even felt the agonising pain.

I stepped up on the shoulder of another branch, then held on for dear life. 'Please! Please don't stab me again,' I sobbed.

The cold-hearted, evil bastard stuck me again. The pain was like a searing hot needle being slowly inserted in my leg. I was almost eating the bark off the tree.

I looked down and saw the demon in Jonno's eyes, the orange cast from the town's lights making them glisten like eggs in jelly. I could see he was literally stoned out of his mind. He was a mean, unscrupulous bastard at the best of times, so what chance did I have now he was as high as a kite?

'Move!' he shouted, gouging me a third time. It hurt so badly I kicked out furiously with my back heel, clocking him in the face. He lost his balance and grabbed my legs, almost wrenching me out of the tree with him. Thank God I'd had a tight grip on the branch, the only thing holding us from certain death.

Down below, I felt the tree shudder as a rush of people began scrambling up the trunk towards us. That must be the rest of the freaks catching up, I thought. By now my whole body trembled with the immense strain of holding our combined weights.

Beneath me, Jonno was whining like a little girl as his legs swung wildly to purchase a foothold on one of the branches. At least I had the pleasure of seeing him suffer too. How do you like it now, you fucker?

I could only hold on for a few more seconds, it was just too heavy. I clenched my eyes, and tasted death in my mouth. It was like burnt matches. Then my grip went. Bye, Mum!

I thought it was branches I'd hit, but they were human arms clutching me, saving me from my fatal plunge. Now I began to believe there were such things as guardian angels, for mine were no other than my two best friends . . . Pete and Simon.

Yes! They had come to my aid, right in the nick of time. Another second, and I would have been lost forever.

The only thing I remember before passing out was hearing Pete's 'Fate or what?'

20

After blacking out, the next recollection I had was waking up in my bed at home the following morning. Instead of taking me back to the tent, Pete and Simon in their wisdom had decided to take me back home. Although how on earth they got me back down off that tree, let alone up to my bedroom without waking my mum, I'll never know. But thank God they did! I never thought I'd be so happy to see my boring striped wallpaper again.

Needless to say, I wasn't so happy when I remembered my butchered leg, and carefully peeled back the covers to have a peek. Thanks to Pete and Simon, it had already been bandaged. They'd used one of my old tee shirts as a dressing, and there was also blood on the undersheets. Well, I suppose that goes to prove that it definitely wasn't a nightmare, I thought.

But what was I going to say to my mum about the sheets, and my leg? I mean, I wouldn't be able to hide them for long.

The excuse I cooked up was that during our early morning stroll, someone's dog bit me. Well, it did look like a dog-bite with three distinctive puncture holes in my calf muscle. That's why the bed sheets were covered in blood.

However, the price I paid for my little white lie was a

visit to the local hospital to have the wound stitched up and a tentanus injection in the arse. All this, plus a finger-wagging from my mother. 'Right, that's it! No more camping! I told you you were to stay in the tent and not go wondering about.'

A small penalty to pay for my life, methinks!

As for Jonno Edwards, things didn't turn out quite so well for him. The last thing I remember was the look of death on his face as he dangled off the end of my foot. Isn't it odd that no matter how stoned you can get, whenever your life is in danger, your head clears up in a flash.

Unfortunately for him, there were no more saintly arms left to save him from his fatal plunge. Death was ready and waiting to greet him at the bottom, arms wide open. His grisly remains were found the next day by a man walking his dog through the woods, who immediately called the police. Then all hell broke loose.

The whole area was turned into a circus of policemen, forensics and reporters. Nobody was allowed anywhere near the bottom of the golfie, it was completely cordoned off.

At first, they all thought Jonno's death was the result of a homicidal maniac at large. There were even curfews set by our anxious parents for us to be home no later than eight o'clock at night. 'You come home any later, and you might end up like Jonno Edwards,' they'd wag their fingers at us.

However, it was a different picture once the autopsy and toxicology report on Jonno's body was disclosed. They revealed he had sustained massive internal injuries to the body. Also, he had taken extremely large amounts of illegal narcotic drugs – e.g. crack, cocaine, acid – probably enough to kill him. (Of course this was no secret to Pete, Simon and me.)

Consequently, the police began to speculate as to how the drugs were administered, how his body received such a battering, and why his body lay at the bottom of a large pine tree.

Nevertheless, the main informants who could possibly shed some light on the incident were his devoted gang members, who apparently turned Judas to their exhaulted leader. What a surprise!

As it happens, they all confessed to taking drugs (they had to) but claimed that the last time they had seen him was a few hours before his death. He had told them he was going off to take his dog for a walk in the woods. Apparently he liked to climb trees in the dark.

Coincidence, or just a convenient story to make it look like an accident?

Likewise, when questioned about his character, they bleated he wasn't very well liked, and the only reason they stayed loyal was because he intimidated them. So much for so-called friends (I bet they were the other balaclava members at the green, although since that night, they never bothered us again).

Next came the routine door-to-door enquiries. What would they reveal? Basically, the consensus was he was a total nutter, an off-his-head delinquent who was often seen wandering into the woods at night with his dog.

Needless to say, the only remaining link that could provide the police with valuable circumstantial evidence was Jonno's carving knife. Thankfully, that was the first thing Pete and Simon dealt with, after they carried me down from the squirrel tree. They picked it up and took it with them. Lucky they remembered.

Later that day, we went to the barren wastelands over the back of the Orme called the Gunsights. (Couldn't chuck it in the sea just in case it washed back up on the beach, and some bloody do-gooder handed it over to the cops.) We dug a hole some two or three feet deep, dropped the fucker in, and covered it over.

Months or years later, it didn't matter if anyone dug it up by pure chance. By that time, it'd be a dirty old rusted knife in a derelict area that used to be a military school for army cadets in the Second World War. I mean, you'd expect the place to be a damn junkyard for metal detector fanatics anyway.

Finally, after exhaustive investigations left the police without any feasible motives or suspects, they had no alternative but to rule out the possibility of foul play. The verdict? Death by misadventure. He got stoned, tried to climb to the top of the tree, and fell to his death ... Perfect!

However, in the weeks and months that followed, many juicy myths and rumours begun as to how Jonno met his mysterious demise. You know how morbid-minded some people are! Here are some of the most gory tales ...

He was chased by a maniac (talk about irony) and fell out of the squirrel tree, landing on the railings, which went straight through his head ... He was thrown from the top of the tree by a madman, and impaled himself on the railings ... He went mad and jumped to his death, decapitated by the railings ... His body was cleft in two and his innards spilt out, steaming and glistening on the damp brushwood ... and so on.

Bearing in mind I never even saw his body hit the ground, the only two unofficial witnesses, Pete and Simon (not including the chap who discovered him), said he was nowhere near the railings.

Still, it makes for a good campfire ghost story, don't you think? ... To this day, the spirit of Jonno Edwards still wanders through the forest at night and chases people who dare to venture into the woods after dark. Sometimes, on a clear moonlit evening, he can be seen as a silver phantom clinging onto one of the tree's branches. So beware!

As for the freaks who held us captive and terrorised us, we never found out who they were. For all we know, they might still be having their weekly macabre raves at Lovers' Green. Creepy.

Yet what of the other haunting enigma that has never been solved – the hidden identity of the person we all owe our lives to, the one who cut us free that night?

At first we thought it was Jonno. Yes I know, why that prick? Perhaps he didn't want the freaks spoiling his long-awaited opportunity to waste some of the Orme scum, who were on his shit-list. He alone wanted to be the one to do the culling, and didn't want any witnesses. If that was true, we guessed his plan was probably to jump us from the bushes on the other side when we made our escape. Sounds a little bit thin I know, because how could he be sure which direction we would run?

But if it wasn't him, who else could it have been? Maybe amongst all those psychotic maniacs there was one, just one rational, human being who woke up and decided to do something about the sickening depravity before them. Maybe we'll never find out (watch this space). We're just extremely thankful to whoever it was.

Also, thank God for Pete and Si, who as it happened, had to outrun the freaks, then sprint back up Llwynon Road, looping back down into the golfie, and up the squirrel tree, just in the nick of time.

That took guts to charge back into the lion's den like that. I owe them my life!

Back in my living room, present day.

'It's hard to believe all that was twenty years ago. What do you think about it, Pete?'

Pete swallowed his mouthful of lager pensively. 'I think we all should have had therapy for what we went through that night.'

'Do you think it would have made any difference about the way we've turned out, though?'

'Well, look at us! Twenty years on and we're still struggling to come to terms with it. We're all having problems with our relationships, that's got to be a side effect of bottling it up for all those years without any outlet.'

Simon chimed in. 'Yeah, but like you've said, Pete, if we had sought help, we'd have opened up a very messy can of worms. If we'd told the truth to the police, they could easily have turned around and said we chucked Jonno out of the tree. The motive was there, we had drugs in our bodies, three kids settling a score that went wrong. We'd have ended up spending the rest of our youth in a detention centre.'

Pete shook his head on reflection. 'The nightmares I've had because of that night, the thought of what they did to us . . .'

'I can still see that fucking old woman lying beneath me,' Simon added. 'It was like shagging your grandmother. Now and again, when I have a shag, I can still see that fucking wrinkly old face cackling back at me. It was like the film *The Shining* when that old banshee rose out of the bath in that hotel room.'

Which I think was a good analogy.

'I still think that's why we're all having trouble with our women today,' I said. 'It must be similar to women who try to get on with their lives after being violently raped. Even with therapy, they still find it extremely difficult to let a man get close to them.'

'Well, if so, even with therapy, we still might not have overcome our mental problems,' Pete shrugged.

'Yeah, but doesn't it feel better to talk about it?' I remarked. 'Isn't this chat we're having the best therapy you can get?'

'Well, let's put it this way . . .' Pete leant forward on the couch. 'If we've all managed to survive this long without any professional help, we can't be doing too badly.'

'I just wish we'd done this ten years ago!' I said, and took another swig of lager.

'What do you think?' Pete nudged Simon back to life, who burped heavily.

'Well, it's just one of those things you've got to learn from, isn't it? Don't they say you can pick up something positive, even from the worst experiences imaginable?'

'The only thing I picked up from that was that curiosity almost killed the cats,' Pete murmured.

'To tell you the truth,' I said, 'until you two turned up after all those years, I'd more or less blocked it out of my mind.'

'I think we all did, to a certain extent,' Pete sighed.

'What about the women?' I asked. 'Have any of you told your women about what happened to us that night?' But both shook their heads.

Pete looked at me warily. 'Why, have you?'

'No! Definitely not! But do you think we should have?

If we told them now, do you think it would make any difference to the situations we're in?'

Pete shrugged his squared shoulders. 'I don't know. Maybe . . . maybe not. Obviously, our relationships with women have suffered. It's definitely poisoned our emotions, hasn't it?'

'And the fact that we've lived with it for so long, and we're still here to tell the tale, says a lot for us as well, doesn't it?' I added.

'Yeah, at least we haven't turned into drug addicts, or alcoholics, or even committed suicide,' Simon pointed out.

'Oh, I don't know about Si with his ecstasy tablets!' Pete looked him up and down dubiously.

'Aw, come on! I only have a few every now and again,' Simon protested.

I took another swig, enjoying the nostalgic comfort of hearing them arguing again, just like when we were kids. 'I just wish you two hadn't lived so far away. We definitely should have done this twenty years ago.'

'Yeah, well, that's going to change from now on!' Pete put his lager can down in earnest. 'I've been away from this place far too long now, it's time I came back home.'

'Really?' I asked excitedly.

Pete began to tell us about how he felt when his parents moved to town. And why, in his early twenties, he moved to Bristol with his wife.

I was right all along, he did it to bury his past and start anew. However, he did stress that the gamble to sacrifice his two best mates in the process turned out to be the biggest mistake of his life.

Likewise with Simon. In a way, I felt proud I was the one who stayed behind. Maybe I was stronger than I thought.

'What about you, Si? Are you going back to Manchester?'

'What have I got to go back to Manchester for?'

I couldn't believe it, I was getting my two best mates back after all that time. Were those dark cumbersome clouds of doom finally beginning to lift?

'Let's have a toast to the three of us!' I announced.

'Hang on, I can do better than that.' Pete rustled in his plastic bag and brought out a Kodak camera. He set the self-timer, and placed it on top of my television. All three of us leant into the frame with our cans raised.

'Here's to the almighty triangle!' Pete proclaimed. 'We're back!'

'A . . . fucking . . . men!' Simon and I cheered.

A flash of white light, and the moment was captured on film forever.

21

Last night with Pete and Simon was definitely the most memorable we've had since we all hooked up again. And to cap it all, I had myself the most restful and uninterrupted night's sleep I'd had in a long, long time. By the way, we've planned another one of those nightmares anonymous sessions, same time next Thursday night.

The following day, I felt so much better in myself, so much lighter, thanks to facing up to all those dreadful past memories. I was also spurred on by the heartwarming news of Pete and Simon moving back to Llandudno – permanently.

Just think of all the lads' nights out we'll be able to have, I thought. All being well, we could even end up going on one of our much talked about trips abroad. Now where did we say we wanted to go when we grew up? Was it Spain? Turkey? The Bahamas? Or Greece? Whichever! What a laugh we'd have.

Perhaps when we open up a tiny bit more about the past, we might even go back to revist Lovers' Green again, as part of our therapy. Only in the daytime, of course.

One down, one to go. The only other hurdle left to get over now is facing Sammy on Friday night. Is it 7 p.m. or 7.30? Whatever, I'll be here waiting.

However, I wonder if that one will turn out just as well.

To be honest, feeling the way I do right now, I think I'd prefer to leave it until next week. At the moment, it's such a relief not to be bogged down by all that ponderous depression, I would like to be able to enjoy it for a little bit longer.

Shame the weather outside doesn't do very much to help. It's so dark and overcast, it's going to be one of those days that never seems to wake up. I bet we have a shower before the day is out.

Still, not even that can dampen my spirits at the present. Suppose I'll just have to stay in and watch one of my favourite videos. This, I have to confess, happens to be one of my great weaknesses. But it is something I can only do when all my chores have been done. Only then can I settle down in front of the box, slip in a film from my copious collection of all-time greats, and disappear into wonderland for the next few hours. You can't beat it!

Oddly, that was a hobby of mine Sammy could never understand. She used to say to me, Once you've seen those films, how can you sit through them all over again?

And I used to reply, Well, if everyone thought that way, there'd be a bit of a drop in video sales at HMV, wouldn't there?

Of course, it helps if you are a film buff like me, but the trouble was Sammy was not. Tirelessly, I tried to explain it to her that it was no different from people who go out and buy music tapes or cds. Don't they end up listening to the same tunes over and over again?

Yes, she'd reply.

Well, it's the same for me, but instead of music, it's films . . .

Yes, she'd argue, but music's different, it's real, it's more alive.

Maybe it is a guy thing, something women just don't understand.

Be that as it may, tonight I think I'll go for something uplifting in the hope it will keep my spirits high. What about *The Shawshank Redemption*? A compelling feel-good drama, something that if it was a meal would satisfy me, while also providing some nutritional value . . .

In the kitchen I turned on the radio, a bit of music to kill the silence. Look, Sammy, I'm playing some real, alive music.

Ring! went the phone in the living room. On my way to answer it, I joked to myself it was Sammy wanting to pick up the argument on films and music.

In the living room, the stale smell of lager from last night hit me like someone throwing their week-old dirty socks in my face. I picked up the receiver, and opened the windows for some fresh air.

'Hello?'

'John?' It was Pete.

'Sleep any better last night?' I asked, taking in a few lungfuls of refreshing air, and smelling rain in the atmosphere.

'John! It's Simon . . . He's dead!'

'Move, you fucker, or I'll stab yer!' Jonno growled, with the knife sticking out of his mouth, like a dog with a bone. But I couldn't move, I was so fear-bound, I couldn't even breathe, let alone move. I'm going to die, I know it! I'll never see my mother again. How is she going to handle losing her only son as well as having lost her husband, my father?

And what about Pete and Simon? I'll never see them again. Never go into the woods with them again. Never have another mug of tea with them, never climb another tree. They're just as much a part of my family as my mum. I don't want to be without them either.

I don't want to go, I'm scared!

I lowered myself onto the edge of the couch hearing Pete's despondent voice pouring down my ear. And I don't know if I was saying it, or if it was in my mind, Just tell me you're joking, Pete. Don't throw this at me now! Say it's a mistake, tell me I'm dreaming – anything.

Pete mentioned ecstasy, and said he'd be over in an hour.

I clicked off the line, and dropped the phone at my feet, which clipped my big toe. My eyes fell on the video time display – it read 10.16 a.m. Outside, grey blankets of clouds provided me with little or no comfort at all, so I turned away.

It was then I realised I was losing it. My soul simply couldn't take any more and was ready to dive out of my body and leave this empty, burnt-out shell.

I got up and plodded back into the kitchen, only to be greeted by the morose tune of Bruce Springteen's 'Streets of Philadelphia' on the radio. That song now, whenever I heard it, would serve as a memory portal straight back to the worst moment of my life. Yes, even worse than that night!

I started to make myself some tea, but stopped short of filling the kettle. I couldn't continue. Ecstasy? I repeated.

Lumbering back into the living room, I dropped into

my easy chair, my mind playing a cerebral video tape compiled of every single memory I ever had of Simon.

Was my brain trying to make me cry, just as it makes you think of everything you hate to eat when you're feeling sick? Cry? ... Not at the moment, I can't even think.

Is there any possible chance Pete could be wrong? Any chance he'd turn up and say, 'John, shit, I was wrong! It was someone else and Simon will call you later.'

No, I don't think so! And what are the chances of Simon ever calling me again? Not even a million to one. In fact there's more chance of the sun not coming up tomorrow. Why the hell should that be? Simon was with me only last night, and that was no bloody miracle ... That's because he's dead, you moron! ... Dead? ... Yes, DEAD! ...

My head sank into my hands, and there it remained until Pete rapped at the door.

Again Pete knocked, and my mind told me to get up and let him in. For a moment, I dreaded the prospect of seeing him. Seeing Pete was seeing Simon. But right now, that voice in my head said, Pete's the only person in the world that can help you ... OK! I'll let him in.

When I opened the door, Pete immediately averted his eyes. His face was deathly pallid, another shocking reminder of Simon's death. I told him to come in, and he seemed to glide into the living room after me.

We sat down, and I noticed that his eyes were a bit red-rimmed. Without further ado, he proceeded to tell me what had happened. His voice was barely louder than a whisper, like the drizzle on my windows outside.

'Remember last night here, when Si said he had to meet Susan, his new girlfriend from the flat? Last week?'

I nodded.

'Well, as you probably guessed when you met her, she's a bit of a nightclubber. Last night, when he met her, she wanted to go to Boulevards, it was open for a one-off special theme night. Si, as you know, is not really into that, but he went along just to make a good impression.'

I interrupted him, half curious, and half stalling him before he reached the bit I didn't want to hear. 'Who told you all this?'

'Susan told me! I was the only one she could call on Simon's behalf . . . I gave her my mobile number the night we were in her flat – we all swapped numbers. They didn't swap numbers with you because they thought you weren't all that interested in them. That's why that girl was trying to loosen you up a bit.' Pete heaved a big sigh. 'So anyway, they went to Boulevards, and you know they were into ecstasy and that?'

I nodded again.

'Well, Simon ended up triple dropping.'

'What's triple dropping?' I asked.

'It's when they take three at a time!'

I dropped my head in despair.

'But the tablets he took were contaminated, some lime-coloured shit that was supposed to be banned. Susan only took a half to warm up, but ended up puking her guts out all night, and still needed hospital treatment. Simon . . .' Pete composed himself. 'Simon took three because, at Susan's flat earlier, he was in a bit of a state after what we'd talked about.'

'Shit! It's my fault!' I said guiltily.

'No, it wasn't your fault!' Pete put in quickly. 'Last night was something that had to be done, Simon knew that and so did I . . . He said to Susan before they went out that he wanted to completely forget about what we'd talked about, and get totally wrecked. He said he wanted to chase the dragon, so to speak. Then in Boulevards he started going wild on the dance floor, and Susan started getting worried when she couldn't get him to stop. Then she started feeling sick, and soon after that, Simon passed out, and went into a coma. An ambulance came and rushed him to hospital. They worked on him all night, but he died about six thirty this morning.'

I erupted with anger. 'You'd fucking think that after what had happened to us that night, he'd steer clear of stinking shit like that, wouldn't you?'

'Obviously for him, taking the thing was his way of escaping from the stress.'

In pure anger and frustration, I could feel my nails almost tearing strips off the arms of my chair.

'Susan rang me about quarter to seven this morning. I thought it was my wife, with something serious concerning Jeremy . . . It was something serious all right.'

I began to calm down a bit, and let Pete finish.

'I rushed over, but it was too late. Fucking hell, John,' Pete exploded, 'he looked like someone who'd just been run over by a fucking truck. It wasn't him at all. It wasn't Si, not the way we knew him. He was all blown up like a balloon.'

I looked at Pete disturbed.

Pete settled again. 'Police were there, they asked me a few questions and I answered them. By the way, I had to give them your name as a close friend, and because we were among the last few who saw him. They may come round and ask you a few questions.'

I nodded.

'And that's all I know!'

For a short while, we just sat silent, realising that this terrible tragedy had cost us our most precious blood . . . Simon.

For the next few days Pete stayed at my house. The weight of our grief was simply too heavy to bear by ourselves. And to be honest, without Pete's company I would have cracked up for sure.

As expected, the police did pop by for a chat, and after answering all their routine questions, they left satisfied, and that was that.

The following day, unfortunately for everyone who knew Simon, there was quite a big write-up in the papers about his death being linked to the drug ecstasy. That was all we needed.

However, now that it was almost front-page news, I thought it best to give Sammy a ring. Although she never knew him, it was just a matter of time before she found out I was in some way connected. Nonetheless, after I'd explained to her who Simon was, and what had happened, she promptly suggested postponing Friday, but I said it'd be all right.

The day after, she even sent me a card of condolence. Nice touch.

The funeral itself was scheduled for Friday, would you believe it? The same day I was due to see Sammy!

The expense for the funeral itself fell upon Simon's next of kin, namely, his mother who apparently was still alive. But in light of the fact that Simon had more or less lost touch with her since she remarried, there was always the possibility she might have reservations about paying the bill.

Had that have been the case, Pete and I were standing by ready to step in. Little did we know that his mother had taken out an insurance policy for Simon when he was young, in the hope it would provide him with some financial help when he was older. Guilty conscience for not always being there, perhaps?

The trouble was, this was something she forgot to mention to Simon himself, and when they did finally drift apart, his mother stopped the payments. However the surrendered value she could now claim would at the very minimum cover two-thirds of the cost. The rest, she agreed to chip in herself.

Christ! It's like neighbours battling over who should foot the bill for the broken fence between their gardens, I thought. How fucking ridiculous!

Still, at least that was settled.

Simon our brother, as we would always refer to him, was buried that Friday afternoon in St Tudno's cemetery on the Great Orme, on a typically cold, gloomy November day. He was laid to rest next to his beloved grandmother.

His mother, an auburn-haired woman in her late fifties, attended with her new husband. She hardly recognised the two people who had been closest to him, standing only a few feet from her, Pete and me.

Saying goodbye to one of your best mates is something I'm not going to disclose right here, right now. It is without doubt a Mount Everest of ordeals, as all who have suffered the same fate will know. And at this time, it is something Pete and I are only able to confide in each other. All I can say is what we put on his wreath:

> 'Friends are the comforting lights that illuminate the path before us. For without them, we are all but lost in this cold black jungle we call life.'

The funeral wake itself was held at one of the local hotels along the North Promenade. But Pete and I didn't go as it was mostly his mother's family, and we'd have felt a bit out of place. Instead, we had a quiet little gathering back at my house, which I'm sure Simon would have preferred.

Earlier that day Pete had told me he was thinking of going down to visit his son in Bristol, but after the funeral, he'd had second thoughts. I think he was more worried about me spending another weekend alone. Especially if my one-to-one confrontation with Sammy didn't turn out so well. Which, I have to admit, was a trifle worrying.

Needless to say, I put on a brave front and told Pete to go. So he did.

As I sat in my living room, watching the seven o'clock news and waiting for Sammy's arrival, I wondered how I'd react at seeing her again. At present, I was so mentally drained, it was hard enough to feel any kind of emotion at all. Yet when I heard the taxi pull up outside, the moths in my chest fluttered, so I must have cared some.

I took a deep breath, and tried to remember all the things I'd been wanting to say to her over the last few weeks. I opened the door and there she was.

Inside, the old ticker cried out like a lost child being reunited with its mother. I was pleased to see her, that I couldn't deny. Looking at her all over, I noticed her hair had grown a bit since the last time I saw her. And the soft light from the hallway, gave her golden suntan an added glow. But what about her new sylph-like figure – had she lost some weight too?

'How are you?' she asked.

Lost for words, I could only make a gesture that meant I was doing all right. I stood aside to let her in, then followed her into the living room. She surveyed the room as if she'd never seen it before, and sat somewhat uncomfortably on the edge of the couch, as if she didn't plan on staying very long. I'd almost forgotten how nice it was smelling Givenchy perfume in the air again.

She asked about how the funeral went and how everyone involved was coping, and I told her it went fine. I asked if she wanted tea, and she accepted. Christ! It was like our first date all over again.

Drinks in hand, we finally got down to the nitty-gritty.

'So what are we gonna do then, Sam?' I asked her point-blank.

Sammy collected herself, and put down her mug. 'When I left here a few weeks ago, I was convinced the only time I'd be returning would be to collect the rest of my things. And when I said I think we both needed some time to ourselves, I was right! Now I've had that time, I've made an important decision.'

Sipping my tea, I eyed her solemnly above the rim of my mug.

'If you're willing to get some professional help, I might consider giving it another go.'

Had she said, it's finished and that's it, I think, under the circumstances, I would have cracked up and begged her for another chance, no matter what she'd done. Instead, what she virtually said was, I still want you, but have set conditions, because you are just as much to blame as me, and I'm not letting you get off scot-free.

The guilty one she may have been, but the storm of relief and joy that almost erupted from me was confirmation that my conscience was willing to forgive the affair she'd had. The point was, she still wanted me, over that person. I was worth something, after all, and that alone made me feel on top of the world.

Yet did I go over and fling my arms around her? No I didn't! Call it selfish pride, call it what you will. I had to set my mind at rest and find out the whole truth. She still had some explaining to do.

'Hang on a minute, Sam. Let's not forget it was you who had the affair and left me.'

Sammy snorted. 'You see! That's exactly what I'm talking about, John. There wasn't any affair, it's all been your own septic imagination.'

Normally, I would have jumped down her throat again, but this time I held back and took a deep breath. 'Yeah, but you didn't deny it though, did you?'

'How many times in the past have I had to deny I was seeing someone behind your back? I just couldn't be bothered to do it any more.'

'Come on, Sam, how can you sit there and say that after I saw you?'

'Saw me with who?' Her shoulders shrugged in annoyance.

'Outside Asda that Thursday night, I was there across the road watching you. You came out with a lad, then he went round to the swimming pool so nobody would see. And you picked him up in my car.'

'You were spying on me?'

'Damn right I was, after what I heard when I crept in the night before.'

Sammy's face wrinkled in bemusement.

'Wednesday night, three weeks ago, when I went to Mike's, and Pamela was here. I came back early because Mike wasn't feeling very well, and I heard you telling Pamela about that chap who kissed you, and you were supposed to meet him Thursday nights.'

Sammy had to think for a second. Was that because I had caught her out? Or was it genuine confusion?

'What night was it again?' she stalled, and I said to myself, Got you.

'Thursday night!' I replied self-assuredly.

Her face began to glimmer with recognition. 'Was that the night I was supposed to give Danny and his girlfriend a lift to Craig-Y-Don?'

'Who the hell's Danny and his girlfriend?' I asked.

'Danny and Tracy work with me in Asda on the checkouts.'

'Well, there was no Tracy there that night, just the two of you,' I pointed out.

More recognition shone in Sammy's face. 'That was the week Tracy had off work, and she'd gone swimming. The day before, Danny asked if I wouldn't mind giving them a lift tomorrow night to Craig-Y-Don because they were going for Tracy's birthday meal. The same meal I forgot to mention to you that we were invited to. That's right! It was the first thing I said to you when I came in the kitchen after you'd been out to God knows where . . . Remember?'

I thought back to that dreadful night again . . .

'You're home late . . . Where've you been?'

'Out!' I had grumbled, turning back to the newspaper.

While Sammy went to the fridge to find something to eat, I had peeked at her slyly from the kitchen table. 'Oh, I forgot to tell you last week we were invited to Tracy's birthday party tonight.' She grimaced as she sniffed inside a tub of coleslaw that was on the turn. 'I didn't fancy going myself, and I know you wouldn't have wanted to go anyhow, so that's why I probably forgot to mention it. Her boyfriend Danny has got her a really nice ring . . .'

I snorted to myself, saying in my head, You should have said to me that you wanted to go. That would have given you the perfect excuse to fuck around with that prick you were with, and I never would have found out . . .

'So if Danny was the person you gave a lift to, where was Tracy then?' I mumbled.

'Tracy had told Danny that if she wasn't either outside Asda or by the swimming pool, she'd already gone home. That's why Danny went there. We both walked to the car, and he said he'd just go and check if she was by the swimming pool, while I got the car from the car park.'

In my mind's eye, I saw them walk to the car park, then the lad left Sammy and crossed the road past me as he headed towards the swimming pool round the corner . . .

'Why didn't you tell me about the lift?' I gulped.

'Well, Christ, John, it was just a bloody lift. What's so important about that? It's not as if I was driving to Land's End with a bunch of naked gigolos. And besides, I didn't know you were waiting outside, did I? It just wasn't such a big thing.'

'Right, fine,' I said, my argument, like the great *Titanic*, having just hit an iceberg but managing to stay afloat for the time being. 'But when I was listening to you talking to Pamela, what was it you said about he kissed you and Pamela saying she bet he'd do more than that if he had the chance. Then you said, He's lovely. I just couldn't refuse . . .'

Sammy thought hard again, but couldn't seem to recall any of this. Had I finally cornered her? I took another mouthful of tea to compose myself.

'Wait a minute!' she announced. 'Was that Harold?'

'Harold?' Now she'd got me confused.

'Harold, that old chap who I told you comes in every week to shop.'

. . . Back to that night in the kitchen three weeks ago, just after she'd mentioned Tracy's birthday party.

'Saw Harold again today . . .' She tried to make conversation.
'Guess what he did when I helped him with his shopping?' She was referring to that old man customer who comes in every week to shop. But I wasn't in the mood to listen, and rattled the paper miserably.

I awoke back to the present again. 'What's Harold got to do with it?'

'Well, that's one of the things Pamela and I were talking about! Usually he comes in on a Thursday, but that week for some reason he came in on Wednesday. And for helping him with his shopping, he gave me a kiss on the cheek. It was so sweet, I told Pamela that night. And she said to me jokingly, I bet he'd have done more than that if he'd had the chance, and knowing that he was harmless, I said I couldn't refuse a kiss . . . Don't you remember me saying Harold came in today, and guess what he did? I was just about to tell you he gave me a kiss, but you didn't seem to be listening to me.'

My *Titanic* was now taking on so much water it was sinking fast, and there was nothing I could do about it, except leap overboard and hope for the best.

Listening behind closed doors is going to be your undoing one day.

'Why were you talking about Danny and Tracy to Pamela then?'

'Because Pamela knows Tracy very well, and was supposed to be going to her birthday party as well, but she declined, like us . . . You can phone her and ask her if you want.'

Talk about a gross misunderstanding. What the hell could I say? I had got it all wrong!

That night, three weeks ago, I had picked up fragments of a conversation I had no business listening to, between my girlfriend and her friend. What I heard, I pierced together, and let my wild, neurotic imagination fill in the gaps.

What a total, major screw-up I was. Why the hell didn't I have the gumption to just confront her about it there and then, instead of jumping to all the wrong conclusions, I could have prevented all this shit from ever happening in the first place. Serves you right you absolute plonker! And if you lose her now, let that be a lesson to you.

Listening behind closed doors is going to be your undoing one day.

I felt so embarrassed, and mortified, I couldn't even look her in the face. The only thing I could think of to get out of there was to make the excuse I needed the toilet. Then I tore up the stairs and slammed the bathroom door behind me.

I stood there, stiff as a board, and broke out in a cold sweat. How on earth can I possibly repair all the damage I've caused through my own stupidity? Maybe I do need professional help.

I slumped down on the toilet, head in my hands.

Listening behind closed doors will be your undoing one day.

Perhaps if I tell Sammy everything that has happened in the past, she may be able to understand why I was so insecure. I have to at least try, it's my one and only hope.

That, and eat a hellava lot of humble pie.

'John?' Sammy shouted from the bottom of the stairs. 'What are you doing up there?'

'Be there now!' I stood up and pulled the chain to cover myself.

I turned to look at my reflection in the cabinet mirror.

Christ, have you got a mountain to climb! I heaved a large sigh, and marched back downstairs.

To tell Sammy everything, I mean absolutely everything that happened, took a good few hours and about half a dozen mugs of tea. At first, I thought she would think I was simply trying emotional blackmail to get her back. But the way she sat rigid in her chair clearly showed she was shocked by what she'd heard. And besides, she knew me well enough to know I wouldn't make up something like that under the circumstances.

When I'd finished, her first reaction was to shake her head and ask why the hell I hadn't told her all that years ago. All I could do was shrug helplessly and say I wish I had.

Catching her while she was still in an understanding mood, I begged her to stay the weekend with me. The full impact of Simon's death hadn't truly hit me yet, and I didn't want to be alone when it did.

'Is that really why you want me to stay?' she asked.

'No! I've missed you so much, and you're the only person I need at the moment,' I told her sincerely.

At first I thought she was going to say no, so I even promised to sleep in the spare room. To my utter delight and relief, she accepted. However, before she even considered the prospect of moving back in, she told me point blank that I was on a month's trial period . . . Fair enough!

In the meantime, she also pointed out, I had a lot of work to do to convince her I was worth the effort.

One thing was for sure: if I did get her back, I certainly didn't intend to lose her again. That was a promise! And as for being insecure, that's something I planned on burying along with all the other unpleasant memories of my past.

22

After the weekend I spent with Sammy, despite the trauma of losing Simon, I felt I was finally getting my life back on track. But what it had cost me.

Sunday, Pete dropped me a text to let me know that he was back from Bristol and was popping over that night.

Sunday evening, Sammy was due to go back to her mother's, but I asked if she wanted to stay and meet Pete, and she agreed. About seven o'clock Pete arrived, and when I led him into the living room, Sammy stood up and gave him a big sunny smile.

'Pete, this is Sammy.'

Despite being surprised to see her there, Pete still managed to raise a refreshing grin. 'So this is the famous Sammy!'

'Nice to meet you! I've heard a lot about you too,' Sammy replied coyly, and gave him a hug.

Pete eyed me oddly over Sammy's shoulder, and I shrugged back at him. Perhaps she was touched by some of the things she'd heard about him from me.

'Right, well, I'll be off then!' Sammy announced, and edged towards the door.

'Your taxi's not here yet!' I said.

'It's all right, I've told it to meet me at the end of the road anyhow.'

'You sure? I don't like the idea of you waiting outside in the dark.'

Sammy tutted towards Pete. 'God, it's not as if I'm standing in the middle of a back street in the middle of the night. There's loads of people about.'

'Give us a few rings then in about half an hour, just so I'll know you got home.'

She tutted again, showing off a bit in front of us, then said her ta-ras. After the door clicked shut, Pete stood there grinning at me like a man who'd just fallen in shit and found 50 quid. 'Obviously a lot has happened in my absence.'

'Yeah, it has! I'll tell you about in a minute. Want some tea?'

Pete hummed his approval and followed me into the kitchen. He stood leaning against the worktop while I filled the kettle.

'So how did it go, down in Bristol?' I asked.

'You first!' he replied, and I gave him an ambiguous glance.

'Well . . .' I turned to him guiltily. 'I told Sammy about what happened to us.'

'Me too!' Pete shrugged. 'I mean, I told Janice.'

'Really?' I asked, astonished. 'How did she take it?'

'No! No! You first.'

'OK . . . I think it made a difference me telling her everything. In a way it was my only hope to get her to understand about the way I've behaved over the years.'

'So you've forgiven about her cheating on you then?'

'Yes, I mean, no! She didn't cheat on me.'

Pete twitched his neck back, confused. 'Come again?'

'I'll explain it to you later.'

'You mean, after all that, she was innocent?'

I nodded in shame.

'And she's still going to take you back after all that?'

'Well, that's the catch. After realising that I'd made the mistake, my only chance was to tell her the whole story. And the upshot of it is, in light of what I've been through, she's now given me a month to sort myself out and prove to her that I'm worth the effort.'

'That's a good start, mate! And if, as you said, she is innocent, don't fuck it up this time. What have I always told you about that bloody insecurity of yours? Told you it'd be your downfall one day, especially listening behind closed doors.'

'I know! I know! . . . So what have you got to tell me then?' I folded my arms in anticipation.

'I'm gonna give it another try with Janice,' he said with a determined smile. 'We were up until about three this morning talking about it.'

'Fucking good on you! What a turnaround for the both of us.'

Pete breathed in a whole lungful of air. 'After losing Si, it made me realise how pointless it is to hold stupid grudges. All that time we waste by constantly playing a game of one-upmanship with the people we're supposed to love . . . I know what she did was wrong, and God knows she's proved she's sorry now. But after all is said and done, all the pain she's caused me was nothing compared to the pain of losing Si and what we've carried around with us for the last twenty years. Isn't it time now to stop moaning about the way we like our meat cooked. Let's just tuck in and enjoy it while its fresh, tender and hot.'

'Well fucking said, mate,' I cheered, just in time for the boiling kettle to click off.

After telling Pete everything about my little *faux pas*

with Sammy, I asked what his intentions were now he'd decided to go back. As I did, the phone rang twice, then stopped. It was Sammy giving me my two rings to tell me she'd got back to her mother's safe and sound.

'The plan is for me to go back to Bristol for a short while, while I get things sorted. I've got some holidays owing to me which I'm going to make use of, then after the new year, we'll sell-up and move back here for good . . . That was one of the conditions I set for us starting over again.'

That's what I wanted to hear. 'So are you going back straight away?' I asked.

'Yeah, tomorrow!' he said, then grimaced. 'Really, I would have preferred to stay a bit longer after, you know . . .'

I nodded that I understood.

'Just think.' Pete suddenly brightened. 'I'll only be gone a few months, then I'll be back, and we'll all be growing old together.'

'Yeah!' I grinned. 'I'll be knocking at your door, and you'll all be hiding behind the curtains, saying, Ah shit, not him again. Wish he'd just piss off.'

'I won't be hiding behind the curtains, I'll be throwing a bucket of water at you from the bedroom window, telling you to piss off.' And we both had a bit of a chuckle.

Back in the living room later on, we ended up watching the tape of Simon on the *Sasha* morning talk show again. What a classic.

Soon after, Pete left with the promise that he'd drop in just before he left for Bristol, tomorrow afternoon, about five o'clock.

However, all day long, the next day, I was dreading the

prospect of seeing him go. It was as if he'd been with me so far through the valley of death, and now we had to walk the rest of the way on our own.

Early evening, Pete turned up as promised, and popped in for a quick brew. We talked, we laughed, we remembered, one more time, and just before he left, he gave me a little goodbye present.

It was a framed photograph of the three of us in my living room on the last night we spent with our best friend Simon.

Finally, Pete and I shook hands, embraced, then I said to him, as he walked over to get into his navy blue Toyota, 'I think the three of us meeting up again was no coincidence.'

Pete looked up from the hood of his car.

'After that night back in '82, we let loose the dragon, didn't we? And deep down I think you and Si knew that one day you'd have to come back and help me slay it for good. Because only the three of us together could do it.'

'Well, I've only got one thing to say to that,' Pete opened the driver's door.

'What?'

'Fate or what?' And he sank into the car before I could respond.

I just smiled to myself, and stuck out my hand in farewell. Pete tossed me a wave, tooted his horn, and pulled off.

I waited until his car disappeared from my view, then closed my door to the world once more. I walked back into the living room, holding the prized picture of the three of us together toasting our so-called futures. That very evening, I hung it up on the wall in prime position facing the doorway, so it'd be the first thing anyone would see when they entered.

Barely a week later, on another cold, grey wintry day, I drove up to St Tudno's Church cemetery on the Great Orme to visit my mate Simon. As I got out, I saw a figure in the far west quadrant standing over Simon's grave. Suspicions aroused, I proceeded through the iron gate, praying it wasn't Simon's ex-girlfriend Joanne.

Thankfully, I discovered it wasn't. It turned out to be Susan, the last person he was with the night he died. Seeing me coming, she said in a dreamy voice, 'Hi,' and as I smiled back at her, I noticed her face was pale and with little make-up. Both of us turned to look over the withering hump of bouquets and floral wreaths beneath us.

Looking down at Simon's grave, I still found it hard to accept Simon was six feet below all that soil. Can't I just see him one more time before the earth claims him? All I have to do is dig down.

Susan turned to me. 'Listen, you don't hold me responsible for what happened, do you?'

I looked hard into her hazel eyes, and recognised the pain that shone back at me. 'No! I don't hold you responsible!' I said, and thought I heard a sigh of relief.

'You three were very close, weren't you?' she asked.

'He saved my life once.' I stared at her solemnly, and she bowed her head as if she was going to say a little prayer.

'I'm actually glad I ran into you. There's something I've been meaning to tell you and Pete about Simon. I was going to wait another week for things to settle down a bit, but as you're here now . . .'

She had my undivided attention.

'The night Simon came to see me, he told me something which he said he'd bottled up for the last twenty years.'

My curiosity was definitely stirring now.

'He said that one night when you were kids, you got caught by some people and they tied you all up.'

'He told you what happened that night?' I became alarmed.

'No, he wouldn't tell me the whole story, but he did tell me the identity of the person who cut you all free.'

'Who was it?' I cried.

'He told me it was a girl called Sharon Roberts.'

'Sharon? Sharon Roberts off the Orme?' I reeled back in shock, horror. 'No . . . Couldn't have been! How the hell could it have been her? How the hell did he come up with that?'

'Simon was going out with her.'

'Going out with her?' I shrieked.

'Yeah, but he didn't want to tell you both straight away in case you might poke fun, because she wasn't very pretty or something like that. He was going to leave it a while and tell you when he was ready.'

What a sledgehammer blow. I just stood there slack-jawed.

'He'd only been going out with her about a week when she let slip about a certain midnight rave that was going to happen on a Thursday night in the woods. And apparently, all sorts of kinky things were going to go on. But Sharon made Simon promise that he wouldn't tell anyone, because her cousin would kill her. And she also made Simon promise never, never to go there, because they were a bunch of maniacs. But Simon couldn't resist it, and not wanting to go by himself, he suggested you all go for a midnight walk or something, to give him the excuse to go.

'Then, to cut a long story short, Sharon later overheard her cousin (Jonno) saying that they were setting a trap for you three. But on the night, Sharon couldn't get back to Simon to warn him in time. (We went camping.) That's when she made the excuse she wanted to join in this particular party, so she could try and help you all. She was the one who ended up cutting you free. Unfortunately for her, though, that was the night she was first introduced to drugs. Simon said she died from an overdose when she was only twenty.'

I nodded sombrely. 'So that's how she got involved in drugs.'

'Since that night he's never been able to forgive himself for secretly roping in his two best mates. He said if he'd had any kind of idea what he was letting you all in for, there's no way in the world he'd have gone through with it. And since then, he's never been able to face up to you two about it, in case you didn't bother with him again.'

Once again, my mind was alight with flashbacks from that summer. The day Sludge was bullying me, and he warned me that Jonno and the others had special plans for us three. Then Pete and I were chased by the gang into the woods. But where was Simon?

He told us he was with his mum, but I was sure she wasn't due down for another few weeks. I bet he was with Sharon. That very same day, he told us Sharon had a boyfriend. Little did we know it was him.

Was that his way of slowly breaking it to us? And remember when I slagged her off, he scolded me for it. That was the second time he'd stuck up for her . . . Also when we were looking at dirty mags in the den he remarked unwittingly that Sharon was going to have a nice arse when she was older. At the time, I thought he was hinting that he knew I liked her. Who would have guessed it was the other way around? Not his two best friends, that's for sure!

'I'm sorry.' Susan touched my arm. 'Has all this been too much for you? I should have waited a bit longer. It's just that I wanted to tell you so Simon could finally rest in peace, if you know what I mean?'

'No! No! It's all right, I'm glad you told me ... Honestly!'

'Do you want me to leave you alone then?'

'No, it's all right.'

She gently tugged on my arm. 'If you don't mind me asking, what did actually happen that night?'

I took a deep breath to compose myself again. 'Nothing! Nothing happened! They just taught us a lesson for spying on them, that's all. But at the time it frightened us.'

She nodded and turned back to Simon's grave, giving me time to absorb everything she'd just told me.

Time? I was afraid I was going to need quite a lot of that to get it to sink in. I just couldn't get over it. Simon was going out with my Sharon? Sharon was the one who cut us free, saved our lives, and I said all those nasty things about her?

I needed to go home and think it through in private. I turned to Susan and told her I was going to make a move and would she like a lift, which she accepted gratefully.

On our way back to my car, I began to wonder how I was going to explain all this to Pete. Should I explain it to him? I stopped and asked Susan for a favour.

'Please don't ring Pete and tell him what you've just told me. It's all water under the bridge now. Pete's got enough on his plate already, and doesn't need that as well. Let's just keep it to ourselves.'

'OK. If that's what you prefer.'

'Thanks!'

We started off again, then Susan nudged me. 'Hey, do you remember my mate Karen, the girl who sat on your knee that night in the flat?'

'Yeah!'

'Well, she thought you were quite cute, you know. Why don't you give her a ring?'

I smiled, flattered. At last I had an admirer.

EPILOGUE

The following day, I visited Sharon's grave at Llanrhos cemetery and laid a fresh bouquet of flowers beside her black marble headstone. I stood there for about half an hour, talking to her, and most of all, thanking her for saving us that night. Finally, I prayed that she and Simon would find peace together, then I tapped her headstone affectionately and left.

In tribute to them both, I decided to take a walk on the Orme, through Haulfrie Gardens, our old haunt.

I started at Sunshine Café and made my way up the stepped footpaths, which were now fitted with metal rail handles instead of the wooden ones I remembered.

At the top, where the path branches off back along the brow of the gardens, or onwards towards the woods, I stopped for breather. At 35 now, going on 36, I was not as fit as I used to be.

I sniffed the keen late November air, and continued. Soon I discovered a wooden gateway, which was a new addition to this pathway as far as I was concerned. In fact, as I reached the golfie, part of the woodlands along the near side was now fenced off. I wondered why.

I carried on along the path carpeted by soggy dead leaves that looked like spring cabbage. All the trees in the glade, pines, whitebeams, limes, ash, were bare to their bones. It looked like a trees' graveyard.

But what about the grand old man himself, the squirrel tree? Would he still be there? And if so, how much had he aged? I didn't look, not for now. I wanted to savour that little reunion later. First I wanted to visit our beloved den, and the infamous Lovers' Green, to see what the ravages of time had done to them.

On the way, I stopped at the footpath leading up to Llwynon Road, where I was met on that fateful night by Jonno's dog. And in the coppice nearby was the leaning pine tree where I sat sobbing after Karen the superbitch had made jibes about my dolphin head.

Karen the superbitch, after what we'd seen in Hayley's window that night, we'd have loved to take the piss out of her. But we couldn't risk it, not as it was so closely linked within the timeframe to what happened to Jonno.

However, years later, I did receive some payback when I saw her and her friends stumble out of the Carlton pub in town, pissed as farts. She puked her guts out right in front of me, and when our eyes met, I'm sure for one moment she remembered me. In disgust, I just looked at her bloated, misshapen body up and down and walked off. Who was looking down at who now?

When I came to where our den used to be, all that was left was a charred barren wasteland, scattered with charcoal. Someone had burnt the whole area down. I shook my head indignantly, and moved onto Lovers' Green, wondering if that had also been desecrated in some way.

To my surprise it hadn't. Basically it looked the same, except for the addition of another pig-sty gate, and an alpine bench, where one could sit and marvel at the views of the town and the surrounding coast. I went over and had a little sit-down and a fag while I reflected.

Strange to me, the place seemed a lot smaller now that I was an adult.

Finally, it was time to meet my old nemesis, the squirrel tree. As I doubled back through the woods, I caught sight of him standing head and shoulders above the other trees. The fucker's still there, I said with admiration. I side-skipped down the sodden embankment and marched down to the mighty trunk, my eyes wandering over every inch of his flaky bark. He hadn't changed much either – just missing one or two branch-teeth, that was about it.

'Hello, old man,' I said, looking right up at him. 'Remember me? It's been a long time, hasn't it? Have you missed me?' And I think he had. How could he forget? Especially after what we'd been through together.

For a moment or two, we stood eyeing each other like two long-lost adversaries. Then he seemed to smile and wink at me, Are you up for one last challenge? So I smiled back at him.

I clasped hold of the first branch just to get the feel, then up I went. Up and up I climbed. I remembered the route so well, and didn't look down once, until I got about two-thirds of the way. Taking a breather, I peeped down, and discovered to my relief that the spiked railings were no longer there. Thank Christ for that!

My clothes were now covered in powdery lime, my body was aching with fatigue, and vertigo was making my head spin, but I didn't care. I looked skyward and continued, one bough at a time.

Soon the branches became thinner and thinner, until I could climb no further. Hands and legs trembling, I slowly raised my head above the pine needles and into the clearing blue sky. I had done it! I had finally conquered the mighty squirrel tree, and the views were breathtaking.

I began to cheer and whoop like the 14-year-old boy I once was. If only Pete and Simon were here to see me now, they'd be proud of me . . . at last. 'Hey Si, can you hear me up there? I've finally done it!' I shouted.

But the only response I got was the fluttering of a white dove landing in one of the trees beside me. Startled a bit, I watched with interest, and saw it tilt its tiny head towards me and blink its oil-drop eyes. Then it hit me, I don't know why but it did. The memory of the pact I made with Pete and Simon, back in '82, our first night out under the stars.

. . . '*If there is life after death, whoever goes first out of us three must come back to let the others know.*'

Yet before I had a chance to ask, the dove snapped back into flight, leaving me to guess whether it was or not.

Maybe Simon had come back to let me know he was with us, and that he was all right. I certainly hoped so! But before the dove vanished from my view, I just had time to ask one more question.

'Si? Now I've finally made it up here, how the hell do I get back down?'